PATIENCE, MY DEAR

PATIENCE, MY DEAR

BOWER LEWIS

PATIENCE, MY DEAR

INFINITE WORDS
NEW YORK LONDON TORONTO SYDNEY

INFINITE WORDS
P.O. Box 6505
Largo, MD 20792

ISBN 978-1-59309-644-1
ISBN 978-1-4767-9343-6 (ebook)
LCCN 2014942326

First Infinite Words trade paperback edition March 2015

Cover design: Keith Saunders/Marion Designs
Cover photography: © Keith Saunders/Keith Saunders Photos
Book design: Red Herring Design, Inc.

10 9 8 7 6 5 4 3 2 1

Manufactured in the United States of America

For information regarding special discounts for bulk purchases, please contact Simon & Schuster Special Sales at 1-866-506-1949 or business@simonandschuster.com

The Simon & Schuster Speakers Bureau can bring authors to your live event. For more information or to book an event, contact the Simon & Schuster Speakers Bureau at 1-866-248-3049 or visit our website at www.simonspeakers.com.

For Jefferson,
who turns my foibles funny
and my strengths into superpowers.

ACKNOWLEDGMENTS

I'd like to acknowledge my parents, Robert and Judith Munro, with profound love and gratitude, and with apologies for the language in this book (and for my adolescence). Also, John Munro, Hilary McLeod, Alan McLeod, Heather Danskin, Ian Danskin, and the ever-indomitable Amelia and Evelyn McLeod.

And my aunt, Penelope MacNaughton, who helped me come into my own. Thanks also to Winifred Lyons and Richard Pettengill, Lucy Lyons, my whole, huge Lyons family, Gillian MacNaughton, Andrew MacNaughton, Heidi Van der Heuvel and Douglas Loyd, Chuck Danskin, the guy who let me turn left onto Cross Street today, and Charles and Linda Austin.

And with all my love, the knucklehead—Danielle Victoria Austin.

Grateful acknowledgment to Kelley A. Swan, who makes me write better and laugh harder than anyone I've ever met. Also, Liane Thomas, Benjamin Leroy, Rebecca (George) Gray, Sara Kriynovich Burton, Eugene and Lynne Cox, Cameron Cox, Douglas Cox, Katie Allen Henderson, Emma Aer, Theresa Stone, Karen Gould, Dr. Yuan-Chi Lin, and Mr. Thomas Still.

I'd especially like to thank my indefatigable agent, Sara Camilli, and my publisher Zane, along with Charmaine Parker, Deb Schuler, Shontrell Wade, Yona Deshommes, Tory Lowy, and the whole team at Infinite Words/Atria.

And finally, I acknowledge my husband, Jefferson Marcus Lyons. Infinite words are not enough. I love you.

CHAPTER ONE

Defenestration was going to be a bitch. Patience didn't like touching unsealed wood, a quirk of hers since childhood, and there wasn't a window frame in the place that wasn't paint-curled and splintered. She didn't care for the sensation of freefall either, and—despite the impression people seemed to form at the sight of her tattoos and fuchsia-streaked hair—she abhorred a public spectacle. Also, she was afraid of heights. She crouched in the living room window frame of her fifth-story apartment, gazing across the neighboring rooftops at the skyline of downtown Boston, and disappointment hung around her like a tuba. Patience didn't want to die.

Patience.

She wouldn't have heard the building explode over the wind in her ears, but The Voice came through as clear as a live mic in an empty auditorium. She fought against the surging air to be just as clear as she told it to fuck off.

It sighed. She ignored it.

Her descent into the Kelleher family schizophrenia had been marked by the intrusion of an auditory hallucination more passive-aggressive than her mother's Aunt Prim. The Voice sighed. It cleared its throat. It complained when she didn't respond and typically ended up insulted when she did. She'd slept little the past few weeks, and fitfully when she did—dreaming of laboratories and boy band singers—despite the double shifts she'd been pulling to exhaust herself beyond its reach. It didn't work of course, nothing ever did. The Voice interrupted as she took customers' orders and followed her into the walk-in freezer. It commented if her plates weren't carried straight enough or if she spilled some juice over onto her tray, always insisting that it was *just trying to help.* Her head hurt all the time now, and she was done. She'd known for years that this was coming, and now that it was here, she could think of nothing but finding some way to make it go away. The culmination of a decade's anticipation and anxiety had turned out to be something of a fucked-up joke, but she'd be damned if she wouldn't handle the punchline herself.

She looked down at the tattered strap of leather she'd worn around her left wrist since her thirteenth birthday—since the night her favorite uncle gave it to her and then packed up his voices and disappeared for good. He'd promised her that she'd understand someday, that his world would make sense to her when the time was right. It had been ten years of ticking since that night. Ten years of waiting in line for a movie she didn't want to see. Like the constant drip from a leaking faucet, it was always there, whether she noticed it or not.

Patience yanked the old cord from her wrist and dropped it over the ledge, then pushed a pink lock from her face.

"Fuck your promises, Uncle John. And fuck you too."

Patience.

"That goes double for you."

It sighed again, and then her cell phone rang inside the apartment. Its chimes sounded clearly in her ears, as impervious to the wind's dominance as The Voice. She glanced back to her cluttered coffee table, then turned forward again and caught sight of a man not much older than her standing at a window across the street. He was dressed in pajamas with a cup of coffee in his hand. She stared for a moment, confused at finding him there, and then he waved.

She tightened her grip on the frame as it occurred to her that her plummet to the street would likely cause a fair amount of danger and discord to the people around her. She'd managed to miss that detail in her distraction and fatigue, and she was curious now whether that sort of disregard for others was a condition of the schizophrenia, or if she'd simply become an asshole over the past several weeks and somehow failed to notice.

She slid her hands back to pull herself inside again as a torrent of wind bent a path around her and drew her forward, breaking her grasp of the frame. She hung suspended over Commonwealth Avenue for one miraculous moment as the shaft of air completed its arc around her body and pulled her back into the apartment. It dropped her onto her living room floor and quieted to a reassuring breeze, brushing the hair back from her eyes as her heart thumped in her ears. She coughed for air, and then, slowly, she began to quiet as well. It was as though a persistent humming she'd never noticed had stopped and a new sort of peace existed beneath the world's general blare. She pushed herself up and dropped her head back against the sill. Her apartment seemed brighter than before, the air more transparent. She turned her eyes up to the light shining from the uncovered bulb and wondered if it always felt this way when an episode passed. The sensation wasn't unpleasant. It was something—she wasn't at all sure what—but the moment was tolerable.

She wondered, too, if it was sensations like this that had fed the one constant thing in her uncle's increasingly inconstant psyche—his staunch refusal to accept any form of help that might quiet the voices he alone could hear.

She looked down to the tan line at her newly naked wrist.

"We're alike, Pax. You and me," he'd said. "Don't worry, I'll be there to help you through it when your time comes."

But, he wasn't. He'd never been heard from again. It was months before her mother stopped crying and accepted that her little brother was gone, just the way their grandfather and one of their uncles were also gone. Patience learned soon enough to stop asking about him and life resumed as a new kind of normal.

No one ever spoke of John now.

The phone chirped beside her pile of unopened mail and she nodded. If she wasn't going to kill herself, she should probably check her messages.

The guy across the street was still at his window, but his mug was overturned and empty now and his coffee was streaming down the front of his pajamas. She waved back apologetically and pulled the window shut.

A text message was waiting from someone who called himself The Biz. Patience frowned at the extra fifteen cents this would cost her and pressed the button. She didn't know anyone who called himself The Biz. She didn't *want* to know anyone who called himself The Biz.

CAN U HEAR ME NOW?

She checked the sender field again and deleted the message. Cell phone spam could get to be a pricey invasion for a girl without a text plan, and Patience didn't care for texting in the first place. There was an immediacy and an expectation about it that she found annoying and harsh, and text speak generally made her want to put her head through a wall. She hit the power button, but the phone lit right back up in her hand.

THER IS WRK 2 DO! :)

It had been a stressful enough morning as it was. She was in no mood for a lecture from some anonymous ass with a cell phone. She had nimble dialing fingers and an excellent vocabulary. She hit reply, fully prepared to spend another fifteen cents unloading her displeasure onto The Biz and his work ethic, but the field was empty where his number should have been.

"Goddamn it!"

HEY!

She stood very still beside the table, staring down at the admonishment. A prickly sensation started at the back of her neck and worked its way up. This would be the paranoia, of course, arriving right on cue. She leaned against the wall and raised a hand to her throbbing forehead.

"Would you at least lay off the caps lock, for crying out loud? It's too early for the noise."

The responding chime seemed more restrained than the last. Patience opened one eye and glanced down.

Sorry.

That prickly sensation turned into a cold sweat. She turned slowly around the apartment and then looked back out the window. Her neighbor's was empty now and she appeared to be alone. But Patience was not alone, she was certain of that. Someone was there with her, watching. Taking inventory. She grabbed her coat on her way to the door and took the stairs down two at a time.

"I'm being followed."

The cop at the front desk looked up and Patience dropped the phone without invitation.

"I've been receiving text messages from someone I don't know. I think he was in my apartment this morning."

"You *think* he was in your apartment? Was there evidence of a break-in?"

"No."

"Did you hear something?"

"Nothing but the phone."

"Miss ..."

"Look," she said, "I'm getting messages from someone who's responding to the things I do and say, as I'm doing and saying them. He was there with me this morning, I'm certain of it."

The officer picked up the phone. "It's probably kids. What they can't do with cell phones these days. I let my twelve-year-old get his hands on mine a couple of weeks ago to set up my voicemail for me, and in the five minutes it was in his possession, he'd downloaded over thirty bucks worth of video games, including something called *Zombie Cop Killers*. I never knew a thing about it until the bill came." He paused and looked up at her. "Did you erase the messages?"

"Why would I ask you to look if I'd erased them?"

"There's nothing here now."

He passed the phone back and Patience grabbed it from the counter. They were right there on the screen, just as they had been. "What are you talking about?" She held it up to show him. "This one at the top, I've already deleted twice and it's still here. Look!"

The officer glanced down and his expression grew increasingly cop-like. "Miss, I am looking at a screen that says zero messages. What's your name?"

She raised her hands and stepped back. She'd come in looking for help and had wound up the remedy for some cop's boredom instead. Unless, of course, the messages she could see as clearly as she could see the suspicion in his eyes weren't really there, and the episode from the morning hadn't passed at all.

"My mistake," she said. "You know, I think it was a different phone I was looking at. Thank you for your help, Officer. I'm sorry to have wasted your time."

She turned away and pushed through the precinct door, praying no one would follow. The phone went off again halfway down the steps and she froze. She glanced back toward the station and then slammed the device ten or twelve times against the frigid iron banister, until there was nothing left but a catastrophe of plastic and metal. She yanked the battery from its remains and shoved the mess back into her pocket before turning in the direction of the wireless store.

CHAPTER TWO

The kid fiddled with his Bluetooth earpiece as Patience refused to let him transfer her previous number to the new phone. He finally gave in after some discussion, and it wasn't until she asked whether it could be programmed not to receive calls at all that he became visibly annoyed.

"Why don't you just keep it turned off?"

"Because messages would still go to my inbox. I don't want them coming in at all."

He chewed on the tape covering his lip ring and frowned.

"I don't think there's a setting for that."

"Well, could you just get rid of the inbox for me? Delete it or something?"

"Delete the inbox?" He scratched his head. "I've never heard of anybody wanting to delete their inbox. I mean, how would you even do that?"

Her patience with the kid was wearing thin. "If I knew the answer to that, Eugene, I'd hardly need to call upon your expertise, now would I?"

He crossed his arms and shook a lock of faded green hair back from his eyes.

"No, I cannot delete the inbox. I also can't set the phone to self-destruct whenever a call comes in, and I can't program it to automatically electrocute anyone who adds your number to their contacts. There could be an update for that one down the road, though, so you might want to keep an eye on the website or something. Is there anything else I can help you with today?"

Patience smiled back at him. "You could disable the texting function for me, right? Or do I need to wait for an update for that as well?"

He tugged on his tie and leaned in a little closer. "Maybe you're not ready for a cell phone, ma'am. Landlines have way limited functionality, and they're a lot less convenient too."

Patience touched the dismembered carcass of her phone on the display case as she stared back at the kid barely two years younger than her who'd called her *ma'am* on the worst day of her life. He straightened and took a half step back as she brushed the phone's pieces onto his shoes.

"Do you have any other recommendations?"

He picked up her new phone and pressed its buttons deftly. "The texting is disabled now." He nodded. "And as an extra special treat, I've set your ringtone to silent and turned off all your message alerts. I'll ring you up at that register over there, if there's nothing else I can help you with."

"Super."

Patience reached to slide the new phone into her coat pocket, but the text and ringtone-disabled beast lit right up in her hand.

I M THE LORD UR GOD! :)

She stared down at the message, paralyzed in her tracks as pedestrians played chicken with the traffic on Harvard Avenue and a car alarm polluted the peace. A bus pulled up and she blinked at the passengers stepping off before looking down at the display again. Her fingers closed around it as she turned back to the brick façade of the store and smashed it until it was virtually unrecognizable from its predecessor. Then she stalked back inside and tossed the pieces onto the case in front of the startled kid.

"Change it again."

Patience sat on a bench in Ringer Park, contemplating her descent into mental illness. Perhaps more than any other facet, she was dismayed to discover such a dearth of creativity at the deepest recesses of her mind. So she was receiving messages from God now, like a million other schizophrenics before her. She'd have thought her psyche would have gone with someone edgier and a little less clichéd. Someone like Kurt Cobain or Dorothy Parker...Lenny Bruce, perhaps.

U DONT WNT 2 GIVE LENNY BRUCE ACCESS 2 UR HEAD!
TRST ME ON THT ONE!

She glared up at a passing cumulus cloud and deleted the messages. It chimed again and her face was hot in a flash. "Stop it! Can't you leave me alone for five damn minutes?"

A woman on a nearby bench looked up as Patience argued with the sky and she took a breath. She smiled back nicely and the woman returned to her book.

"Would you at least cool it with the texting?" She kept her voice low now. "It's obnoxious. If you won't get lost, then why don't you speak normally, like a proper hallucination, until I find someone to prescribe me something that'll make you go away?"

I DID SPEAK! U WUD NOT LISTN!

"You're right. I'm sorry. Mea-fucking-culpa! You've got my attention now, though, so you can go back to your regular voice anytime you're ready."

The phone remained dark and silent for a moment. Then it chimed at last.

NU IPHONE! GRATEST THNG SNCE YO-YO MA!
SRSLY...DID I DO THIS???

She dropped her face into her hands as it chimed away like a babbling toddler. Patience didn't care what intricate perversities were involved with mental illness, this was unconscionable. "You cannot be serious," she prayed. "Please tell me that you're joking."

ABOUT THT LAST PART, YEAH ...
WUDNT WNT 2 PISS OFF JOBS! ;)

The woman across the path stole another glance as Patience cursed and snapped the phone shut. Then, without a thought to what she was doing, she was on her feet with it thrust before the startled stranger's face.

"I'm very sorry to bother you, ma'am, but I need an outsider's opinion on something. This is too much, don't you think? I mean, I don't care if the guy does think he's God, it's bordering on harassment. I really don't feel I'm being overly sensitive or anything..."

The woman drew back. She appeared apprehensive about her role in the conversation.

"I'm sorry, I don't understand. Were you expecting a call?"

"God, no! I want the calls to stop!"

Patience pleaded silently with her to understand, and then, just as quickly, lowered the phone and backed away. She'd never understood why Uncle John hadn't kept his voices to himself. He knew that no one else could hear what he did, but he never seemed able to refrain from upsetting everybody by answering back. And now, here she was in a public park, demanding validation from a perfectly polite-looking stranger, and there seemed no stopping the momentum.

She closed her eyes and pressed her palms into her temples. She *could* stop the momentum; she *would* control this. She turned away before opening her eyes again, afraid of what she'd find in the woman's expression.

"I'm very sorry I disturbed you, ma'am. I'm sleep deprived and a little out of my mind at the moment. I'm pretty sure I'm not dangerous, or anything. I'll leave you to your book now." She left the park and waited until she was out of sight before pulling the chirping phone back out and hitting the power button.

"I'm done talking for today."

PATIENCE!

"Bite me, Biz."

She may be hearing voices, but that didn't mean she had to listen to them, and she sure as hell didn't have to do their bidding. Her will might be slightly fucked up at the moment, but it was still hers and it was still free.

PATIENCE!!

"What did I just tell you?" She stalked up Allston Street, shutting down text after text as she fumed at her hallucination's disregard for her personal space and boundaries.

PATIENCE!!!

HOLE!!!

She looked up just in time to avoid tumbling into a massive ditch in the sidewalk, six feet deep and more than two feet across, with nothing but a string of yellow tape attached to a few skinny sticks to protect the distracted or disabled from plummeting to a broken leg or worse. She stared down at the hole. She stared at the tape. She really wasn't sure how much more of this she had left in her to take.

She glared up at the sky and shouted. "What about *blind* people?!"

A man at the mailbox at the corner of Commonwealth Avenue gawked at her as she turned back to the street.

"I'm going to get drunk now," she warned the cloud. "Do not fucking follow me."

THER IS WRK 2 DO!

"I mean it."

CHAPTER THREE

Patience turned her glass in its condensation on the bar, her face propped in her hand. A guy approached from a few seats away, but she wasn't interested enough to look until he paused beside her and gaped.

"You're the girl..."

He looked a bit stunned, and she realized that she knew him. His familiarity seemed associated with some vague sense of guilt on her part. She shrugged back, wondering if maybe she'd cut past him on the train some night to grab the last seat—or one of the other crimes of impoliteness she was prone to committing when she was more tired than fair-minded—and had then felt badly enough to look in his direction more often than she might otherwise have. Whatever it was, she was certain about two things: She had been in the wrong, and he had not been nearly this inebriated.

"I'm what girl?"

The phone chirped and she stabbed a finger at the power button. The tequila wasn't having nearly the amnesic effect she'd been hoping for, and she was about ready to throw in the towel on the evening. She was mildly curious, however, and decided to give him another thirty seconds to illuminate her about how, precisely, she'd done him wrong.

He listed to one side and she grabbed him by the arms.

"Thank you."

"Look, if we're going to have a conversation, you're going to have to drop in something I can work with pretty soon, okay? Because, this really isn't doing it for me."

He reached for the back of her stool and smiled down into his glass.

"You're the girl from the window this morning."

Patience considered him seriously for the first time. She hooked her foot around a leg of the stool next to hers and slid it back from the bar.

"Right," she said. "I think I owe you a drink."

She shook her head as she signaled to Frank for another round.

"I'm sorry, but you really don't look like a Zane. Are you sure you've got that right?"

"My name?" He drained the last of his vodka and glanced sideways at her as he set the glass on the bar. "I'm pretty sure, yeah."

"Maybe you've misheard. Maybe your parents actually named you Wayne and they've been too polite to correct you all these years."

"My parents have not been too polite. Your phone is ringing again."

Patience lined up a row of cocktail nuts and flicked them, one by one, at the tip jar. She missed one hundred percent of the shots, but spotted herself two points for the peanut that plinked cleanly into a BU undergraduate's beer. The guy beside her was still trying to sort out what he'd seen that morning, even as they both avoided the question of what she'd been doing on the window ledge in the first place. She didn't begrudge him his need to work through it any more than she begrudged the undergrad the dirty look he shot her just before he hurled the dripping nut back and nailed her companion squarely in the forehead, but she really couldn't help either of them just then.

"But, if you didn't fall," he persisted, "and you didn't jump, and you weren't pushed, then how on Earth did you—"

"It's just that Zane sounds like a cowboy name or something."

He sighed and wiped at his forehead with a napkin. "Zane Grey," he said. "The author of about a thousand Westerns. My father couldn't get enough of them when he was younger. Getting tagged with the name Zane Grey Ellison doesn't follow a kid during his formative years, let me tell you." He dropped the napkin back onto the bar. "I suppose it could have been worse, though. My older brother's given name is Steve McQueen."

"Well, I still think you look more like a Wayne."

"That's not polite!"

Indignation sparked life into a face alcohol had rendered nearly incapable of maintaining an expression up until that point. She smiled at him for the first time and lifted her hands in surrender. His ire evaporated as Frank approached with their round.

"This is her, Frank; the one I was telling you about. This is the girl from the window."

The bar owner set their glasses down and crossed his arms over his chest. Patience shrank on her stool as he looked down at her.

"You're what's at the bottom of this, Patience? Christ, I mighta known."

She shoved a shock of pink back from her eyes and pulled her drink closer for protection.

"What have I done now? Damn, Frank, this is a hard room tonight."

"You've had this man so far off his mark today, I nearly had to bounce him twice, just to get some peace. No offense, Zane, but you've been a bit longwinded."

"None taken," he said. "You've been a pal, Frank. Really."

"I really haven't. And if you're hoping that being my goddaughter will save you from getting bounced yourself, Patience Abigail, think again. Well, my dear, seeing as you've been the cause of Zane's mysterious angst, I'm making him your responsibility. Quit with the theatrics and practical jokes and see to it that he gets safely back to wherever it is he goes at night. I've little faith he'll make it in one piece on his own."

Patience's phone lit up then and her godfather narrowed his eyes. "And whatever it is you've got cooking, you keep it out of my pub."

She lifted the phone from the bar and dropped it into her drink. A halting chime garbled to the surface, turned whiny, and then died.

"I'm trying, Frank. So help me, I am."

He closed his eyes for a moment and pointed to his cheek. She rose dutifully up onto the rungs of her stool and gave him a kiss.

"Call your mother tomorrow. You're way overdue."

Zane just blinked as she settled again and stared down at yet another hundred and twelve dollars she didn't have, resting at the bottom of her seven-dollar margarita.

"Frank is your godfather." It was more a statement than a question.

She sighed. "And he never forgets it for a second." She looked up again with a slight shrug. "My father was killed by a poorly secured truckload of kegs behind the pub when my mother was pregnant with me, so Frank takes this business of watching out for me pretty seriously."

"Jesus Christ."

She smiled at that. "He's a little overzealous, if you ask me. Especially when you consider the fact that my father shouldn't have been in that alley in the first place. Frank was constantly threatening to brain him with an andiron if he didn't stop picking up 'sweet deals' in Southie and supplementing the pub's inventory with them. But my family's always been a bit cracked when it comes to loyalty, and my father was extremely loyal to Frank. It had been that way since they were kids in Belfast. So he just ignored the threats and kept on helping him out, against Frank's wishes."

Zane sat quietly with for a moment, with his fingers curled around his glass. "I'm sorry about your father," he said. "My mother died when I was twelve. That's a hard thing."

Patience shook her head. "That's real loss. To me, my father's always just been someone who was missing from the lives of the people I loved. My mom did just fine with me, and I'm really not sure how much more of a father figure I could have taken beyond what I've had in Frank."

He laughed, and then a message alert chimed and her eyes flew to her drink. She exhaled as Zane pulled a sleek-looking phone from his coat and she reached over to steal his vodka.

He was quiet too long, so she set his half-empty glass down and looked up. He met her glance and then turned on his stool, as if checking the room for something or someone. Patience watched with a growing sense of apprehension as he turned back with a puzzled expression.

"I think it's for you."

She took the phone and dropped it into his drink, and then she stood up and reached for her cash. Zane stopped her and tossed a couple of bills onto the bar. He rose clumsily beside her with a side-long glance at the submerged phones.

"Bad breakup?"

She just grabbed him by the elbow and turned him toward the door without a word of goodbye to her godfather.

CHAPTER FOUR

Patience sat on her living room floor and considered the heap of mismatched linens on the couch. Somewhere in that pile of cotton and fleece was a Wayne—or a Zane as the case may be—and he seemed to be the only other person on Earth with the ability to witness her great hallucination, the Lord her God. Whether this development was evidence in support of her sanity or against his, however, remained to be seen.

"Zane."

She pressed her fingers to her temples. The room was silent, apart from the haranguing of her inner self for having chased copious amounts of tequila with vodka. She repeated his name a little louder and resigned herself to standing up.

As she approached the couch, she discovered that it wasn't so much that Zane was a quiet sleeper as it was that he was an absent one. She stared down at the blankets, and then her eyes darted to the still-bolted door. She turned next to the window above her fire escape, but nothing aside from the blankets seemed out of place. Could she have gone so far as to pull out linens for a man who didn't exist? She pushed them aside and dropped to the couch, searching her mind for some proof that she hadn't hallucinated their stumble back from O'Malley's. She could still feel the pressure of his arm around her shoulder and smell the booze and soap in his skin, but the memory of him wasn't enough. It wasn't reliable. She fought against surrendering to her mounting panic as she lqwered her face to her hand.

On the floor beside the couch lay a pair of men's sneakers. In the distance beyond the kitchen, she heard the toilet flush.

She closed her eyes and exhaled. Three weeks before, she'd at least have considered the obvious before assuming the fantastic, but those three weeks seemed like a lifetime ago now. The unreliability of her reality was crushing her.

Zane came barefoot through the kitchen and paused in the doorway. She lifted her face to look back at him and frowned. He was taller than she'd thought, and his T-shirt and jeans hung a lot better on him now that he wasn't slumped against a bar. He reminded her of a less emaciated, less twitchy Ian Curtis—if Ian had grown his hair out a bit and made it to the age of twenty-five alive. The inebriation had cleared from his face and was replaced now by a slight squint and tightening at his brow that suggested a headache on par with her own. He nodded a half-smile and she breathed a curse at the water-stained ceiling tiles. The Wayne of the previous evening had seemed a manageable enough dolt to contend with. The Zane of this morning, however, had an appreciable intelligence to his expression. He also had a runner's build, well-defined arms, and dark eyes that made her bite down on her lip a little too hard as they met hers from the doorway. This guy was the last thing in the world she needed.

He approached and she pushed the blankets aside. She kept her gaze forward as he sat down beside her and stared at the knees of his jeans. An embarrassed smile slid onto his face.

"I don't usually drink to make a fool of myself," he said. "I also don't make a habit of conning strange women into taking me home with them just to spare me the indignity of waking up behind the Twin Donuts covered in cat piss. That was out of character for me."

Patience laughed. "You were never going to make it to the Twin Donuts last night. Hell, you couldn't even tell me your apartment number. The alley behind O'Malley's was about as far as you were going to make it on your own." He glanced down again and Patience felt like an ass. His contrition left him toothless in the discussion and they both knew it. "Anyway, it was obvious that you weren't a habitual offender. You're pretty bad at it, for one thing."

"I suppose that's hard to argue."

She went to the kitchen for some aspirin, hitting the coffee maker on her way past. She paused before the sink, taking more time than necessary to fill the water glasses. She was feeling a bit toothless, herself, and hoped it didn't show. She had no intention of letting her guard down around this guy until she figured out who he was and what, precisely, his connection to her delusions was.

She returned to the living room and he took the aspirin from her gratefully.

"Now that I've been duly chastised for my behavior, would you please be so kind as to tell me what the hell is going on?"

It seemed a reasonable question, considering what he'd been through on her account over the past twenty-four hours.

"No," she said. "But I will buy you a new phone."

His eyes sparked and she backed up half a step. "I couldn't care less about the phone, Patience. Whatever it is that's bothering you, it's got my number now too. I think that entitles me to some information."

She was thrown by the directness of his appeal. And by his apparent confidence that it would be responded to. The confidence struck her as peculiar, however, rather than arrogant, and there was something unusual about the way he spoke as well. It was sort of as though he had an accent, but it wasn't exactly that. Zane Grey Ellison seemed less like the man she'd met at the pub with every passing moment, but she couldn't put her finger on the change.

"I couldn't help you if I wanted to, Zane. I'm sorry, but this is beyond my control."

"This isn't some sort of prank, is it Patience? You're not just entertaining yourself, or screwing around with me for kicks or the attention?"

She choked back a gasp and a laugh together. He didn't sound hostile or accusing, nor did he appear to be joking. "What on Earth are you talking about? I'd never laid eyes on you until yesterday morning. What could I possibly have against you?"

"Nothing, I hope. Actually, I was hoping you might help me put some things into perspective, but it's often been pointed out to me that I'm not as careful as I ought to be. So, if you are having a laugh at my expense, I'd appreciate it if you'd let me in on it now and I'll be on my way."

She didn't know how to respond to that. He shrugged and reached for his shoes.

"What kinds of things?"

He turned back and set the shoes on the table. That look of total confidence from just moments before seemed to have evaporated, but he didn't appear to miss it. Patience was starting to feel disoriented.

"Like how I can be absolutely certain that what I saw you do outside your window yesterday morning is impossible. Also, I still can't put that call to my phone into any context that makes sense to me, and I'm a reasonably intelligent person. I graduated *summa cum laude* from Harvard with degrees in philosophy and religion, and I am about to feel like a complete ass for telling you that. I was a pretty decent guy until yesterday morning, Patience. What the hell have you done to me?"

She reached for his arm and he stopped talking. He looked so earnest, and she wanted so much to help him. But how could she explain what she couldn't understand, or help him understand what she couldn't accept?

"If you can't work it out after four years at Harvard, Wayne, I don't think there's anything more I can do."

He nodded and removed her hand from his arm.

"Fair enough, Patience. Goodbye. Thank you for the use of your couch."

She tried not to watch as he got himself back together and started for the door. She was glad that he was leaving and sorry to see him go.

He paused with his hand on the knob and looked back. "Please do me just one favor, though, would you? Watch it around the open windows."

"You bet."

A tortured bleat emanated from his coat as he pulled the door open. He froze at the threshold and turned back, reaching into his pocket with equal parts suspicion and trepidation in his expression. A brick of lead formed in Patience's gut as he withdrew a margarita-sticky cell phone and his lips fell apart. Then he closed them and returned to set it on the table between them.

"What the hell is that?"

She glanced up, and Zane Grey Ellison looked confident of nothing in the world. She gestured down to the cell she'd made damn sure was still submerged when they'd left O'Malley's the night before.

"That, Zane, is the physical manifestation of my schizophrenia. Either that or it's God. Take your pick."

Zane ignored the periodic chirps and bleats as he scrolled back through the messages.

"God likes emoticons."

"Yes," she replied. "He does."

He shook his head at some of The Biz's less decipherable stabs at text speak and turned it off when he came to the end at last.

"Who do you think is doing this?"

"I think I am."

He raised an eyebrow at her. "If you were schizophrenic, you'd just be schizophrenic. You wouldn't be trying to bully yourself and your hallucinations into believing that you were, and I certainly wouldn't be able to see any of this."

"I've been thinking about that." She tugged at a torn bit of the blanket, wrapping the errant threads around her index finger until its tip turned as purple as her mood. "I believe you might be schizophrenic, too, Zane. I'm really sorry about that."

He laughed and set the phone back down. "I'm not schizophrenic, Patience, and neither are you. Which brings us to your second theory."

"Don't be absurd."

"I think I earned the right to be as absurd as I like the moment your hallucination called my cell phone."

He leaned back as the threads she was tugging ripped a gash up the side of the blanket.

"What the hell is wrong with you? You noticed a girl on a window ledge yesterday morning and you *waved* at her. Now you're sitting here, calmly trying to determine whether it's reasonable to assume that I've been receiving text messages from an iPhone-obsessed God— as if that's no more unexpected than spam email or a fundraising call from the Fraternal Order of Police. Does none of this strike you as even a little over-the-top? Because, frankly, Wayne, it's freaking me out."

He glanced up for the briefest moment, and then a strange look passed over his face. "I suppose I might be slightly more accustomed to the over-the-top than the average person," he said. "My life, until recently, was spent in an environment most would probably consider fairly surreal."

He appeared uncertain about elaborating further.

"Were you raised by circus performers or something?"

"No." He paused. "My father is Rutherford Ellison."

Patience busied herself with collecting the aspirin and water glasses from the table.

"You've heard of him, then?"

A few drops of water sloshed from a glass as she turned back to face him. "Of course I've heard of him, Zane. I may not be the most tuned-in person in the world, but I'm not unconscious."

He dropped an arm over his eyes and leaned back, then caught her wrist to prevent her return to the kitchen. Patience exhaled and turned back again. She hadn't meant to be rude or to make him feel self-conscious, but he kept catching her off guard. She was also a little intimidated by him now, and that irritated her as well. It was just money, for crying out loud—that and the inalienable power and prestige that fortressed the Ellison name. As if the guy wasn't trouble enough already.

"I wasn't trying to impress you," Zane said. "Which is good, of course, because it's obvious that I haven't. I was just trying to clarify that if I seem a little less thrown by unusual occurrences than others tend to be, it's probably because I'm still acclimating to the everyday world. I've only just moved up from Hyannis, and at least half of what I encounter tends to strike me as somewhat unusual. I'm learning to roll with the punches when the dots don't seem to connect, Patience, because nine times out of ten, the piece that's missing between those dots is with me."

She just stared back at him. "I thought you said you went to Harvard."

"I did."

"You weren't able to get some sense of the everyday world after four years in Cambridge?"

"I didn't live in Cambridge. I lived in Hyannis, where I pretended to manage banks in my off hours. That was the deal I struck with my father—I could live anywhere I liked while pursuing a field of study that would advance me toward an MBA or law degree or I could live at home and commute while gaining work experience if I insisted upon studying inane drivel like philosophy and religion."

Patience pulled on a smile and sat awkwardly beside him again. There was too much about Zane that she couldn't understand, and she was trying so hard not to like him.

"Well, it was admirable of you to stick to your convictions."

He shrugged.

"It was the single stupidest decision I've ever made in my life. I threw away four years of freedom over a pissing match with my father. I could have studied all the philosophy and religion I wanted through elective courses and free access to the world's largest academic library. No one's ever died from understanding business or the law. In fact, a degree like that might even come in handy someday, if I ever figure out what I want to do with my life."

She stared down at the gummy mess on the coffee table. She'd really liked this response from him, although she wasn't entirely clear why. Finally, she stifled a sigh and looked up again. "Is it strange that I didn't recognize you?"

"Not at all." He didn't sound terribly convincing. "There's a lot to be said for juxtaposition. Allston can be pretty good camouflage when I want it to be." He paused and looked down as a wry smile slid onto his face. "My name tends to ring a bell with most people, though."

"I'm sorry."

"Don't apologize."

She chewed on her lower lip. Something wasn't coming together for her. "If that's true, Zane, and you're trying to fly under the radar here in Allston, then why on Earth did you make such a big deal out of telling me your name last night?"

He shrugged at the threadbare rug with a sheepish expression.

"Because last night I *was* trying to impress you."

She turned back to the kitchen, heartless to his dismayed expression. Members of the Ellison family didn't get caught sunbathing nude on remote islands or fall down in VIP rooms. They sat on the boards of humanitarian organizations and donated art to museums. The sons of Rutherford Ellison most certainly did not move out to dingy apartments in Allston, and they didn't trouble themselves about the opinions of a waitress on the verge of a mental breakdown. Patience had never been a gullible girl, so the fact that she hadn't yet doubted a word this man had said seemed proof enough that she was insane.

At least he wasn't texting her.

She paused before the sink. "What happened to it, if you don't mind me asking? Did you lose it in the stock market or something?"

There was no response for a moment as she stared down into the two-day-old dishes. Then he appeared in the doorway.

"To the money?" he asked. "Nothing's happened to it. It's safe and diverse and being very well cared for, I can assure you of that. I turned twenty-five recently, and a greater degree of freedom has become available to me. I've chosen to exercise it, that's all."

"You've chosen to exercise it in Allston?"

"Why not?" He glanced at the untouched coffee mugs on the counter. "I didn't want to live on Beacon Hill, and other than the really dodgy parts you read about in the papers, I wasn't familiar enough with the neighborhoods of Boston to know which areas I might find interesting enough to want to live in. So I opened up the *Apartments for Rent* section in the paper and set my finger down on a listing. It's worked out pretty well, in my opinion. The apartment is right on the Green Line and O'Malley's is just around the corner. What's not to like?"

She laughed, despite herself, and poured the coffee at last. He pounced on his mug like a starving man on a free filet mignon.

"Well, it gets way too much wireless coverage for my tastes." Patience sighed. She was quiet a moment, and then she turned back. "So how long has it been, exactly, since you ditched the family compound for the mean streets of Allston?"

"It's an estate, actually," Zane replied. "It's not a compound. There are outbuildings, of course, but just one primary residence." He squeezed his eyes shut then, as the pink crept up from his collar. Then he shook it off and continued. "It'll be three weeks ago tomorrow. I'm starting to feel like one of the locals."

She took the cup back from his hand and turned to the sink again. Three weeks ago tomorrow was the very day a strange voice had broken into her head and refused to go away. She didn't know what was happening, but she needed Zane to leave.

The phone bleated and she ran past him to the living room. A picture of Joey Forsyth appeared on the screen, shimmering in all his Plasticine and porcelain glory. And that's when Patience broke.

"That is it! I'm out. I can't take this one second more!"

She threw the window up and leaned out into the wind. Zane leapt and pulled her back, stumbling as his foot caught the corner of the table and they fell together to the floor. He lay frozen above her for a moment, breathing into her hair as his wits returned, and then he scrambled back with his neck glowing approximately the color of her hair.

Patience pulled herself up to sit with the sticky phone still in her hand. She stared down at it and then held it up for him to see.

"I was only going to litter."

CHAPTER FIVE

Patience sat alone in a booth at Murray's Diner, thumbing impatiently through a gossip magazine. Zane had promised to be quick, but he'd been gone over thirty minutes, and it had been at least twenty-five since she'd lost interest in her reading material.

The bell above the door jangled and a pristine new cell phone skidded across the table.

"What the hell is that?"

He slid onto the bench across from her, grabbed a menu from the holder, and opened it.

"That's your new phone. Please try not to break it."

He ignored her glares, keeping his attention on the breakfast choices as a look of wonder spread over his face. Patience slapped her hand down in the middle of his perusing.

"I never agreed to a new phone, Zane. What's going on here? Are you on His side, now?"

"Am I on His side?" He nudged her hand away with the backs of his fingers. "He's the fucking Lord, for Christ's sake, so yes, Patience, I suppose you could say I'm on His side. What is *hash*, exactly? Would I like it?"

"Do you like greasy lumps of starch mixed in with your mutilated meat products?"

He looked back up without a trace of irony in his expression. "I really couldn't say. I've never tried either."

She tossed the weekly toward him. "You're not even in this one."

He didn't even glance at the magazine's cover. "I should think not."

"For crying out loud, Zane, what is wrong with you? Even if I accept that it's the Lord or God or Whoever-the-Hell that's been harassing me these past few weeks, His great plan, thus far, seems to be hinged upon torturing me with text speak and beaming me pictures of douchey, has-been, boy band singers. Schizophrenia is the lesser evil, as far as I'm concerned. How can you support this?"

"I know Joey Forsyth." Zane nodded. "And douchey doesn't begin to describe him. Joey and Alexander Rockwell have been trying to get in thick with my family since his unfortunate Boi II Boi heyday, and they've been particularly gross about it since their attention shifted to politics."

"Who is Alexander Rockwell?"

He looked up from the menu. "Alex was Joey's business manager and the mastermind behind Boi II Boi. Now he's his business manager, campaign manager, chief strategist, and primary spokesman. The common term for Alex's role in Joey's life, I believe, is puppet master. Joey doesn't take a piss without Alex's say-so."

"Oh." Patience looked down. "That makes me feel sort of sad, actually."

"Well, that's a waste of a perfectly good pout. Someone's got to tell Joey what to do, and at least with them always together, I can avoid them as a unit. Alex's aspirations toward my father's endorsement run toward pathological, and Joey's not far behind him there. I need a spatula to scrape the ooze from my clothes whenever I run into either one of those guys. I will say this for Alex, however—he's good at what he does. I don't care how many pockets they're living in, I'd have bet my entire trust fund that Joey's first run at the state senate was going to end in spectacular defeat. Good thing for me I'm not a betting man, because, clearly, I was wrong."

"Joey Forsyth is a state senator?"

Zane closed the menu at last and leaned in across the table. "Former boy band sensation is elected to the Massachusetts State Senate, and this is the first you're hearing of it? He's in his second term, Patience, and he's making a pretty heated run at the U.S. Senate as we speak. These have not been media-quiet campaigns."

She shrugged.

"Politics bore me. And so do boy bands."

"Well, you might want to get interested in this. Joey Forsyth is a moron, but Alexander Rockwell is anything but. They're connected to a lot people with a lot of money, and they haven't got a scruple to split between them. If God wants you on this, I think you'd better—"

"Didn't Joey Forsyth claim to be from the projects, but it turned out that he grew up in Needham or something?"

A resigned look set into Zane's face. He shook his head and signaled for their waitress.

"Your geography's off, but I believe you're thinking of Vanilla Ice. The members of Boi II Boi were very rich and very white, and they weren't at all shy about getting up in your face about either of those things. It was pretty devious packaging, considering what was coming out of Boston at the time. That's Alex for you, though. He's been slapping a new label on Joey and selling him off as the latest thing ever since they were kids."

The waitress set their coffees down and Patience ordered her omelet. She sighed, then, as Zane started in on the first of a hundred questions, and she resolved to be more responsive to his inquiries in the future, for the sake of expediency. She did note that the waitress didn't seem at all put off by the grilling, despite the busy lunch rush.

The phone chimed as he finished, and Patience shut it off. Zane reached across the table and closed her fingers around its case. "Joey could very well win this thing next Tuesday," he said. "I, for one, would like to know why God is putting him on your radar. Please stop screening His calls, Patience. You need to answer the damn phone."

She pulled back and he released her hand.

"I disagree."

"Well then." He shrugged. "Maybe we've finally figured out why I'm here."

If The Biz wanted her attention, He had it now. Even Zane's enthusiasm for the fare of the common man expired as they studied the messages He sent between the corned beef hash and his order of Eggs Ala Murray. Joey Forsyth might be a douche bag, but he was a douche bag caught in the eye of a perfect storm of selfishness, stupidity, and influence—a lit match hovering at the tip of a long and inextinguishable fuse, the other end of which lay embedded in the Powder Keg of Doom. Or, to put it more succinctly, the world would end in ten years' time and Joey Forsyth started it.

Patience pushed the phone back across the table.

"No," she said. "Sorry, Wayne, but I'm out. This one's all yours."

He picked it up again and slid around to her side of the booth as she locked her eyes on the world passing outside. She'd never regretted an omelet more.

"This is serious."

"This is a lie. It's a sick prank, being pulled by a sick person. If you fall for it, Zane, you're even more delusional than I am."

"You wouldn't be the first to suggest that."

She glanced back at him and was surprised to see that he'd turned a little gray himself. His face was determined, though, and he kept at it, catching the texts and images as they came in. As hard as she tried, Patience couldn't quite keep her eyes from wandering back to the multimedia horror show unfolding between them.

As his first official order of business, U.S. Senator Joseph M. Forsyth would add an amendment to an already sponsored, publicly popular, miraculously bipartisan, renewable energy bill. The amendment called for the construction of a revolutionary new type of power plant, the first of which was currently in development by SolarTech Industries (the same SolarTech Industries that had been channeling money into the Forsyth Campaign's hopper through third party donations since his first term in the Massachusetts General Court). The success of these plants would exceed even SolarTech's expectations, harnessing more energy by the second than any previous source of solar energy, for a fraction of the cost of fossil fuels.

The waste being emitted into the Earth's atmosphere by the process they'd developed to separate the electrons from their atoms in the composition of the solar cells would not be detected until the damage was irreversible. The first casualty would be the polar ice caps, resulting in tsunamis and flooding across all seven continents. The receding waters would leave pestilence and disease behind, and earthquakes and fires would come next. By the time the Earth finally burned itself out, there would be no one left to mourn for it. The changes in the planet's atmosphere would render it incapable of sustaining life within seven years of the first plant's grand opening.

And God was looking to an ill-equipped, short-tempered, twenty-three-year-old waitress from Allston to do something about it. His recommendation was a grenade launcher to get the job done quickly and efficiently (an M32 ought to do the trick), and He was even so helpful as to text her the address of the corporation's exploration and development laboratory.

Patience pushed herself into the corner of the booth as nausea menaced her equilibrium. Zane sat very still beside her, staring down into the screen with the look of a man who'd just been bitten by his own dog. She shook her head at his expression, her throat constricting with the sting of angry tears, and then the phone was in her hand again, thrust up toward the ceiling.

"What the hell is wrong with You?" she demanded of the grease stains. "I'm a waitress, for crying out loud. And not some radioactive, ninja waitress, I'm just the regular kind. Last time I checked, we didn't store grenade launchers in the cellar, Biz. We need that space for the pickles."

RADIOACTVE NINJA WAITRSS! LOL!

I SHUD MAKE 1 OF THOSE! :)

She cast the phone to the table with a look usually reserved for mean drunks and bad tippers. "Joke all You want, but You've picked the wrong girl to try to get Your Old Testament on with. As far as I'm concerned, the fact that You'd even request a thing like this is proof that I've been right about You all along." She ducked beneath the table to free herself of Zane and the Agent of Destruction on the tabletop before him, pulling herself back up on the other side. "There are plenty of people in the world who'd be happy to kill for the Lord, Zane. I'd expect Him to know who they are. Whatever it is in that phone, that's not my God."

PATIENCE!

She grabbed it again and Zane took her hand before she could hurl it to the floor.

"That's not my God, either, Patience. I think you may have been right about this being a prank. I had no idea I was so easy to get one over on." He looked down. "It's useful information, I suppose, if humbling."

The phone cut her off from responding.

WHO SED ANYTHNG ABOUT KILLNG?

THOU SHALT NOT KILL!

Zane straightened as Patience gaped down at the screen.

"What the hell? But He said..."

THOU SHALT ALSO NOT PUT WORDS INTO MY MOUTH!
NOT A DROP OF BLOOD SHALL B SPILT BY UR HANDS
I NEED UR HELP, BUT NO BLOOD!

Patience thrust the phone back at Zane and grabbed her bag from the bench. "You know what, Zane? I think I just might be sane, after all, and it's God who's the fucking schizophrenic."

He stared mutely down at the screen, but some of the color seemed to be returning to his face. Patience looked away.

"Leave it alone, would you, please? It's not healthy."

"Just stay a little longer, Patience, please. I want to see what else He has to say."

"Do you have any idea what it's like in a lab like SolarTech's? People work around the clock. When I blow up a building, I try to respect the fact that I'm blowing up everything and everyone inside it as well. Not a drop of blood shall be spilled? Christ, Zane, does He know what a grenade launcher does?"

There was a faintly strained quality to the phone's next chirp.

IT LAUNCHES GRENADES, IIRC
NUTHNG IS IMPOSSBLE UNLSS U DO NOT TRY

She backed away from the table. "That's an excellent point, Biz. And what I'm trying to do right now is walk out that door."

"Patience," Zane said. "Please?"

She turned back and leaned low over the table to look into his eyes.

"Has it occurred to you that this could be something else altogether? We're talking about politics and big business, here. Those are two things I know nothing about, but those who do know about them seem to find your family very compelling. This could be the work of people we really don't want to screw with. We need to get rid of that thing and just leave this whole mess alone."

He shook his head.

"I'm sorry, Patience, but I can't. I don't expect this to make sense to you, but I don't remember a time when I've ever gotten worked up about somebody trying to mess with me. When I've had a problem in the past, I've tried to take care of it myself. When that inevitably didn't work out as I'd hoped it would, I went and had a conversation with Ed from my father's security force about it. Then, I ate a sandwich. That's the way problems are handled in my family, and it'd been one-hundred-percent effective until I met you. I don't think I can walk away from this. I can't explain it, but there hasn't been a moment since we met when it's occurred to me that I should go and talk to Ed. I just don't believe this is something he can help me with."

She crossed her arms and looked away.

"What's this Ed's number? He sounds like a handy guy to have around." He didn't respond and she nodded. "Frankly, Zane, I don't care if this is big business at work, or the Big Guy, or some twenty-eight-year-old sitting in his mother's basement. I'm sorry, but I'm out. I hit my limit a grenade launcher ago."

She paused at the exit long enough to glance back at him before she pushed the door open. "You seem like a really good guy, Zane, and you've got that trusting thing going for you. I'm sure you'd make one hell of a martyr. For what it's worth, though, I hope you don't."

"One, please."

"Which movie?"

Patience glanced up at the endless list of titles, until they blurred together in her fatigue.

"I'll just take whatever's starting next."

The girl behind the counter wore a bored expression and a name tag that read "Bradley." She scratched at a bit of chipped purple nail polish and waited, so Patience sighed and ceded Bradley the battle. She stepped back for a better look and screamed. The titles were all the same.

Are You There, Patience? It's Me, God.

The crowd behind her stared as she raised a hand to her forehead. "I'm sorry," she said. "I think I just ate a bee."

Bradley recoiled in her booth, finally showing some sign of life. Patience noticed a small child at the feet of the woman behind her and turned to her. She looked smart enough, and she was at least polite enough not to be glaring.

"Hi, Honey." Patience crouched down. "You seem pretty advanced for your age. Do you see a movie about God up there in those pretty red lights? Or how about a message for me? My name is Patience. Do you see anything like that?"

"Mommy!"

The child's mother whipped the whimpering toddler up into her arms and charged to the ticket window, demanding to see the manager.

The front door of the Boston-West Mental Health Center fell closed behind her and Patience blinked into the late afternoon sun. Then she straightened at the sight of Zane, sitting halfway down the steps with his arms at his knees and the phone dangling from one hand.

"Couldn't go through with it?"

She'd waited nearly two hours to be seen emergently by the psychiatrist on call, only to walk right back out again the moment her name was called. She felt it was impolite of him to know that.

"I will," she said. "When it gets bad enough. And I don't appreciate you following me."

He laughed and held the phone up without turning back.

"If this isn't it, Patience, I hope I never find out what your definition of 'bad enough' is. Come on, you must have figured out by now that you're not crazy. And I didn't follow you, I found my way here the same way I found myself compelled to take in the scenic wonders of Comm Ave with my coffee yesterday morning and the same way I found myself compelled to get drunker than I've ever been in my life at your godfather's pub, only to be placed in your custody. Losing control's not my thing, I don't do that. Do you really believe it's an accident that when I finally did, it occurred at O'Malley's?"

"I can't think of a more suitable place, actually."

He kept his back to her. "I sat for a while after you left the diner, having no Earthly idea what I should do next, and then I started walking. I came upon this staircase, and I sat down to wait for you. Here you are, end of story."

She dropped down onto the top step and he crawled up to sit beside her. A couple of women in scrubs stepped from the center and they moved aside to let them pass. Then Zane held the phone out.

"I don't want That. You've got a lot more patience with It than I have, and It likes you better, anyway. We'll probably all live longer, happier lives if you'd just hang on to It."

He shook his head at her with a sigh. "You do understand that it's not the phone that's communicating with you, don't you, Patience?"

"I'm not the one with the fancy degrees from Harvard. This is your area of expertise."

"That's religion, Patience. This is God."

She looked away. The women in scrubs had turned down Brighton Avenue, laughing over a shared joke. It occurred to her then that she didn't want them to die in some massive SolarTech flame out. She pushed her hair behind her ears and held a hand out for the phone.

"I accept and agree to nothing."

"Understood," he said. "But we really do need to talk. Can we go somewhere?"

She groaned. "What, now? Sober?"

Zane's eyes widened and he took her by the arm. He turned his sights toward the pub.

"Good God, Patience. I'm not a monster."

CHAPTER SIX

Patience dropped her hand onto the bar and fought the urge to let her head follow. She was exhausted from explaining herself, and doubly so from repeating herself.

"I'm sorry, but I can't accept that a plan this irresponsible could be by the Lord's design. It reads like a special Apocalypse episode of *I Love Lucy* or something. I hated that fucking show, Zane. I want nothing to do with this."

He started to respond, but she cut him off with an accusing finger pointed at the phone.

"How can He not understand that I'm the worst possible choice for this? I don't know anything about politics or solar power technology or grenade launchers, and I don't want to know about them. I'm not even religious. He's God, for crying out loud. He's got armies. He's got zealots. He's got armies of zealots. He doesn't need an agnostic waitress from Allston. What the hell is He thinking?"

The phone chimed in and she turned it face down on the bar. Zane sighed and took a drink of his vodka.

"Have you considered asking Him that?"

"Asking Him what?"

"What the hell He's thinking? Why He wants you? He's right there, Patience."

She lowered her eyes as the tequila sanded down the sharper edges of her mind. When she looked up again, he was still watching her, and he appeared disproportionately sober. Then she remembered that she was ahead of him by nearly two-drinks-to-one, so that was all right. She was glad he was sober, actually. Zane Grey Ellison was turning out to be a pretty responsible guy, for a guy who'd never had much of anything to be responsible for. He was nice too, and getting nicer by the margarita. She was certain he'd never replace the word *to* with a 2 or LOL at her. Patience liked that about him. That and his ass.

"I'm sorry, what were we talking about?"

He touched his fingers to her hand to prevent her from lifting her glass again. "We were talking about what it is that's preventing you from asking The Biz why He's tagged you for this mission."

"Oh, that." She shrugged. "I'm not speaking to Him."

"Why not?"

"Because I'd like to avoid getting smited, if at all possible. I'd also like to skip the eternal fires of hell, or waking up in a bed full of locusts."

"I'm pretty sure you made that last one up, but I hear you. I'm not sure I see how ignoring Him is going to help you—"

"Just look at our history so far. Look, I'll do my best to respond when I can figure out what He's getting at with all this texting nonsense, but I sincerely feel that it's safest for everyone involved if we restrict our personal contact to the barest minimum."

He stared back for a moment, then released her hand so she could take that drink at last.

"Let me see if I've got this straight. You're comfortable talking back to Him and smashing up His designated means of communication whenever you don't like what He's got to say, and you certainly aren't the least bit shy about taking His name in vain, even when speaking directly to Him, but you won't ask Him why He wants you to blow up the SolarTech Industries Exploration and Development Laboratory, and you won't ask Him why He feels so strongly that you, specifically, are the best girl to prevent the Apocalypse?"

"We all have our comfort zones, Zane. As far as I'm concerned, the less I know about His motivations, the better off I'll be."

He sighed and Patience smiled down at her margarita. Zane's face was so sincere, and his hair was so floppy. With a little more hair gel, and a lot less money, he'd make one hell of a Calvin Klein ad, sitting there with his hand on his drink and a thousand-and-one unasked questions swimming around in those dark-brown eyes.

"So, I gather that prayer is out of the question?"

She smiled and bumped that count back to a thousand.

"Of course not, Zane. Knock yourself out."

Her voice trailed off as her attention was captured by something down the bar. She squinted through the haze and a whole new countenance came over her being. For the first time in weeks, Patience felt something close to hope.

Zane followed her stares and worry lines deepened in his forehead. She ignored them and grabbed him by the arm.

"What are the odds of that? It's a sign, Zane. The Biz finally realizes that He dialed the wrong number after all, and now He needs our help to forward the call. Now, that is a job I'm up for. Let's not keep Him waiting."

Zane's back remained turned to the priest in his clergy shirt and clerical collar sitting a few stools down the bar. He pulled his arm from her grasp as Patience jumped down.

"Patience, this is Boston. Two things you'll find in abundance here are priests and bars. There's no reason their paths shouldn't cross on occasion. That's not a sign; that's a man reading his paper over a beer. Please, leave him alone."

The phone chimed and Patience took it from him and shoved it into her coat pocket.

"The Biz hasn't exactly been cryptic with you thus far," Zane said. "A detail that would have the College of Cardinals tying nooses in their rosaries if they knew. Would you at least see what He's got to say before you charge up to an unsuspecting priest and try to rope him into doing your chores?"

She shook him off and turned away. He'd already killed her buzz, she wouldn't let him kill her conviction. "Everything's going to be all right, Zane. I'm nauseous and my ears are ringing, and that says God to me. Stay here if you don't want to help."

She pushed her way through a throng of Boston College students and paused beside the freshman sitting next to her target. He looked up with an expression of optimistic surprise, until she whispered something into his ear and he slid his fake ID back toward his pocket and pretended to notice someone more interesting across the pub.

"Excuse me, Father. May I speak with you for a moment?"

The priest was youngish—perhaps in his mid to late forties—and he appeared to be in reasonably good shape. He turned to her with a bemused smile and refolded his section of newspaper.

"Of course, my dear. Please, have a seat."

Zane approached as she was introducing herself. She ignored the cautioning hand on her shoulder and introduced him as well.

"Rick Conner," the priest replied. "It's nice to meet you both."

"Do you work at one of the churches around here, Father Rick?"

He shook his head and took a sip of beer. "I don't have a parish, Patience. I run St. Mark's Shelter in Dorchester."

She beamed at Zane and he gestured no. Father Rick cocked his head at the exchange.

"Are you interested in the Church, Patience?"

"No, I'm interested in you. Running a homeless shelter sounds like very demanding work—physically as well as mentally and spiritually. You probably have to keep in pretty good shape to do a job like that, right?"

"I'm sorry, I don't think I understand what you're—"

"Well, you must get all kinds down there. I figure it probably gets a little dicey at times, with so much hard luck bumping up against itself at such close quarters, day in and day out. I was curious whether you receive any special training to do what you do."

He raised an eyebrow at the question, but then shrugged it off. "We have our moments. There are generally a couple of challenging cases around at any given time, but that's an important part of our role, Patience. St. Mark's doesn't exist just to nourish and shelter the body, we nourish and shelter the soul as well. Anyway, I've found that people generally mean well, even when they're at their worst. They're usually just depleted. It's our job to help them locate the enrichment they need."

"That's nice," Patience said. "But say you had to protect yourself from some maniac with a knife, or to save a room full of nuns or something, before you could hit him with the religion and the nutri-ents. You could bring it, right?"

Father Rick paused with his glass midair. Then he lowered it and glanced around the room before beckoning her closer. "The Vatican frowns upon priests sharing classified information with civilians, Patience. I'm sorry, but I'm sure you understand." He winked at her. "My divinity school did have a fight club in the basement. But, of course, I can't talk about that either."

She turned back to Zane and said, "See?" before returning her atten-tion to the priest. "I think what I admire most is your faith. Not every-one has that, or would know what to do with it if they did. Take me, for example. I just can't seem to figure that sort of stuff out. I definitely don't think I'd be a good instrument for God's will, if you know what I mean."

"We all have our purpose, Patience. If God sees fit to—"

Her phone chimed and she silenced it with an apologetic wave. Then she took the priest by the arm. "Here's the thing, Father Rick. God's been a little...up in my business lately. He's got it stuck in His head that I should perform a specific task for Him, and it's not some-thing I feel at all qualified to do. I'm better suited for what I'm doing now, which is waitressing. Being a soldier of the Lord is serious busi-ness, and it should be handled by a serious person. So, when I noticed you sitting over here, I couldn't help thinking that what He *really* needs is help locating a better candidate for the job, someone who's maybe prepared for this sort of thing all his life, and who's already got a positive working relationship established with Him. Then I could go back to waitressing, which is an area where I feel I can actually do some good."

From the ruckus in her pocket, she might well have stashed a tiny marching band inside. Zane stepped between them and reached a hand for her arm.

"Patience, please. It's time we stopped."

The priest pulled him back and studied Patience with a heavy look on his face.

"When you say that God has been 'up in your business lately,' what do you mean by that?"

The chimes died mid-tone as Zane crossed his arms and looked down at her alongside the priest. She felt a third, omnipresent, set of eyes staring as well and the scrutiny was unbearable.

"Miss Kelleher, are you suggesting that God speaks to you?" She reached for her drink, but he stopped her hand. He was turning a bit pale as he recaptured her gaze. "Do you mean to say that He speaks to you directly?"

Patience's heart fell and her lip followed in its wake as she stared up at the need to know—and the desperation to dismiss—stamped so candidly into his face. She nodded and pulled her hand free of his grasp. Zane had been right, of course. This wasn't going at all as she'd intended.

"In the beginning, He did, but I ignored Him because I thought I was only schizophrenic. So now, He's a little more creative with His methods, but, yes, He speaks to me directly. I'm sorry I bothered you with this, Father Rick. I'm pretty confused about the whole mess, and I've had more than my share of tequila. If I've been rude, or blasphemous in any way, I sincerely apologize."

She turned to go, but he reached for her arm again. His aftershave mingled with the scent of beer and honest work as he pulled her back to face him.

"I have prayed my entire adult life to discover God's plan for me and sought new ways of serving Him. I have taken a vow of poverty. I have taken a vow of chastity. I've devoted my whole life to the Church. And now you're telling me that when He needed something here on Earth, He overlooked my devotion and years of steadfast servitude, and turned instead to the pink-haired non-believer in the Buzzcocks T-shirt sitting three stools down the bar from me?"

"Oh."

His grip tightened and Zane stepped forward again. This time, he blocked the priest's attempts to hold him off and it was Patience who held him back. She looked up to face Father Rick's incredulity full on, but he just laughed and released her.

"The only thing more absurd than what you've just told me is the fact that I believe you." He turned his face to the bar. "Can either of you explain that part to me? Your story is clearly absurd, and I'm not a stupid man. Why on Earth do I believe you?"

A bead of sweat broke free of his hairline and Patience looked back at Zane. She looked to the phone next but, for once, neither seemed to have any advice for her. She touched the wrecked clergyman's sleeve and he flinched.

"You shouldn't believe me, Father. I'm a liar, that's all. I'm sorry."

The swinging door banged at the end of the bar as Frank pushed through with a keg in his arms. He nodded hello to Father Rick, then stopped in his tracks as the priest's expression registered. He set the keg down on the floor mat and turned to face his goddaughter.

"I've been gone less than ten minutes, Patience. What have you done now?"

She looked from Father Rick to Frank, and then she turned her eyes down to her hands.

"We were just having a conversation. I wasn't trying to upset anyone."

The priest touched a napkin to his forehead and drained the last of his beer as the three stood by helplessly. He rose from his stool and turned back to Zane.

"You seem like a fairly forthright man. Would I be wise to believe that this young lady is a liar?"

Frank saved Zane the trouble of responding.

"You would not, Father Rick. My goddaughter is truthful to a fault. It'd be a blessing if she'd learn to lie on occasion, quite frankly. It would save the rest of us a lot of anguish and confusion. Whatever atrocity she's been confessing to you, I'm afraid she's got to own it."

The priest dropped a couple of bills onto the bar and turned toward the door without another word. Patience felt like a murderer, watching him push his way through the crowd.

"Have you considered that I might just be insane?" she yelled after him. "I lied about being a liar, didn't I? And to a priest! What kind of a person does a thing like that?"

The pub's door slammed shut behind him, and Father Rick was gone.

Patience stared listlessly down at the water Frank had set in place of her confiscated margarita. She'd been trying to end the evening forever, but Zane kept right on talking and The Biz was more revved up than ever about SolarTech and its lab.

He chimed in again, and a new image appeared on the screen. She pressed her lips closed and banished it with the others.

"Would You cool it with the Apocalypse shots? If You're that hot for a Jerry Bruckheimer finale, go make nice with Father Rick or something. I'm sure he'd be delighted to set off Your pyrotechnics for You, as long as You supply the firepower and free passes through the Pearly Gates."

NO FREE PASSES! AND NO X-PLOSVES 4 FR RICK!

She raised her glass to the priest. "Well, kudos to him. It's nice to hear I'm not the only one around here who's too rational to believe she can launch grenades into a busy laboratory without spilling a drop of blood."

HES NOT 2 RATIONL! HES 2 DRUNK! ;)

She whimpered and dropped her head onto the bar. "He was in uniform, Zane, practically paraded in front of me. What was I supposed to do?"

"I think it's time we settled the tab."

U CULD HAVE TALKD 2 HIM

U CULD HAVE SOT HIS COUNSL

U CULD HAVE ASKD HIM ABOUT HIS FAITH OR HIS JOB

U CULD HAVE TALKD ABOUT THE RED SOX 4 ALL I CARE!

U WERE NOT SUPPOSD 2 BREAK HIM!!!

"I was simply offering him an opportunity I felt he was better suited for than I am. I never meant for it to—"

I TRIED 2 STOP U BUT U WULD NOT LSTN!

U R MORE OBSTINATE THN JONAH!

Zane grabbed the phone, his eyes flashing with startling intensity. "Look, You must have known that she'd be difficult when You came to her. It's not as though she hides it well. I'm doing everything I can to help You out, here, but if You're going to toss around allusions to characters You've allegedly coerced into compliance via some rather smitey techniques, then I'm sorry, but this is where I step off."

Patience just stared at him for a moment. Then she took the phone back from his hand.

"I'm sorry about Father Rick." She sighed. "Please don't smite me."

There was a pause, and then a chime.

NO SMITING

"Thank You."

She set the phone down on the bar again.

"What if I decide that I can't do this, and I honestly mean that I cannot do it? What then?"

ITS UR CHOICE 2 MAKE & URS 2 LIVE WITH

"You still won't smite me?"

WHT DID I JUST SAY ABOUT THT???

She pushed it back, half-wishing her interaction with Father Rick hadn't been such a sobering experience. She pressed her lips together and looked up at Zane.

"The grenade launcher is out, but if He really feels this strongly that it's got to be me and not, say, the Armed Forces, who needs to do this, I suppose I could try to find another way."

Zane glanced down the bar to check Frank's location, and then he slid his vodka over. "Wouldn't you rather tell Him this?"

"He can hear me just fine. The election isn't until Tuesday, right? So, why don't we just knock Joey Forsyth out of the race and cut out SolarTech's connection? That should be easy enough to accomplish, and no one needs to get hurt."

He raised an eyebrow and leaned back on his stool. "Define 'easy enough,' please."

"Any task that doesn't involve hordes of people flailing and screaming through the massive ball of fire we've just lit up in their workspace."

He shrugged and handed her the phone.

STOPPNG FORSYTH IS A BAND-AID

SOLARTECH IS A DEEP WOUND

"But a Band-Aid will stop the bleeding, won't it? Isn't that what it was designed to do?"

There was another pause. They held their breath as the screen lit up at last.

UR WAY WILL NOT B EASY

She exhaled. "Story of my life."

She shut the phone off and took a long sip from Zane's vodka, then pointed a finger down to the darkened screen.

"Do You think we could finish our drink now in peace?"

U BET

CHAPTER SEVEN

Patience frowned at the Valentino that was hugging curves she was certain hadn't existed before she'd strapped herself into it. The dress and the curves were equally disconcerting—even more so than the buffing she'd endured at the salon that afternoon—but there was no time to dwell. She checked the time and turned away from the mirror, fastening the bag Zane had sent over with the dress as she crossed to the door. She dropped it to the floor and turned out the lights, and then she returned to the window to wait. She was as ready as she knew how to be. It was time.

A whine, like a jet engine, accompanied by a throaty rumble, approached from the street and diminished into an authoritative, guttural sound resembling the purr of a Bengal tiger. Patience stared down in dismay as a red car, sleeker and more intimidating than anything she'd seen in her life, glided to the curb below in perfect choreography with its resonance. She crossed her arms and willed the driver to get his GPS programmed back to Beacon Hill. The car demanded attention simply by existing, and she was determined to make as surreptitious an exit as possible.

The driver's window lowered and a pair of brown eyes caught hers through the darkness.

"Son of a bitch!"

Patience grabbed the bag and her keys and flew downstairs in her calamitous heels. The passenger door opened from the inside and she dove in as Zane hit the gas. The force of acceleration slammed her door shut for her and pressed her back into the leather seat as she struggled to straighten herself out.

"What the hell is this?"

He appeared perplexed by her reaction. "Whatever do you mean? I told you I was going for the car."

"Yes, but you never said it was a... What in God's name is this thing?"

"This 'thing' is a Bugatti Veyron. It's got over a thousand horses under the hood and a top speed of more than two-hundred-sixty miles per hour. It's certainly a lot more accustomed to impressing women than it is to repelling them. It's my car, Patience, and it's quite a good one. Why are you yelling at me?"

She shook her head, speechless for the moment. She tugged at the dress, hoping to avoid wrinkling it, but gave up on that soon enough. "We are about to abduct a Massachusetts state senator, Zane. Don't you think a little stealth might be in order?"

He didn't respond to that. He looked indignant. And insulted. Patience turned to the window until the cranky silence between them was interrupted by a burst of organ music from her bag. She grabbed the phone at the sound of her latest ring tone and turned an accusing eye to Zane.

"What?" he said. "It's funny."

"It's hilarious." She pressed the button and glanced down at the screen. "Whatever His thoughts about this latest development are, they're all yours. I am not touching this one."

PT ON UR SEAT BLT!

"That's it?" Patience was aghast. "That's all You've got to say right now?"

There was a pause, and then another half note from the pipe organ. *PLEASE?*

She shot Zane another look as she reached back for her seatbelt. "Well, I certainly hope you know how to drive this thing."

He kept his eyes on the road ahead. "I do, actually. It's one of the few things I do very well."

Patience brushed her expensive hair back from her face and sat with that for a moment. Her irritation dissolved and she reached over to touch his arm.

"I don't believe that there are few things you do well, Zane. Anyway, how would you know? To hear you tell it, a hell of a lot had been done for you until now."

He just shrugged, leaving her to stew about the absurdities of God and man, the fact that she'd been AWOL for two days now from a job she actually liked, and the fear she'd been able to neither squelch nor give in to, despite her best efforts. They were risking everything in the hope of saving a world that irritated her just about every moment of every day—a world that seemed determined to burn itself out soon enough, anyway—because, no matter how hard she'd tried, she'd been incapable of doing nothing.

Zane glanced over as she scowled at the phone. She thought she heard him say something, but the words had been devoured by the Bugatti.

"What?"

He paused and eased up on the gas. The engine quieted to a moderate roar.

"I said it gets from zero to sixty in two-point-five seconds. It's a better car than you think."

She just stared at him for a moment and turned back to the window. God help her if he was going to start rambling about turbochargers and torque. The Bugatti itself was surprise enough.

She was pulled back by another blast from the pipe organ.

HE SED HE HOPES U NEVER TURN UR HAIR BACK 2 BROWN

UNLESS EVRYONE ELSES TURNS PINK

"What the...?" She gaped in dismay at the smiley winking up at her from the screen. "I can't believe You just ratted him out like that! What the hell is wrong with You?"

The Biz was unabashed. Zane looked over and Patience hit delete. The messages disappeared as he touched a finger to the screen.

"How have you two been getting along since I left you today? Are things starting to smooth out, now that you've agreed to help?"

She turned the phone over in her hand. "He's discovered rickrolling," she grumbled. "And He's started inventing His own emoticons. They don't even make sense."

"Oh."

"I swear, it's like having my dad follow me everywhere I go. Showing up at parties, dressed in plaid shorts and sandals with tube socks, and then trying to be cool in front of my friends. He's not cool, Zane, and this texting business isn't helping Him. Why can't He just speak to me like a normal human being?"

Zane didn't reply to that. The phone chimed again and she held it up.

"This one's all yours. I'm officially out for the night."

He glanced down and raised an eyebrow. "A punk rocker with acne and a very tall Mohawk?" he guessed. "Or, perhaps it's a zombie wearing a top hat?"

She shrugged and silenced another blast of *Toccata and Fugue in D Minor*.

ITS A BNNY RBBT WEARNG SNGLSSS! U DONT SEE IT?

Patience deleted the message, along with the SNGLSSS wearing BNNY RBBT.

"I'm turning You off now. I can either attempt to stop Joey Forsyth from destroying the world tonight or I can play along with Your iPhone nonsense, but I can't do both. And please, don't just turn the phone back on whenever You feel like chiming in—unless Your true goal is to watch me blow this thing straight to hell and spend the rest of my days awaiting the Apocalypse from the confines of the federal pen. Okay?"

KTHXBAI :)

"You bet'cha."

She shook her head at the house, and then she shook her head at Zane. The opulence was oppressive. Patience had never seen so many wings and levels and walls made of glass, in real life or on television. It didn't fit with any of the neighboring Brookline mansions, nor did it appear to want to.

"What will we do if he won't let us in?"

"That's not a concern."

"But what if he isn't—"

Zane cut her off with a smile and gunned it up Forsyth's runway of a drive. It was lined with gold leaf bricks and flanked by a number of statues, most of which depicted naked women of indeterminable origin or era. When they arrived at the top, she looked at him again, but that only intensified her apprehension. He appeared at ease in his tailored trousers and silk fitted shirt, and so different now from before. She could barely watch him as he stepped from the Bugatti.

The manner in which Zane carried himself charged the air around him with an aura of indomitable wealth. It intimidated Patience more than the house above them. She pushed a lock of hair behind her ear and tried to ignore the tendrils of inadequacy creeping up from her gut as he opened her door for her.

"I can't go in there," she whispered. "Look at that house, Zane, and look at you. He's never going to believe that I'm with you. No one would ever believe that I'm with you."

He reached down to release the lock of hair she'd exiled from the others and smiled as he smoothed it back over her face.

"He'll believe it," he said. "You're a knockout, Patience, and a shock to the system. There isn't a woman in the world I could show up with here tonight who would better satisfy Joey Forsyth's expectations of me than you do in that dress. You look smokin' hot in it, by the way. I'm not sure if I mentioned that."

She frowned down at it. "It's so tight, and these are definitely not my boobs. What the hell have they got woven into this thing?"

"The crushed hopes and dreams of a million would-be starlets who can't afford the ten-thousand-dollar price tag. Let's put them to good use."

Patience choked and pulled back. "Ten thousand dollars? Christ, Zane! Do you have any idea how clumsy I am? What on Earth were you thinking?"

He just smiled and remained maddeningly silent as he reached again for her hand. She looked up at this new Zane—this controlled, commanding, moneyed Zane—and wondered how he could possibly be the same man she'd first seen in flannel pajamas at his window only two days before. She could barely find a trace of that guy in the titan standing before her. The same slight clip to his speech and occasional stiff word choice that came across as awkward and quirkily endearing in Allston were anything but in his native habitat. As he stood beside the passenger door of his insane car, below Joey Forsyth's garish mansion, Patience finally understood what he'd meant about juxtaposition. There was nothing awkward or quirky about him here. He was completely alien to her, and he was stunning.

"I prefer you in your jeans," she whispered as she stepped a stiletto onto Forsyth's chaotic driveway.

He looked her over once and nodded his approval. Then he slipped an arm around her waist and turned her toward the house.

"Ditto," he replied. "But I'm really not complaining."

CHAPTER EIGHT

"Tex!"

Joey Forsyth appeared at the door in a cologne-infused cloud of forced bravado. He clapped a hand on Zane's shoulder and ushered them inside.

"It's good to see you, man. I'd heard that you'd gone into the Peace Corps or something."

Zane glanced at his shoulder, as though checking it for spray-tan residue, and drew his mouth into a smile of sorts. "It's good to see you as well, Senator. I've recently moved to Allston. I believe that's the report you're referring to."

"Allston?" Forsyth laughed. "What the hell is in Allston?"

"I am."

The senator closed his mouth, covering his unease with a fractured laugh as he motioned them toward the study. "Vodka martini still your drink?"

"Patience prefers gin," Zane said. "Old Raj, if you've got it."

Forsyth straightened slightly, then he winked and turned toward the bar. Zane said nothing more; he just stared at the artwork on the study walls with an expression of bored disdain. Even with his back turned, Forsyth seemed to grow an inch smaller every moment Zane was in the room.

Patience didn't dare look at him at all. She kept her eyes and her voice low.

"I don't even know what 'Old Raj' is."

"It's just a brand I happen to know he never keeps on hand. Don't worry about it."

Forsyth clapped his hands twice and turned back with a tray of martinis.

"Sorry about the simplicity, folks! Normally, the staff would serve such distinguished company, but you were so cloak and dagger about us needing to be alone tonight, Tex, I've sent them all home for the evening." His fake, folksy twang grew more pronounced by the sentence. "They were happy enough for the night off, of course, but clearing out my advisors was no easy feat. Especially with the race heating up the way it is. But hell, man, when Zane Grey Ellison himself calls up and asks to come by for a visit, how can I possibly refuse?"

Zane didn't respond to that. The senator laughed at nothing and handed him his drink.

"I've got to tell you, buddy, it sure caused a buzz when word got around that you'd left All Things Ellison and moved out to the wilderness. I hope your trust fund kicked in before you embarked on this crazy adventure."

"Of course, Senator. I left Hyannis because I wanted the freedom to do as I pleased and to interact with people who don't hang lithographs of themselves on their study walls. I didn't leave out of any great desire to be poor."

Forsyth's face turned the color of the bright pink lithograph of his younger self dancing with his arms in the air and his shirt blown back from his chest that was hanging on the wall behind him. He turned his attention to Patience next, acknowledging her for the first time since they'd arrived. He lifted a second martini with a wink.

"I'm sorry, little lady, but I seem to have run out of Old Raj." He flashed her his best teen magazine photo shoot smile as compensation. "Some of the domestics may be overdue for a firing, I'm afraid. Will Bombay Sapphire suffice?"

She took the drink from his hand, smiled slightly, and said nothing.

"Well, Tex! I see you haven't lost your taste for exotic-looking women. She certainly is a colorful little thing, isn't she? But then, you always did buck convention." Forsyth turned back to Patience. "Young Zane, here, would always go sneaking off at the club when he was a tyke. They'd find him hiding out with the kitchen staff or the grounds crew when the day was through, but it drove his father insane. Of course, I suspect that was the point, wasn't it, Tex? Speaking of Rutherford, how is the old man? Still roaring cracks into the plaster?"

"You'll have to tell me, I'm afraid." Zane took Patience's untouched drink from her hand and set it back down on the bar. Forsyth watched in frozen-smiled agony as he returned and slipped his arm around her waist again. "I haven't spoken to my father in weeks. And how are you getting on with him? The election is next week and I've yet to hear anything. I'd have expected Alex to have leaked his endorsement to a dozen different news outlets by now."

"Well, Tex..." Forsyth flushed. "You know how Rutherford is..."

"Yes," Zane said. "I do. Well, we don't want to waste any more of your time, Senator. Why don't we dispose of the silly nicknames that never caught on and the buoys about my father, and get down to business?"

Forsyth licked his lips.

"Rutherford's not the only Ellison with cache in this election. I think you'll find the conversation Patience and I would like to have with you interesting. But first, I'll have to ask you to show us to your control room."

"My control room?" Forsyth glanced toward the door. "I'm not sure what you're thinking of, kiddo."

Zane turned back to the lithograph. "I'm here on private business tonight. I'm not interested in attracting the sort of attention a photograph of me shaking hands with the next U.S. senator from the Commonwealth of Massachusetts would generate if it found its way into the wrong hands. I'm perfectly aware that you've got more cameras installed in this house than the Louvre. It's a quirk that you're sensitive about, obviously, as you've managed to keep it from Alex, but this is one aspect of your life I happen to be better informed about than Alexander Rockwell."

Forsyth made a mess of pretending to tidy up the bar. "Aw, Zane, that fundraiser Rutherford attended was three years ago. I didn't see any need to reinstall the cameras his agents disabled. Things are different for me now. That was an old system, installed during my days with the band, when I attracted a different sort of fan. My groupies are a lot less crazed now. Hell, I was grateful to your father's men. They saved me the time and aggravation of taking it all down myself."

Zane set his drink on the mantel and reached for Patience's arm. "Thank you for your time tonight, Senator. Best of luck in the election."

Forsyth stepped before them with his hands in the air. "Now, Zane, let's not be hasty. A man in my position can't be too careful. But hell, buddy, I've always thought of you as a little brother. I guess it's okay for me to let my guard down with family." He gestured toward the door. "You two just come along with me."

Zane appeared hesitant, but Patience looked up at him with a frown. "You know how concerned I am about the environment, honey. This is important to me."

She managed half a pout and he turned back to Forsyth. "What concerns Patience concerns me as well. Give her any further cause for alarm and our next stop will be at Jake McEvoy's camp, where I'm confident that she'll be greeted with respect and his undivided attention."

Forsyth wiped at his lips with a cocktail napkin. "You don't want to do that, Zane. If it's the environment you're concerned about, Joey Forsyth is your man." He gestured to the door again. "I'm not sure this Allston adventure's been too good for your mental hygiene. You seem to have developed a bit of a paranoid streak since you left Hyannis."

"That sometimes happens."

Forsyth led them down a series of hallways, stopping at last before an enormous, ornate, full-length mirror. He smoothed his hair back at the sides and then pressed at a spot behind the frame. A door released and swung forward and he stepped into a concealed room, waving to the bank of monitors that lined the far wall.

"Make yourself at home, kiddo. I can't wait to hear what this is about."

Zane stepped up to the monitors and removed the disc from each tray. He passed them back to Patience, and when their set was complete, he reached to his ankle holster and pulled out his revolver. "I'm sorry, Senator, but it looks like we're backing McEvoy in this one after all. Politics just isn't a good field for you."

Forsyth stood there for a moment, laughing like the man who doesn't get the joke. "What the hell is going on, Zane? Is it some sort of campaign gag? Did Alex put you up to this?"

"No, Sir. Alex will have to wait his turn to take a run at you."

He nodded to Patience and she stepped behind the senator to search him for weapons. She pulled a revolver from his coat and another from his ankle, followed by a whale's-tooth-handled hunting knife from his belt and an unsettling-looking set of metal balls from his trousers' pocket. Then she relieved him of his BlackBerry and pulled a pair of handcuffs from her bag.

"I'm sorry if this seems a bit crude." She cuffed the senator's hands behind his back. "We didn't have time to plan anything snazzier. Now, we don't intend to hurt you, if it's not absolutely necessary, so just relax and try to behave if you can. Everything should be fine."

"Tex!" Forsyth shouted. "What the hell is this?"

"It's our duty to mankind."

"It's nothing personal," Patience said.

"It's a little personal." Zane shrugged. "Let's go."

Patience pulled the passenger door open and spun back with a hand to her forehead. "Damn it, Zane! There's no back seat? What the hell are we supposed to do with him?"

Zane paused a moment, scratching his head as his shoulders lowered slightly.

"Oh," he said. "Wow, I never even... I'm sorry, Patience. I somehow lost sight of that detail in our rush to get here. I don't know what to say."

"Is there a trunk?"

He tapped his gun against the side of the senator's head as he glanced down at the car's interior. "Not as such. Do you think you could sit on the console?"

"Do you plan to shift the car into gear at all?"

"Good point," he said. "Sorry."

She stepped back from the door and looked away. "Let's get this over with. Put him in."

Zane beckoned for her to take the gun as he unlocked the cuffs. He wove them through the headrest and waved the senator inside.

"Try not to tug too hard on that chain, okay, Joey? I'll be pretty put out if you damage the leather."

He turned back to Patience, but she just shook her head and refused to look at either man. She leaned across Forsyth to drop her bag beside his feet, keeping her eyes fixed ahead.

"Please believe me when I tell you that *this* isn't personal."

She climbed carefully onto his lap and pulled her legs inside as Zane closed the door. He came around and slipped into the driver's seat with his gun still pointed at the senator.

"If you try anything over there, Joey, you can forget about Patience's promise not to hurt you. If I get the impression that you're even considering something funny, she'll get that seat back to herself at one-hundred-sixty miles per hour. Do you understand what I'm saying?"

"Zane, don't be an idiot!" The arrogance in Forsyth's voice disintegrated into a whining, nasally drone as his dampening, low-buttoned shirt added injury to Patience's insult. "You must realize that people will be looking for me. Alexander Rockwell will tear this city apart."

Zane fired up the engine as Patience reached down for Forsyth's BlackBerry. He winked back at the senator as she opened a fresh email.

"I've no doubt that he'll be pretty testy, but that's a hazard of the job, Joey, working with you. It seems you met a dental hygienist tonight, and you know how unreliable that sort of thing tends to make you. It's nothing Alex hasn't dragged you out of a thousand times before."

"That was different! Nobody runs off with a dental hygienist anymore. You have no idea what's at stake here. I'm warning you, Zane, you're in way over your head. You'd better listen to me!"

Zane winked back at him and glanced up at Patience.

"Leave out the occasional vowel and go heavy on the exclamation points. Sign it, 'J-Force' and you're home. There's really not much else to know."

She nodded and he threw the car into gear. When they reached the bottom of the driveway, she held the Swarovski-encased Black-Berry up for his approval and he laughed. She hit send and powered down the phone, and along with it, the senator's GPS. Zane turned the Veyron down the hill as a smile formed at the corners of his mouth.

"'Gigantastical' is a very good word. Is it yours?"

"It just struck me as something he might say."

Zane's approval pleased her more than she'd anticipated, his screw-up over their seating arrangements notwithstanding. She kept her face low as she stashed the phone again, hoping he wouldn't notice the slight flush creeping into in her cheeks.

Something stirred beneath her then, and she froze. She closed her hands around the seatbelt, trying not to agitate her surroundings any further as she ignored it as hard as she could. Finally, the ignoring became unbearable and that flush in her cheeks turned molten.

"Pardon me, Senator, but are you joking?" He turned his face to the window, but not quickly enough. A bead of sweat broke free of his hairline. He did appear genuinely miserable, but Patience wasn't feeling particularly sensitive to his plight. "What is wrong with you?"

"What's wrong with me? You're the culprit here, sweetheart. I'm the victim. You're strapped to my lap wearing a dinner-and-domination dress, while I'm handcuffed to the seat of a goddamn Bugatti Veyron. I'm just a man, for Christ's sake. If you're not equipped to deal with it, you should have called a cab."

Zane fishtailed onto Harvard Avenue and slammed to a stop in a fire lane, leaving unspeakably expensive strips of rubber behind in his wake. He grabbed Forsyth's collar, upsetting Patience from her precarious position as she lunged for his arms. She managed to push him back again as the senator's face turned from retching red to air-way-distress purple.

"Stop this," she said, with her fingers still gripping his forearms. "I need you to shed Alpha-Zane now. I have no idea what I'm doing here, and I'm about one misfired erection away from hiring up an Arma-geddon of my own and calling it a night. I need Allston-Zane back to help ensure that I don't do that. Please bring him back."

Zane released the shreds of dress shirt from his fists and pulled his arms free. He turned back in his seat and stared into the taillights of the bus stopped ahead of them. Then he looked over at her finally, with a hurt expression on his face.

"Whatever made you think that response wasn't from Allston-Zane?"

"Oh..."

She looked down at him from her perch atop Forsyth's unfortunate lap, and then she grabbed his face without warning and kissed him. He was still for a moment, his brain catching up to what his lips had going on, and then he slipped his arms around her and pulled her as close as the already taxed passenger seatbelt would allow.

Forsyth groaned and shifted toward the window. "Are you two fucking kidding me?"

Patience barely noticed as Zane pulled the revolver from his seat and pointed it at the senator, never disengaging from the most gigantastically exhilarating kiss of her life. Over a thousand horses stamped impatiently beneath the hood of the Bugatti as Senator Joey Forsyth muttered and cursed. His complaints grew increasingly lurid and whiny, until Patience pulled free of Zane at last and turned back to glare at him.

"You're incredibly disruptive."

He turned away and she brushed the hair back from her face. There was no mending the break in the magic, so she took a breath and nodded to Zane.

"I think we'd better get home now. This is starting to get complicated."

CHAPTER NINE

"You threw out the coffee maker?"

Zane stood before her with an empty mug in his hand and a destroyed look on his face. "You can't still be angry about the seating in the car last night, Patience. I've told you how sorry I am about that."

She stared back at him, trying to connect the dots. "This isn't retribution, Zane. It broke, as things often do. You do understand that things break, don't you?"

He leaned against the wall, sleep deprivation dropping his shoulders and taking his powers of cognition down with them. Senator Joey Forsyth, however, appeared alive and alert for the first time since they'd cuffed him to the crossbar of Patience's sagging sofa-bed.

"He has no idea," the senator volunteered. He plumped up his pillow and settled back to enjoy the show. "Zane's not from around here, honey, or hadn't you noticed? He's got no clue how anything you can pick up for less than ten grand works."

Zane turned on him and Patience took the mug from his hand to prevent it from rocketing into the good senator's cranium. She shot Forsyth a look of warning and pulled Zane back again.

"Of course I understand that things break," he said. "I'm not an imbecile, Patience. I just haven't had any coffee yet this morning, which is the crux of the problem, and I was thrown to discover that it wasn't going to be remedied anytime soon. Joey didn't shut up for

a second last night and I've got a crick in my neck you wouldn't believe. I wasn't thinking, that's all. I misunderstood you."

"Okay."

"Please don't let an idiotic moment turn into some larger statement about my ability to subsist beyond the gates of my father's
estate. If I don't happen to know the price of milk at the moment, it's
simply because I haven't gotten around to purchasing a quart and
not because I can't figure out how to find out where it's sold."

"No one is doing that, Zane."

"Speak for yourself, sweetheart!"

Zane pulled his gun from his waistband and Patience caught him
by the arm.

"No one who can't be silenced by a quick trip down the dumb-
waiter shaft is doing that. There's a 7-Eleven up the street. You can
get a cup of coffee there, and you can pick us up a quart of milk, as
well, while you're at it."

He pointed his revolver at the couch.

"Are you mad, Patience? I'm not leaving you here alone with him."

She released his arm and stepped back, stunned and damned insulted by his implication. "I should think that I'd be able to resist the
senator's exaggerated charms for fifteen minutes, Zane, but thank
you so much for your confidence. Is making girls feel cheap and un-
trustworthy after you've made out with them normal operating
procedure for you or is this something special just for me?"

He groaned and let his head fall back.

"Stop it, Patience. That's not what I meant. My point was that some
dangerous people must already be looking for Joey, and God only
knows what's going to happen next. So, no, I'm not leaving you alone
with him. But since you've introduced the topic, are we ever going to
talk about what happened last night? You've deflected every attempt
I've made to bring it up, and I've been patient about that because I

understand that things are hectic right now. But at this point, it's bordering on insulting."

She looked down and he crossed his arms, awaiting her response. She didn't understand why he couldn't just let it go. Dating was complicated under the best of circumstances. It took care and attention to make a relationship work, and starting something up now—while they waged war against Armageddon—was just begging for disaster.

"I didn't mean to insult you, Zane. I just thought we could deal with that when we no longer had an elected official handcuffed to the sofa."

He slid his gun back into his waistband.

"I guess I hadn't realized that kissing me was something you'd have to 'deal' with. My mistake."

The senator roared. "Buck up there, Zany-boy! I'm sure there's a purple-headed girl out there somewhere if you need to work off the sting. Try over in Brighton, maybe."

Zane was at the couch again before Patience could do a thing to stop him. Forsyth's hoots turned to hollering as Zane dragged him sideways by the ankles and folded him up into the sofa bed. He gave it a shove, and the bedraggled piece of furniture took on the appearance of an extremely stubby snake that had just swallowed its dinner live.

"Let him out, Zane. He might suffocate in there."

Forsyth's unbroken stream of threats and profanity seemed to satisfy him that her concerns for the senator's air supply were unsupported. He tossed the pillows back into place and turned toward the kitchen. She heard him rummaging, and he returned with a roll of duct tape in his hand. He lifted an end of the sofa off the floor, and as Patience stood helplessly by, wound the tape around it with a focus that seemed almost otherworldly. Finally, the tape broke free of the spent roll and he dropped the sticky silver cocoon back onto the floor.

"That ought to keep him out of our hair for the moment."

The couch shook and thumped before spitting out a muffled insult directed at Zane's dead mother. He reached for his gun again and Patience pulled him to the kitchen by the belt.

"This is a different side of you."

He set the revolver on the counter and stared down at his fingernails. He appeared far from penitent. If anything, the project seemed to have relaxed him a bit.

"I've never had any patience for Joey. You try listening to the man dissecting the voting patterns of Billerica and Chelmsford for Caroline Kennedy sometime without clocking him on the head with a croquet mallet. It's a lot harder than it sounds."

Patience didn't know how to respond to that. Zane rubbed a hand over the back of his neck and their uncomfortable silence was broken by a blast of The Biz's ring tone. She pulled the phone from her pocket and set it beside the gun. "This is private, if You don't mind." Then she turned back to Zane. "I wasn't trying to deflect you about last night. It's just that I think we need to know each other better before we try to figure out what that was."

"That's fine," he said. "What do you want to know?"

"It's not that simple. Take the guy you were last night, for example. We've been through a lot together these past few days, but I'd never have believed he existed if I hadn't witnessed it myself. Don't get me wrong, you were amazing and effective, and it was sexy as hell to watch, but honestly, that guy scared me a little."

"Is that what this is about?"

Her phone chimed again and he dumped it into the sink. He flipped a switch at the splashguard and a thwumping-clonking sound thundered from the garbage disposal. The *Toccata and Fugue* died horribly and took the ancient motor down with it. Patience gaped at the plastic shards spewing from the basin as it coughed out a burning smell and then she gaped back up at Zane. He turned off the disposal and crossed his arms with no discernible change in expression.

"I only behave the way I did last night with people who demand it of me. I don't enjoy it and I don't enjoy spending time with those who won't respect anything less." He shook his head at the ceiling. "Please don't be upset that I can do that, Patience. Be happy I choose not to."

She stared down at the remains of their latest cellular catastrophe, awed a little bit by the carnage. A smile twitched at the corners of her mouth.

"That is so much worse than anything I've done. At least I was mostly in denial when I smashed up His phones. You just really went for it, didn't you?"

He glanced at the sink and then nodded. "I'll probably feel wary about wayward lightning bolts for a while."

She sighed and he lifted his gun from the counter. It appeared they were in agreement, even if neither was entirely clear about what it was they'd agreed to.

The couch lay motionless when they returned to the living room and the blood drained from Patience's face. Zane crossed over to it and nudged it a few times with his shoe, but he was met by no response. Patience turned back to grab a knife, but he reached for her arm. He circled to the rear of the overtaxed piece of furniture and tipped it forward over its front legs, and it let fly a string of profanities. It came down with a thud, exposing a wedge of the scowling senator's face from behind its torn underbelly.

"How ya doing in there, Joey? Feeling snug?"

"I am going to sue the shit out of you, Zane. I'm going to sue your girlfriend and your father, and then I'm going to have your ass tossed in jail for kidnapping and extortion. And that's just the beginning, kiddo. You are going to be very sorry you fucked with me."

Zane smiled at Patience and yanked the sofa upright. "He's fine."

She sighed and turned back toward the bedroom. "Nonetheless, I'm going to scare up a pair of scissors to keep on hand. Will you please do your best not to shoot him while I'm out of the room?"

She heard him mutter something about dumping the whole couch out the window and being done with it, but she knew he'd never fit it through the frame, so she chose to ignore it. She turned to her dresser in search of the scissors, then froze as a high-pitched whizzing sound shot through the front door. A second pierced the frame, followed by the unmistakable crack of a heel splitting wood.

Patience ran into the living room as Zane shouted her back. She froze and gaped at the stern-looking stranger who stepped in through her broken door carrying a revolver with a silencer attached. He was tall and slender, dressed in a business suit. He took one look at Zane, who stood over the misshapen couch with his own gun pointed down at it, and turned his weapon on Patience.

"I'll take that revolver now, sport."

Patience shook her head, but Zane dropped his weapon and kicked it under the couch.

"There!" the couch shrieked. "You two thought you were so smart with that ridiculous email, but I told you Alex wouldn't be fooled!"

Rockwell never turned his eyes from Zane as he reached to his belt for a black-handled Buck knife. "So help me, Joey, I'm having a god-damn LoJack installed on your ass."

Zane stared at the knife with a disapproving air. "Christ, Alex, this weapons thing really has become a fetish for you two. I'm not sure that's healthy."

The bed burst apart with a few long slashes, expelling the sweat-soaked senator as though it couldn't purge him quickly enough. Rockwell's jaw tensed at the sight of his candidate, but then a stark smile etched across it as he turned a cold eye back to Zane.

"Let me tell you what's not healthy, sport: attempting to fuck with me, or this campaign, again. If you or your girlfriend tries another stunt like this, it won't make a bit of difference who your father is, because your bodies will never be found. Do you understand what I'm saying?"

Patience stiffened, as chilled by his manner as by his words, but Zane appeared to find the speech amusing. His smirk wasn't lost on Rockwell, who squared his shoulders and stepped his gun closer to Patience.

"I'll take the key to those cuffs, now."

She shook her head from the doorway. "Don't do it, Zane. You're an Ellison. He can't touch you."

"You'd be wise not to underestimate me, Pink. I know how to clean up a mess."

She shook her head again, but Zane reached into his pocket and tossed Rockwell the key. "I couldn't take another minute of his yapping, anyway. Now, lower your goddamn gun, Alex."

Rockwell released Forsyth from the bar and dragged his still-gasping candidate down by the scruff of his neck. He stared back at Zane as he pushed him toward the door.

"I wasn't ever with a dental hygienist last night," Forsyth complained, keeping close to his handler. He pointed to Patience as they passed the bedroom door. "She's the one who sent that e-mail from my Black-Berry. They were only supposed to come over for a minute. I was planning to stay in and rest up for Marblehead, just like we agreed."

"Shut up, Joey."

"But, Zane said he wanted to talk about the election. I was just try-ing to pull my own weight, like you've said I should start—"

Rockwell stopped and turned back to the senator. "I have just spent the entire morning tearing your house apart, Joey, in search of some clue to where you might have gone, because I somehow failed to understand that you can't be left unsupervised for a single night. What kind of imbecile meets alone with a man who's never shown him anything but contempt, mere days before the biggest election of his life? It's a miracle you actually remembered to synch your BlackBerry to your computer for once, or you might very well have stayed stuffed in that sofa until Tuesday."

Forsyth sulked back at him and Rockwell turned to Zane.

"I'm afraid I may have left your place in a bit of a mess, sport, but I was in a rush. I'll give you credit for having done a decent job covering, but you and Pink might want to give some thought to window treatments. Imagine my surprise when I looked out your window this morning only to discover you here, shoving my candidate into a sleeper bed."

Patience sighed apologetically. "I've really got to be more conscientious about those shades."

"You and me both, I suppose."

Rockwell waved them onto the mattress and wove the cuffs back through the bar that had been so effective at keeping Forsyth contained. He locked them together and slipped the key into his pocket. Then he looked back down at Zane.

"It appears that we can finally take a break from pretending to tolerate each other for the sake of appearances. So while we're having this moment of honesty, let's get one thing straight. Joey Forsyth is going to be elected to the United States Senate next Tuesday, and nothing you or your girlfriend can do will stop me from making that happen. There's been a lot of speculation about your mental state lately, owing to this radical lifestyle change you've embarked upon. If you were to just go *poof* tomorrow, I don't think it would be very long before your disappearance was accepted as the predictable end to a tragic slide into mental illness. And your girl, of course, is unlikely to be missed by anyone who matters at all."

Patience kicked at him, but Zane just laughed.

"That was a hell of a speech, Alex. It was almost as off-base as it was overwrought. It was also an excellent illustration of the fact that you don't, and won't ever, understand my father. Rutherford doesn't lose his car keys without hunting down every last person who's touched them and holding their feet to the fire until they're returned. That's why his car keys never go missing, regardless of where he leaves them. Don't try to intimidate me with your threats and hyperbole. You sound like an ass."

"You think so, do you?"

"I know so. Now, I have no doubt that in that dark little heart of yours you'd be happy to make Patience and me disappear, but you'll never do that. The simple fact of the matter is that you've only ever cared about one thing in your sad, sociopathic life, and that's Alexander Rockwell. Well, Alexander Rockwell would be crushed to dust and sprinkled as mulch into my father's flower beds if you so much as threaten my lunch money and that's just a fact. And what's bothering you most right now, Alex, is that you know I'm telling the truth."

Rockwell grabbed Forsyth's collar and pulled him to the door. "The smartest thing you can do right now, sport, is stay the hell out of my way."

"We'll see how that goes."

He pushed his candidate through the broken frame and Zane let his head fall back. He turned to Patience with a heavy smile as their footsteps disappeared in the stairwell and she tried to quiet the thunder in her ears.

"I thought they'd never leave."

"Have you lost your mind, Zane? You practically dared that man to shoot you. And not two minutes after giving up your gun!"

"I had to give up my gun, Patience. He might have shot you other-wise. As arguments go, I found that one to be pretty persuasive."

"But you said—"

He grabbed her by the hand and wrapped his fingers around her wrist. Then he started tugging at the chain. "Let's see if we can bust through this poor wreck of a couch. The sooner we get after them, the better."

She turned away and kicked the heel of her boot against the cross-bar. "I noticed that Rockwell's gun didn't deter you from slipping back into Alpha-Zane. For a minute there, it looked like he couldn't decide whether to shoot you or send the senator outside to wash your car."

She looked back at Zane and he glanced down. He appeared appre-hensive about the topic. "It's just a thing we learn to do in my family. Look, Patience, Alex has just upped the ante. This is going to become a whole other mess to clean up if we don't get after him soon. We'd probably have had some advance warning that he was on his way if I hadn't lost my temper with the phone the way I did. I'm sorry."

She pretended to search the crossbar for weak spots. "The Biz can reach me without the phone, Zane, and He damn well knows it. It's like He's entrenched. So, please cool it with the self-recrimination, would you? It makes me itchy."

He nodded and went back to work on the cuffs. Patience watched him for another moment and turned her attention to the sky.

"We really are sorry about that phone," she whispered. "We'll get You a new one. In the meantime, could You maybe help us figure out what to do now some other way? We're sort of in a bind here."

The sky didn't seem to be in a chatty mood, so she turned back and resumed her assault on the crossbar. She got in a few more good kicks before a thundering bang rattled the apartment. They spun to look as the broken front door flew back on its hinges and the frame was filled by an enormous man in combat boots and full camo. He stepped inside and stalked toward them. It was clear that he meant business.

Zane threw himself across Patience as the soldier pulled an automatic assault rifle from his back and fired a single shot. The cuffs blew apart as the bullet exploded against the chain and ricocheted into the window frame behind them. Then he stepped forward and lifted Zane from the mattress. He dropped him onto the floor and Zane grabbed his gun from beneath the couch. He jumped between them as the intruder turned back to Patience, but the man just pushed him aside again and Patience burst into tears.

She threw her arms around the soldier's neck as the fear and fatigue of a decade swelled up inside her. "Uncle John," she hiccupped.

He stood very still for a moment, and then he set the rifle beside the couch and folded her into a crushing bear hug. "Well, hey there, Pax. You got big."

"Of course I got big, you asshole. You've been gone for over ten years."

John grinned and set his niece down onto the floor. Then he turned back with a hand outstretched. "That must make you Zane. You can put your little gun down now if you like, Zane. I didn't come here to fight ya."

Zane just stood there with his mouth agape, his gun hanging in the air between them. John shrugged and turned toward the kitchen, where a muffled sound startled them from their stupor. It was odd in tone and vaguely unsettling, like the cry a gagged Barbie doll might make if she'd been brought to life only to be jabbed repeatedly with a hat pin. Patience followed her uncle to the silverware drawer, where—pushed to the back with the unused serving utensils—he unearthed the senator's forgotten BlackBerry.

"I understand that you two sometimes overlook what's right under your noses," he chided. "We'll have to work on that. Now, this ought to sort out your mobile phone predicament."

Patience felt dizzy as she took it from his hand. It went off unexpectedly and she dropped it with a crash back into the drawer.

Oh!

Forsyth's message alert was a sound bite from an old Boi II Boi tune, the telltale cry that signified the chorus was imminent. She looked up at her uncle, trying to make sense of his presence and his apparent association with The Biz, and then she shuddered as the BlackBerry squealed again. She stabbed her finger at it to silence it.

She stared at the display as the lights began to dim. The message was an address. John spoke again as he took the phone from her hand. His voice sounded distant.

"He's asked me to request that you to be more careful with this one. And to keep it out of the sink, if you can."

CHAPTER TEN

Patience opened her eyes to find her uncle grinning down at her. Zane was on his knees beside him, holding something cool to her forehead. He most certainly wasn't grinning.

"What happened?"

Her tongue felt heavy and uncooperative, and her skin was hot and wet. Her head pounded like John's boots against the door.

"You went down, kid." He winked. "You went down hard."

She pushed Zane's hand back and sat up, fighting the blotches in her vision and the sick, uneven feeling that was the last thing she remembered before everything went away. She tried to stand up, but Zane laid a hand on her shoulder.

"You need to take a minute, Patience. Come on."

She pushed him away again. "I can't take a minute, Zane. We have to get out of here. Once the police show up, we're done. Get your things."

"Joey and Alex aren't going to the police."

She just stared at him for a moment. "What are you talking about? We've just abducted an elected official, insulted his intelligence and his hair, and duct taped him into a beaten-up piece of furniture. You don't think they'll let that all slide just because you're an Ellison, do you?"

"They definitely will not, but they're not going to the police."

John raised an eyebrow at him over Patience's head. "Okay," he said, as they helped her to her feet. "It sounds like you two had better fill me in on the mission, so we can be on our way."

She took the cloth from Zane's hand and pressed it against her throbbing forehead. "So, all this time you've been a...whatever the hell it is we are? You're not sick?"

John laughed.

"Hell no, I'm not sick, Pax. Never have been. I'm a SCUD—a Special Commando Under David—and I was redeployed to Boston just this morning by the Good Lord God, Himself. So, catch me up on the job, would'ja, kid? Time's a wasting."

Patience frowned as her uncle scrolled through the few select messages The Biz chose to set the scene for him. "He just speaks to you directly?" she said. "Like an adult, with no text speak or emoticons?"

John glanced up with a smile. "I don't even have a mobile phone. By the sound of it, I'd say this is His special thing with you."

"That's just super."

"Cherish it."

She raised a hand to her aching brow. "Special Commando Under David," she repeated. "Uncle John, are you suggesting that the Supreme Being is a Judeo-Christian God?"

He stopped scrolling and looked back. "Well, of course He is—to the Jews and the Christians. He's got SCUDs of every religion, though, and they're all called by names that make sense to them. Sometimes He's One; sometimes He's Many. Oftentimes, He's She. It's nothing to get your head too muddled up about, though, and it's not what's important now." He handed Zane the phone and brushed off his fatigues. "I've seen enough. What makes you so sure this Rockwell corpse hasn't dragged his boy off to the cops?"

Zane glanced at Patience before turning back to her uncle. "Because going to the cops ensures that they'll never get what they want most in the world and not going to them pretty much guarantees that they will. We need to stop Joey and Alex before they get to Hyannis. Nothing else matters now."

"What's in Hyannis?"

He shrugged, but failed at looking casual. "My father."

Patience looked up again. He declined to meet her eye.

"Is that honestly what you believe will prevent them from turning us in, Zane? You think they'd rather tell on you?"

"In a manner of speaking. My father's support for Joey's candidacy would open some pretty tightly closed doors once they get to Washington. More importantly, SolarTech's entire financial infrastructure has been built upon loans and lines of credit from Ellison Bank and Trust. If they're about to become publicly aligned with the senator, you can bet that Joey and Alex want his support now more than ever. They want it because SolarTech wants it. They *need* it because SolarTech wants it. My father would never touch a candidate who's in bed with a company that owes his company billions. The bill amendment alone would force him to keep his distance, so if they want him, they'd better get him now. They're taking it to a slightly higher level, but this isn't an uncommon dynamic in Rutherford's life."

"I don't understand. What do SolarTech's business loans have to do with their political shenanigans?"

"Nothing in the world. This is one hundred percent about image, and there's no currency on Earth my father values more. Even with the federal stipends attached, what SolarTech is proposing to do is insanely risky, financially. The goal is to make any impending failure as uncomfortable for Rutherford as possible."

Patience felt like she was trapped in a Fun House. Everything he said seemed like a distorted reflection of the reality she recognized.

"Would your father actually forgive a company's debts over some random, shared connection to a senator?"

"Of course not."

"Is there anything illegal or improper about it? Would he be investigated, or accused of anything underhanded?"

"No, not at all."

"Then would it really be such an ordeal for him if he found out about it after the fact?"

"Yes, it would."

Patience rubbed her eyes and her uncle stepped in.

"So, they intend to coerce your father into backing the senator by exposing what you kids did last night?"

Zane shook his head. "Alex and Joey lack the subtlety required for coercion. They'll go straight for full-scale blackmail. Keeping a story like this from hitting the press would be persuasive stuff to my father. If they get to him before we do, they'll have his support in this election, and in every race for the rest of Rutherford's life. Come Tuesday, we'll be trying to take down a sitting U.S. senator, and that's going to be a hell of a lot harder to pull off."

"Is your father really that powerful, Zane?"

"Yes." He sighed. "He is."

"Then why are we standing here? They could be halfway to Hyannis by now."

Zane laughed at the thought. "You don't just drop in to see my father, Patience. Not even Alex is brash enough to try that. You can't get in to see Rutherford without an appointment, and you can't get an appointment without... Well, you can't get an appointment. There are ways that things are done, extortion notwithstanding, and Alex won't blow it by disrespecting protocol. This is his one shot at the whale." He looked down. "Anyway, I'll know within seven minutes that the call's been placed, and as of seven minutes ago, it hadn't been. He's going somewhere to think and plan."

"What does seven minutes mean?"

He pulled her to the window, with John in their wake, and pointed down to the carriage road below his apartment window. "Seven minutes is the longest it will take the Boston team of my father's security force to clog up that lane with armored SUVs. It's been clocked under every imaginable hazard and traffic condition, and trust me, it'll be quicker than that. I'm on furlough from the imposition of my father's protection right now, and that's a detail no one but me is happy about. My independence will be revoked the second there's a perceived threat against any member of my family, and it won't be pretty. Rutherford's chief of security will have eight men on top of me before Alex has hung up the phone."

"Jesus Christ."

"Ed O'Brien," he corrected. "But I wouldn't screw around with either."

Patience shook her head at the carriage road. An armored security detail descending on a nondescript apartment building on Commonwealth Avenue and blocking arbiter access would definitely put an end the low-profile aspect of Zane's Allston experiment. The thought of that made her indescribably sad.

John tapped Zane on the shoulder and they turned back from the window.

"I mean no disrespect, and I get that you're not exactly on food stamps, but it's not like you're one of them Hilton kids. I'd never heard of you before I got the—"

Patience held a hand up for her uncle to stop. Zane smiled uncomfortably at his shoes. "New money employs people to get them into the papers, Sir. Old money employs people to keep them out."

"The Hiltons are new money?"

"My father would certainly say so."

John appeared convinced. He grabbed his rifle up from the floor.

"Where are they now?"

Zane leaned back against the wall. "That's difficult to say. Joey's family has several properties within an easy drive of here, and Alex has the two—"

John waved him off and cocked his ear upward. He winked at the ceiling and slid the rifle back into its holster. "They're traveling west on the Mass Pike, headed toward the address our boss beamed to your mobile phone before my beloved niece, here, took her siesta. They plan to stop there and get their ducks in a row before making the trek down to Hyannis." He turned to Patience. "It looks like your friend has called this one, Pax."

Patience's jaw dropped, but Zane nodded.

"Wellesley," he said. "That's Alex's place. It's in the Hills."

"All right then." John smiled. "Let's go take 'em out."

Patience froze a moment and looked up at Zane. He appeared equally perplexed. She leapt at her uncle as he reached for the door and pulled him back to face her.

"When you say, 'take 'em out,' Uncle John, what exactly do you mean by that?"

His face softened slightly as he shook his head at her.

"You saw those pictures, kid. There's no room for fooling around here. I know this sort of thing can be upsetting in the beginning, but the hard choices get easier with time. God loves the world that grieves Him, and He's doing what He can, but a little power in the hands of a narcissistic attention-junkie like your senator or a depraved domination-loving goon like his handler can ruin the fun for everyone. Well, He's not ready to throw the towel in yet, Pax, so He needs us to help Him out."

John turned back and Patience grabbed his arm again.

"We can't kill them, Uncle John. Are you mad? Not a drop of blood can be spilled by our hands!"

"Sure it can, kid, and a hell of a lot more behind it. Come on now, time's a wastin'."

"No!"

He tossed her off again as Zane lunged for his other arm. John just pushed him aside and pulled the rifle from his back. He pointed it at them as Patience scrambled to her feet, but Zane pulled her down and held her to the floor.

"Understand that I love you like sunlight and smog-free air, Pax. There's not a day that's gone by these past ten years when I haven't thought about your sweet face or that crazy-intuitive brain of yours, and I will never hold one bit of this against you, because it's who you are. You've grown up beautiful, and I'm real proud of you. I have to go now, though. It is what it is. I'll see you on the other side."

"You can't kill them," Patience cried. Her voice echoed in the empty hallway as her uncle disappeared down the stairs, just as ghost-like as he'd appeared. She sobbed into Zane's shirt until the slam of the first-floor foyer door confirmed that John was gone and he drew her up from the rug.

"We can make this right," he said. "We can stop them all. Come on."

She shook her head as her tears threatened to choke her into incoherence. "It's too late, Zane. Rockwell and Forsyth are minutes from Rockwell's house, and my bloodthirsty uncle is after them with a double-dealing God as his personal GPS. They're dead already."

"Bullshit. I may not understand why your uncle's been sent here, but he has been and we can't worry about that now. We'll deal with Uncle Rambo as the occasion requires. The promise we made was to stop Joey and SolarTech, and that's all that matters. They may all have a head start, but we've got a goddamn Bugatti, so grab your coat and let's go."

She caught Zane by the arm as he collected Forsyth's weapons and his keys. "What if it's not The Biz my uncle's been working for all this time?" she said. "What if it's something else?"

He looked down at her for a moment, but didn't respond. Forsyth's phone cried *Oh!* and a single word appeared.

GO!

CHAPTER ELEVEN

Patience covered her eyes as the Veyron topped one-hundred-sixty miles per hour on the Pike. Zane eased up to scream through the FAST LANE at the toll booth he had no transponder for and hit the gas again as they cleared the merging lanes. They were a quarter-mile south on 95, weaving in and out of traffic like a ballerina dancing across a minefield, before the bells had even rung. They'd already outrun a couple of State Police cruisers, and it was starting to look as though the troopers might be throwing in the towel.

"I can't feel my face."

She said it to no one in particular, which was good, because Zane couldn't hear a thing over the engine. He glanced over as he came off the highway, blowing through a red light as he accelerated onto Route 16. He navigated effortlessly around the slow left turners and double-parked cars that Patience barely even realized were there until they'd left them far behind. He hadn't been overstating it when he'd told her he could drive the car very well. He had, in fact, been outrageously modest. She kept her gaze fastened on the phone and tried not to look at him. This was getting really complicated.

He pulled up to the base of Rockwell's driveway and she let her head fall back against the seat, indulging in a sigh as the world finally stopped whirring past.

"Is there really this much money in politics, Zane?"

"In Boston?" He laughed, seeming to think that was answer enough. "Alex and Joey do come from money, though. Particularly Joey. They've always been pretty gross about it, and their subsequent celebrity and influence have only made them grosser. That's all that is, though, and there's nothing about a large house that should intimidate you. You're twice as intimidating as the two of them together, Patience, and a far more formidable person. You need to watch out for Alex because he's devious and ambitious, and because he's a soulless son of a bitch. Not because he's rich."

She nodded, feeling anything but certain, and held her breath as he killed the engine and let the Bugatti glide up the last half of Rockwell's drive. He eased it to a stop behind a mud-splattered Hummer SUT with a gun rack attached to its bed.

"John."

They were greeted by muted strains of shouting as they pulled their guns from their coats and slid past the truck to the busted front door. Zane nudged it open with his foot and they followed the clamor to the basement. They crept down with their backs to the wall, but their caution proved excessive to their situation. They could have driven the Bugatti down those stairs without being heard over the unholy racket rising from the farthest corner of the basement.

John was hanging upside-down, tied by his knees to a rafter and hollering the hymn "Onward Christian Soldiers." A seething Rockwell stood below him with a polo stick in one hand and a Beretta 9mm pistol in the other, shouting for him to shut up. Forsyth was padlocked into a sturdy-looking wooden stall behind them, along with the garden equipment and a couple of barely broken-in dirt bikes, and he was yelling as well—although what, or at whom, the senator was yelling was difficult to ascertain over the more dominant voices in the basement.

Zane slid up behind Rockwell, who responded to Forsyth's warning shouts with a poke of the stick through the slats before turning back and punching John with his gun. The skin above the SCUD's temple split, and judging by the condition of his cranium, it hadn't been the first blow of the afternoon. Zane pressed his gun to the back of Rockwell's head and the campaign manager froze. He relinquished his Beretta and the stick and Zane pushed him toward the stall. He held him there a moment while Patience relieved him of an arsenal that left Forsyth's in the dust.

"Nunchucks." She sighed. "The three guns, the Taser, and the Buck knife weren't enough for you? You felt compelled to carry nunchucks, as well?"

Rockwell didn't respond to that. Patience found the key to the stall and opened the gate as John grinned down at her.

"You two sure did take your sweet time getting down here, Pax. Damn near gave myself laryngitis covering up the racket of that rocket engine your friend's got."

"How did you know we were ...?"

He pointed a finger upward past his knees. "We're really not totally on our own here. Maybe if you'd stop smashing up your mobile phones, you'd start to understand that."

"Or maybe He could try speaking to me properly—in plain English, using actual words." She pulled off her sweatshirt and pressed it to his temple. "I'm no happier with Him than I am with you at the moment. We had an agreement, and He's broken it by sending you here, with all your zeal and ammo." She paused and looked away. "That's assuming, of course, that it's really Him who's sent you."

John just shook his head as a drip of blood slid past the sweatshirt into his hair. "Come on, now, Pax. You can't believe a thing like that. It's more than biology that connects us and always has been. I'm upside-down and bleeding. This is no time to lose your faith."

Patience turned back to him. "Faith is something I've never had,

Uncle John. I'd expect you to know that about me if you've really been where you say you have all these years."

He closed his eyes for a moment.

"You've got faith, Pax." He sighed. "You've got more than most. Your problem is that you don't know what it is. You're a bit of a perfectionist and you have a tendency to be a touch judgmental in some regards. What some consider searching, you call doubt. What some consider questioning, you call disbelief. Hell, you've even got faith in things you've already rejected, but you have no Earthly concept of what lurks at your core because that rigid brain of yours scares your better angels into hiding. Well, your angels ain't so defenseless as they might seem. They keep right on working behind the scenes. Still, it's no day at the spa, living in that head of yours. Is it, kid?"

She thrust the sweatshirt into his hands, unable to listen to any more. She turned back and approached the stall. "Why is the senator locked up?"

Rockwell crossed his arms through the slats with a malevolent smile. "I've got a senate race to win, sweetheart. If my candidate isn't intelligent enough to avoid getting duped by a pampered fucking poodle and his working-class distraction, I'll just have to monitor his movements more closely."

Patience caught the look in Zane's eye just in time to grab his arm as his fist came within millimeters of Rockwell's jaw. He slammed it into the gate instead, eliciting an appreciative nod from the SCUD.

"Stop doing that!" he shouted. "Drilling these two in the face is the only reasonable response to just about anything either of them says, but you keep getting in the way. Would you please knock it off?"

Patience honestly intended to diffuse his anger when she reached for his arm, but the sparks in his eyes disoriented her like solar glare and she inadvertently slipped her fingers into his hair and kissed him. Her uncle's approving smile froze in his face before disappearing altogether. He gaped, slack jawed, as his arms uncrossed from his chest.

"What the hell are you doing, Pax? You can't behave this way on a job! Stop it!"

Forsyth glowered and muttered to Rockwell about the horrors he'd endured the night before as Zane struggled to hold onto his rancor. He lost that battle fairly quickly, though, and pulled her to him.

"Damn it to hell," John growled. "Someone let me know when they come up for air."

Forsyth and Rockwell stared up at him, but neither responded. Patience's phone let out a disapproving squeal finally, and she released an out-of-breath Zane.

"I know," she said to the screen. Heat spread into her face like lava. "Yes, I understand!" She dropped it like it was on fire as Zane came to stand beside her with his head bent low.

"You've really got to find a better time to do that."

"I realize that."

"It's just that you seem to have developed this compulsion to kiss me at the most complicated moments. It's not that I'm complaining, mind you, but it can be a little inconvenient when I'm trying to concentrate."

"I said I know." She avoided eye contact with everyone in the room. "It was an accident, Zane."

The basement was unified by awkward silence, with the sole exception of Rockwell, who appeared perfectly at ease as he stared back through the gate with a wry and twisted smile.

John coughed finally and clapped his hands once.

"Well then, let's get me down from here, so we can finish our business and move on to something else. Someplace far, far from here."

Patience turned back with a heavy expression on her face.

"I haven't decided what to do about you yet, Uncle John. Your solution is as big a problem for us as our problem is, and we haven't got time to fight you both. If what you're telling me is true, then that's a whole other problem of its own. Is He with us or against us? Because, right now, I really just don't know."

John's expression turned uncharacteristically pensive.

"Well hell, kid, you've got His number. What are you asking me for?"

She shook her head and looked away again. "I've only ever asked Him for one thing directly, and you came crashing through my door thirty seconds later with your bloodlust and your assault rifle. I knew better than to do it at the time, and believe me, I've learned my lesson." She took the sweatshirt back as his wound began to drip again and pressed it to his head. "You never once let us know that you were all right, or gave us any reason to believe you weren't dead or locked up somewhere terrible, having God only knows what done to you. As far as I'm concerned, Uncle John, you can hang up there all night."

His eyes lowered upward toward the ropes binding his knees. "Hurting you and your mother was the last thing in the world I ever wanted to do, Pax. I'm real sorry about that."

Rockwell cleared his throat. "I'm sorry, but are you all out of your goddamned minds? We're in the middle of a hostage situation here, and you're behaving like the panel of a Jerry Springer reunion special. Do you think we might return to the crime in progress, or is working through Pink's angst and family drama really our first priority tonight?"

Zane reached through the slats and grabbed him by the collar. Patience started for his arm, but she caught herself in time and jumped back as his fist cracked against Rockwell's jaw. The campaign manager's head flew back and to the side, and then it fell against his chest. He groaned and slumped sideways and Zane dropped him to the floor of the stall with a bead of drool hanging from his chin.

"Thank you." He shook out his knuckles and glanced down as the whimpering senator scrambled to the back of the stall. "I still owe Joey a few, as I recall."

Patience pulled out the phone and held it up. "You can make it up to him later, Zane. We need him conscious for this. Anyway, it'll be a lot easier to get through while Rockwell's out."

"Fair enough." He took the phone from her hand. "But allow me to do the honors. Why don't you go sit with your uncle for a while?"

"Photoshopped," Forsyth cried, in what had become his mantra during the minutes Zane stood over him, BlackBerry in hand, as he scrolled through The Biz's photos. They'd pulled up a folding chair and offered him a seat, but the senator was making himself a less than gracious audience, nonetheless. "Photoshopped! Photoshopped! Photoshopped! It's so obvious that this is a joke, Zane. Do you think I'm a complete moron?"

Zane declined to answer that. Patience just rubbed her eyes and nodded toward Rockwell, now sitting half-upright in the corner of the stall.

"Do it," she said. "That one won't stay down forever."

"Are you sure?"

"Unless you'd rather I did."

"Oh, no!" A smile sprang to life in the corners of his mouth. "I've got this." Zane pulled a chair up next to the senator's and held up a picture of a man with a few more lines etched into his tanned face, and a few new streaks of gray mingling with his expensive gold highlights, but it was undeniably a picture of the partially charred, lifeless remains of U.S. Senator Joseph M. Forsyth.

"What the hell is that?!" Forsyth yelled. "Oh my God! You sick fucks!" Zane jumped back just in time as Forsyth turned and vomited onto the floor before his feet. Patience grabbed some rags and a bin of water from a sink beside the workbench and returned to stand before him.

"It's good to know that when the images of starved children and demolished cities aren't enough to get your attention, a picture of your own dead self will do the trick." She cleaned him up as best she could and dropped the rags onto the mess on the floor. "You're not evil, Senator, not entirely. But you're disastrously stupid and such a sucker for the influence of others, not to mention the neediness of your horrendous ego, that I could just weep from contact-shame. Those character flaws don't mix well with power. In fact, they'll get the whole world killed if you ever make it to Washington. Don't worry about that, though. We don't intend to let that happen."

Forsyth stared up at her as beads of sweat trailed over the sides of his face.

"But you don't understand what's going on," he whispered. His eyes traveled back to the BlackBerry, so Zane raised it higher for him to get another look. "There are powerful people involved here, people who will never let me out of this election. They've invested epic amounts of money into Tuesday's outcome, and they're not the kind of people who'll let you live to disappoint them twice."

"Yes," Patience said. "SolarTech Industries. We know all about them, Senator."

He recoiled in the chair, his eyes wild and staring. "You don't know anything! I don't know where you heard that name, little girl, but SolarTech, most definitely, is not the company I was referring to. Measures have been taken to ensure that no link has ever existed between the Forsyth campaign and the company I *was* referring to, so don't bother trying to figure it out. Whatever you're trying to pull by dragging this SolarTech into this, it's not going to work."

Patience shrugged. "Then you're fine. It'll be just another day at the office when Zane contacts the local media outlets and accuses SolarTech of coercion and illegal third-party campaign contributions."

"You can't do that!" he shrieked. "I'll be dead in an hour!"

It was almost discouraging how poorly he performed, considering how much trouble he'd caused them over the past eighteen hours. She turned to say as much to Zane, but was cut off by a squeal from the phone. He checked the message and cursed into the screen.

"Troopers," he said. "They're at the bottom of the driveway."

She grabbed the phone as it squealed again, then pointed a finger back at him. "There's an APB out on you, *Mario*. It seems the troopers have found their Bugatti." She turned her frown up to the ceiling. "Of course, a little more notice would have been helpful."

THYVE ONLY JUST FOUND THE CAR!

I DONT NO WHICH PATH A MAN WILL TAKE UNTIL HE TAKES IT

FREE WILL... WHT WAS I THNKNG? :-(

She ignored that last bit and looked back to Zane.

"What should we do?"

He grabbed the ladder Rockwell had used to run John up onto the rafter and started working at the knots around his legs. The SCUD swung recklessly forward and reached for him, nearly knocking Zane to the floor as he grabbed hold of a wrist.

"We can't risk the troopers poking around the basement windows and finding your uncle hanging here, Patience. Help him."

She climbed up behind him with Rockwell's Buck knife in hand and slid the blade beneath the ropes. John battled gravity with brute obstinacy as Zane held tight to his arm. Then he dropped like a stone, pulling Zane over the beam as Patience dove for his legs. Her weight and Zane's together barely matched her uncle's as John centered his feet beneath him and let go. He dropped to the floor as easy as a playground stunt and plucked his niece from Zane's legs.

Zane exhaled and swung himself over the beam, dropping to the floor beside them with his gun already trained on John. The soldier just clapped his hands once with a grin on his face.

"Well, that got the blood pumping. What's next?"

Patience took Zane's gun so he could return Forsyth to the stall and collect the rest of the weapons. John reached a hand out for his rifle and she shook her head.

"The Lord's got no beef with those troopers up there, Pax, so neither have I. I don't kill for sport. You can't send me up there unarmed, though. That's reckless and damn stupid."

Zane nudged him with the rifle and she pointed toward the stairs.

"Take it up with your boss, Uncle John, and be glad that I don't trust you. If I did, even just a little, you'd be locked in that stall with the other two. Now, quit griping about your gun and let's go."

He shrugged and started up the stairs. Patience and Zane followed, until Forsyth rattled at the gate with a protracted sob.

"I don't want to be senator anymore," he cried. "I'm in deep shit, here, don't you understand? I don't want to have my pancreas fed to me before I'm chopped into little pieces and tossed off the side of a yacht, but I don't want to kill the world, either. Please don't rat me out to SolarTech, and please don't make me burn up in a fiery flame pit of doom. Come on, Tex, this is me. My mother referred your mother to her nanny service, remember? Please, man! I don't want to die!"

Zane pulled the BlackBerry from his pocket and stepped down a few stairs.

"What was that, Joey? I didn't quite catch that last bit."

The senator sobbed some more about the unfairness of his predicament, until Zane had heard enough and closed the video capture on the phone. He emailed the file to Rockwell and nodded as he passed Patience on his way back to the door.

"That ought to get Rutherford off the hook for the moment. Where were the troopers?"

"Circling the Bugatti," she said. "One of them was at the back when I looked, checking out the airbrake."

CHAPTER TWELVE

John was effectively, if oddly, cleaned up by the time the troopers' boots thudded against the porch. He'd pilfered a Stetson from Rockwell's wardrobe and pulled it low to cover his forehead, and his blood-stained camo jacket had been traded for an overtaxed, chartreuse V-neck sweater.

Zane locked the weapons in the liquor cabinet, then answered the door at their knock. He led the troopers back out to the driveway—once they'd checked everyone's IDs and were satisfied that he was, indeed, *that* Zane Grey Ellison. They'd looked askance at the soldier a few times, but there wasn't much they could say about him once his record came up clean, so they just patted Zane down and directed him to the car.

He smiled back at Patience as the door closed behind them. She hurried to the window and the phone squealed.

IT WONT HELP HIM IF THEY CATCH U SPYNG

JST HAVE SUM FAITH AND LET HIM DO HIS THING

She glared down at the text, angry and frightened about what would happen next.

"Let him do his thing? Zane shouldn't even be here, Biz. All he was trying to do was settle into a new life, which was disorienting enough, but You wouldn't take *no* for an answer. You hauled him into the middle of Your problem with me, and now he's likely going to jail for something he shouldn't have been involved in at all. Zane can't go to jail, for crying out loud. He's still figuring out how the microwave works!"

John pulled her back to sit beside him. He turned his eyes to his banged-up knuckles with a heavy sigh. "There's so much wrong with what you've just said, kid, I don't even know where to begin. Your friend is here today because he chooses to be. Don't diminish what he's doing by pretending he's got no place in it."

Patience didn't respond to that. Being ganged up on by Uncle Uzi and The Biz was a bit too much to take, given their situation. She turned away from him, until her brooding was cut short by the roar of the Bugatti's engine, followed by a rush of footsteps. She started for the door again, but John grabbed her arm and held her there as Zane sped down the driveway with the cruiser in pursuit.

"If you're not ready to trust the man upstairs," he said, "then trust your man on the street. It's not your place to decide his role in this. That's up to him." He glanced to the window. "And Him." He took her chin in a calloused hand and turned her face back to his. "You don't have to be here, kid. God gets told *no* every second of every day. Your resistance doesn't make you special; it makes you a pain in the ass."

She just looked back to the door and he nodded.

"If your friend needs busting out tonight, then we'll go bust him out. In the meantime, you've gotta learn to relax and roll with the punches. You're throwing away good energy that could be used for better things."

She pushed his hand away and stood up.

"Relax? Zane's being chased by troopers in a beast that can get up to a third the speed of sound and we've been sent here by a duplicitous God. You can relax all you like, Uncle John. I'll hold on to my anxiety a bit longer, thanks."

John stared back with an expression of sincere confusion. For once, he had no glib reply.

"What do you mean by 'a duplicitous God'?"

She turned to Rockwell's bookcases. "We agreed that there'd be no bloodshed if I did this for Him. Sending you here clearly shatters that agreement. He betrayed us."

"Ah ha!"

He glanced to the window with the smirk of a man who'd cracked the code at last.

"So that's what You're up to, is it?" He slapped his hands down onto his knees and shrugged. "Well, it seems awfully labor-intensive, if You ask me, but who am I to argue?"

Patience turned back at that. "What are you talking about?"

He clasped his hands behind his head and relaxed back against the couch. "God's been giving me just the scantiest bits of information about this mission, and that's unusual for Him. He's actually a bit of a micromanager, if you want to know the truth. But this morning, He showed up and said, 'John, get your ass up to Boston and help your niece out.' So, up I got and here I am. You two definitely need the help, there's no question about that, but I've been curious about why He's been keeping me handicapped. That answer seems clear enough now. He's trying to honor His agreement, while sending you the help you sorely need."

Patience looked back to the bookcase and stared at the rows of uncracked spines, trying to digest as little as possible of what her uncle had said.

"That doesn't make sense. If you two are as tight as you've claimed, why didn't you just ask Him what He was up to instead of hassling me about the way I've been doing things?"

"Because when God tells me to do a thing, kid, I do it. I don't question Him, and I sure as hell don't call upon Him to justify Himself. You've still got some work ahead of you in that regard, from what I've observed."

Her brows drew together as she stared back at him, sitting comfortably and complacently, and ready for whatever might transpire. She couldn't imagine ever feeling so sure of herself, but it quieted her mind a bit to see that he did.

"Does this mean that you're with us now?"

"I've been with you every day of your life, Pax. Always will be, come what may."

She smiled for the first time since he'd arrived. John noted the look and held a hand up.

"I've got your back, and I can even appreciate what you're going for here, misguided though it may be. I can't risk playing it your way though, kid. The stakes are just too high. I'm real sorry about that. I do promise to be around if you need somebody to talk to, though, and nobody's getting near you with malicious intent without having a good look at his intestines from the inside. You can count on that."

She turned away, exasperated by his gruesome pledge and irate with The Biz all over again. "I don't understand you, Uncle John. If you know what His intentions are, here—"

"He gives me what He gives me, and I work with what I've got. But, at the end of the day, I serve Him with all the best that's in me and I don't hold nothing back. To do so would be to fail Him, and I won't do that. Not even for the niece I love."

She glared back at Rockwell's untouched books, and they bothered her, suddenly, as much as her uncle. The phone had been too quiet, and Zane had been gone too long. Then she felt those omnipresent eyes again. They made her anxious and restless, like she was trapped in an aquarium. It was all too much to ignore.

"Just spit it out, Biz, for crying out loud!"

The BlackBerry squealed.

I TOLD U THE CHOICE WAS URS 2 MAKE & UV MADE IT SO GET IT DONE & STOP GIVNG ME SUCH A HEDACHE OTHERWISE, Y DONT U JUST GO HOME?

She spat out a laugh and tossed the phone at her uncle.

"Nice try, but You're the one who loaded me up with the apocalyp-tic images and then loosed Kujo on the scene. Sorry, but You're stuck with me for now. If You're not enjoying the experience, then per-haps You'll exercise a bit more caution the next time You tag a new-bie for a job of this magnitude."

There was a pause, and then another squeal. John raised an eye-brow at the screen and held it up to show her.

ATTA GIRL!

She dropped back onto the couch and they let silence take the room, waiting in fractured solidarity until a whine arose in the distance. It was buried by the engine's roar as the Bugatti grew closer and then dropped to a rumble at the base of the driveway. John placed a hand on her arm as it revved and then cut out. A door clicked shut and Zane came in alone a few moments later. He looked spent.

"We're good," he said as Patience flew across the foyer and threw her arms around him. "I apologize for the delay. I had to take them each for a bit of a test drive before they'd forgive and forget. It'll take some doing to get the gears back into fighting form and all four tires will certainly need to be replaced, but the APB is lifted and the troopers seemed cheerful enough when they left."

She just stared at him, trying to wrap her mind around the fact that he hadn't been hauled in or roughed up, and then she turned back to her uncle.

John winked and stood up, and then he smashed the liquor cabinet door with his elbow and broke for the basement with his rifle. Zane leapt after him as Patience grabbed a gun and fired a warning shot. The recoil knocked her back as he dove against the wall and then ducked Zane's right hook. He pushed the smaller man aside and reached for the basement door.

"You've really gotta learn how to shoot, Pax. We'll put that high on the list of things to work on later."

Zane grabbed the gun from Patience, but John ignored it. He froze before the door for a moment as the BlackBerry squealed. Then he turned back and ran straight at them, grabbing each under a muscular biceps and the phone cried again.

DUCK!

Two shots blasted through the basement door as they rolled across the living room floor, lodging in the wall where John stood a moment before. Alexander Rockwell stepped into the hall carrying a Smith & Wesson .44 Magnum and dragging a quaking Joey Forsyth—who appeared uncertain about the Colt .38 in his hand—behind him. John rolled back and raised his rifle and Patience hollered at the ceiling.

Her uncle's finger reached his trigger first.

The rifle jammed and John cursed. He shoved Patience and Zane behind the bookcase and dove for the couch. Rockwell's shot exploded behind them and he stepped into the living room. A sniffling Forsyth tugged at his arm.

"Thank you for handling the troopers, Zane. Cops are always messy."

Forsyth broke then, dissolving into tears. "I don't want to be senator anymore. Come on, Alex. Let's just go to Palm Beach. It's safe there."

"Shut up, Joey."

John raised his rifle's sights to the senator. "I can take care of that for you right now, champ. One shot and you'll be out of politics forever. What do you say we solve this, once and for all?"

"Uncle John, no!"

Rockwell laughed and pointed his candidate toward the door. "Go get in the car, Joey."

Forsyth just stood where he was, staring down at the weapons in everybody's hands and shrinking further behind his handler. "But I told you, I don't want to be senator. I want to get drunk, and then I want to go to Palm Beach. Come on, Alex, the weather in D.C. sucks."

"I told you to get in the car."

Patience watched as her uncle's face hardened, and she knew then what it looked like to prepare to kill a man. She also knew then what it was she had to do. She felt some interest in what would happen next as she slipped from behind Zane and placed herself between them, but not much beyond a detached curiosity about what it was going to feel like.

From nowhere, an old Peggy Lee song floated through her mind.

Is that all there is to a circus?

Zane shouted as he and John both leapt and Rockwell grabbed her arm. There was a crack and a flash, and then nothing.

CHAPTER THIRTEEN

Patience opened her eyes, but they fell closed again despite her best efforts. The lights were searing, and the headache was more searing than the lights. She tried once more, curious about the tears that blurred her strange surroundings as she attempted to sort out how she'd landed in the eye of a tornado with a hippopotamus on her chest. Tornadoes were rare beasts in Boston, and hippopotami were rarer still. She breathed in too suddenly and choked on the air as a hand came down on her shoulder. The roaring registered then as a strangeness that wasn't completely unfamiliar. She was back in the Bugatti.

"What's happened?"

Zane glanced over and she knew that something wasn't right. Some elusive, yet charged, change had come over him, and a trace of something that didn't belong hung in the air between them. It tasted like the Fourth of July.

"Who's been shot?"

He didn't respond; he just pulled her hair back and looked down into her face before returning his attention to the road. The lights in her eyes were relentless. She repeated her question.

"No one's been shot," he said. "Well, no one of consequence. Alex took a bit of lead to the arm, but I'm not counting that."

"What?"

The twister touched back down in her head and pulled her straight up in her seat. Her eyes burned as she tried to focus through the blur of oncoming headlights, and then she noticed the streaks of reddish-brown emblazoned across his shirtfront and the streak of *do not fuck with me* emblazoned across his face.

"Oh God, Zane. What happened back there?"

"Stop it, Patience. Everything's okay."

"It's not okay. You've got blood on your shirt."

He glanced down at his Oxford, then shrugged and changed lanes. "It's nothing you need to worry about now. You've been hit on the head, and I'm more concerned about that than anything else."

She grabbed his arm and he pulled their speed back to eighty-five. He untangled himself from her grasp with a look of warning against further driving interference.

"I was an idiot not to have checked that basement for weapons before leaving them alone down there," he said. "I mean, what is Alex, besides a sociopath with a weapons fetish? He hit you with his gun and then he reached for you again after you hit the ground. The look in his eyes wasn't good, Patience. He was lucky to only get shot in the arm, believe me. He's fine, but I'm not sure he'll stay that way if your uncle gets to him before we do."

Her head fell back against the seat and Zane stopped talking. She touched her fingers to the blood-snarled mess matted behind her hairline and he nodded.

"I really am concerned about that. You've likely got a concussion. You need to be seen by someone."

"Would you forget about my head, Zane? All I want is to know what's happened."

A device in the Bugatti's console blipped twice and he eased off the accelerator. He slid onto the ramp at a rest stop and maintained an easy pace as he circumnavigated the parking lot, cruising past a drive-through into the relative darkness of the dumpster slalom behind the food court, then emerged again into the brighter light of the filling station at the far end of the plaza. A couple of state troopers sped past on the highway above as Zane came back up in their wake and resumed a quieter traveling speed.

He touched a button on the radar detector and eased the car back to ninety, having uttered not a word. Finally, he glanced over and nodded.

"There's not much more to tell. It was all very fast and very loud, and it was clear that discussion wasn't an option as far as Alex was concerned. He should have left you on the floor and made his getaway while we were looking after you, but he didn't. Something had to be done. Do you understand what I'm saying?"

"Yes."

She dropped her forehead into her hand, trying to resign herself to this turn of events she'd set in motion but hadn't witnessed. She looked up again as the lights of an overpass appeared in the distance and disappeared just as quickly into the discarded world behind them.

"So, that's when John shot him." She couldn't imagine why her uncle hadn't killed them both while he'd had the chance.

"No," Zane said. "It isn't."

"I don't understand."

"John's rifle jammed again."

The world slammed on its brakes inside a head already engulfed by pain and confusion and the life drained from Patience's face. All she could see now were those stains on Zane's shirt—the incontrovertible proof that he'd defied The Biz's command not to spill a drop of blood—and her world increased from a hundred to a thousand times too loud.

"Take that off."

The stains appeared to be glowing now, larger and brighter than before. She grabbed his shirttails and yanked them back, snapping the buttons across the interior of the car. The Bugatti swerved as Zane pushed her hands away.

"Are you insane, Patience? My God!"

"Get it off!"

"Jesus Christ."

He muttered a selection of accompanying explicatives as the last button popped from his Oxford and he pulled it back over his arms. She yanked at the cuff as it caught on his watch and tossed it from her window. The shirt floated aloft over the highway and tumbled a few times in the rear view mirror. Then it rose on a torrent of exhaust and disappeared from view.

Zane was still for a mile or two, silent except for his breathing. Finally, he ran a hand through his hair and looked over.

"Well, now I'm convinced you've got a concussion. Don't ever do anything like that while I'm driving, Patience. You could have killed us both."

She kept her eyes forward and he glanced down to ensure that he wasn't in immediate danger of losing his T-shirt as well. Then he turned his focus toward finding a place to pull over. A clearing appeared in the distance, and he drove like it was the mothership sent to save them from a hellish planet where gods waged wars against boy band singers.

He killed the engine and turned to face her, but she wouldn't return the look. "Listen, Patience, I'm not going to apologize for what happened back there. It was Alex or you, and I believe The Biz understands that. Even if He doesn't, you're not going to hide my crime by destroying one of my favorite shirts and nearly killing us both in the process."

"I wanted his blood out of this car."

"Well, it's gone now."

She touched the lump on her head again as she stared at an errant button on the floor.

"I had a hard choice to make," he continued. "I'm satisfied with the result. If He's upset with me, then I'll just do whatever it takes to make things right."

"Can you unshoot a man?"

"No."

She pulled the BlackBerry from her pocket and dropped it onto the console between them. "Has He spoken to you at all since you did shoot a man?"

"No."

She picked it up again and its silence felt ominous. There wasn't a thing in the world that didn't scare the hell out of her. She looked at Zane, finally, and noticed that he appeared more determined than scared. She wondered how he did that.

She closed her eyes for a moment and took a breath. "Do we know where we're going?"

He nodded. "Brockton. Joey's scheduled to swing by a Boys and Girls Club in the morning, and then it's over to Milton for one of those Town Hall meetings he's so crazy about. They won't alter the schedule again after missing the North Shore this morning, especially with Brockton and Milton still very much in play. Your uncle mentioned something about Alex berating Joey about their schedule in the basement today, so I'm certain he's headed there as well."

"That's super," Patience said. "A rogue SCUD with a military assault rifle facing off against the architects of the Apocalypse in a packed Boys and Girls Club gymnasium. What more could the world possibly ask for? My God, Zane, what if you'd missed that shot at Rockwell? He could have killed you."

"I wasn't concerned about missing."

She stared down at the lifeless phone, and then she was done. She jumped from the car and slammed the door. Zane followed, picking up the pace as she spun toward the traffic and started her windup. He caught her wrist in the midst of what looked to be a half-decent slider and took the BlackBerry from her hand. She stalked up the shoulder, pouring what was left of her strength into her fury and he let her go, catching up with her as she was at the brink of collapse.

"This is a joke, Zane. I can't control these people. I can't stop them from doing what they're hell-bent on doing, and I certainly can't anticipate what they'll do next, because I'm not a fucking psychopath!"

"Patience."

"You were set up today. Do you get that? He let us run right into a situation where you'd have no choice but disobey Him, so now you have. He's the omniscient one, Zane. He must have known this was likely to happen. Do you understand that you're screwed? You were set up."

"Patience!"

He held up the glowing screen, but she just shook her head.

"I'm sorry, Zane, but I'm out. I can't work this way. I'll do what I can to stop SolarTech and the senator, but I'm working solo from now on."

"I'm not."

He touched the button and then swallowed a cough. Patience grabbed it from his hand.

I TOLD U UR WAY WULD NOT B EASY
FAR B IT FROM ME 2 SAY I TOLD U SO...

She clenched her fists and Zane recognized his error. He took it back and held it above her reach.

"His way was the grenade launcher! His way was to say no blood and then throw my uncle into the mix. If we wind up caught in my dear Uncle John's crossfire tomorrow or torched in some massive SolarTech flame out, that's on Him as far as I'm concerned. That's smiting by proxy."

The phone squealed and she pulled Zane's hand down before her face.

I SED NO SMITING, I MEANT NO SMITING!

WHY MUST U QUESTION EVERYTHNG I SAY?

I M THE LORD UR GOD!

"Oh, for crying out loud! Are we back to that again?"

There was a zapping sound and a whiff of alkaline in the air. Zane dropped the phone as its screen turned to black and he shook out his hand. Patience grabbed his wrist and looked down, but he closed his fingers over his palm and pulled back.

"It's fine," he said. "It felt as though I was holding a lit charcoal briquette for a moment, but the sensation's gone now. Perhaps you might consider cooling it with the recriminations, though, so close on the heels of my crime against God and Rockwell? Would you do that for me, Patience? Please?"

He retrieved the BlackBerry from the dirt and turned toward the car. It lit up almost immediately and she caught a glimpse of the message before he turned it from her view.

I CANT TALK 2 HER

Zane sighed and shook his head without breaking his stride.

"Please try to remember that she's been unconscious twice today. She's really not herself at the moment. Anyway, her concerns about what happened this afternoon aren't entirely baseless—"

He was cut off mid-sentence and Patience stepped closer as he bent over the message. He flinched toward the delete button as she took the phone from his hand.

"What did He say about that?"

The text dissolved and she looked up. There was something in Zane's expression she'd never seen there before.

"It was nothing important."

She kept an eye on him until the phone squealed again.

I M THE LORD UR GOD!

She thrust it back at him and turned toward the car.

"He's like a broken record with that. Let's go."

CHAPTER FOURTEEN

Zane pulled her beside him on the bed and leaned close. He looked down into her eyes and Patience caught her breath. She felt shy suddenly, and a little flushed under the intensity of his gaze. A tingling sensation ran up her spine as he brushed a lock of her hair back and turned her face to his. She was starting to feel lightheaded.

"What are you doing?"

"I'm not entirely sure," he said. "Looking for some sort of weirdness, I think. I don't know much about concussions, but I believe there's supposed to be something odd about the pupils."

"Get away from me." She pushed him back and stalked over to the window, her hair taking on a surreal glow beneath the neon *VACANT* sign outside. "You're not looking for weirdness in my eyes, Zane. What the hell kind of a thing is that to say to a girl?"

He stood beside the bed with his arms crossed and didn't respond until she turned her glare back to him. "I wasn't looking to create a moment, Patience. The fact that I find you recklessly distracting ought to be apparent enough to anyone—even to a girl of your ornery and suspicious nature—and I really don't care to belabor that point. Now, your brain has taken one hell of a beating today and you need to stay awake until you've been seen. I'm going to stay awake as well, obviously, to make sure that you do. There's no way I'm letting you check out on me in some manner that I'm totally unprepared for, so please don't give me any more grief. I'm tired and I'm not screwing around. Do you understand what I'm saying to you?"

His eyes were bright and his jaw was set. The white T-shirt that was all he'd been left with upon the destruction of his Oxford was doing little to conceal the cut of his tensed arms. Patience came back to stand before him.

"Yes."

"No!"

He jumped back with his hands in the air between them.

"I don't care what happens tonight, Patience—I don't care how many guns are drawn, or how inappropriate the situation may be— you are not going to kiss me. In fact, I want you to stay at least five feet away from me until I tell you otherwise."

She frowned and looked down. "I guess I hadn't realized that kissing me was such a problem for you."

His expression cut off anything she might care to add to that.

"I shot a man today. That's a stressful thing to do, no matter how badly the guy had it coming. I've had my clothes ripped off at ninety-five miles per hour and I've defied the will of God. That's on top of the fact that there were several minutes in there when I wasn't certain I'd ever see that distrustful look in your eyes again or hear the scoff in your voice when you're flabbergasted by something I've said. And now we're here, holed up in a cheap motel in Brockton, instead of at the hospital where you ought to be."

"Would you give it a rest, Zane? My head is fine. I've told you a hundred times."

"I wasn't finished. We've still got your uncle and the impending Apocalypse to contend with and I have a lot of fast talking to do tonight. Please go over to that bed and sit down. And try not to get too comfortable. I'll be in this chair over here, and if I see so much as an eyelid droop, I'm pulling the fire alarm."

She turned back to the bed and did as she'd been instructed. Zane's tirade had the odd effect of making him even more attractive to her, but he seemed pretty serious and more than a little tense. She decided not to press her luck.

"Do you really find me recklessly distracting?"

"Don't speak to me."

He reached a hand for the phone and she passed it over, then settled back against the headboard to pout. He dropped into the desk chair and leaned forward with his elbows on his knees. Zane Grey Ellison was the most confounding man Patience had ever met. This thing was getting complicated as hell.

"It's Zane," he said, turning the chair so his back was to her. "Can you put me through to Mason? No, not Ed. I need Mason. Just Mason."

Zane's expression was one of studious concentration as he fiddled with the television. He'd still eye Patience warily whenever she shifted too abruptly or moved too close from the bed, but his attention to his task had given her some time to think.

"What did you mean earlier, when you said you weren't concerned about missing your shot at Rockwell?"

He smiled wanly at the screen. "I meant that I was careful."

"But, he was a moving target, wasn't he? I thought that sort of thing was pretty hard to be sure about."

"It is, but I'm pretty good at it."

"Oh." Her eyebrows drew together and she looked up at him again. "You are?"

He glanced back and nodded, then returned his attention to the remote. "My father is an avid shooter and an expert marksman, so I spent a lot of time around guns growing up. You don't do anything with my father without learning to do it very, very well if you want to maintain a shred of self-worth. More importantly, I knew that once I could outshoot him, I'd be allowed to do something else with my time. So, I can and I was. You were in less danger from me today than you were from Alex, Patience, I promise. I wouldn't have taken the shot if I wasn't sure about what I was doing."

Her eyes widened in disbelief.

"Hold on a minute, Zane. Did you just inform me, in an insanely round-about manner, that you're an expert marksman? Because, that's the sort of thing I'd have expected to come up before now."

"I'm sorry." He shrugged. "I just really don't care very much for guns."

She continued to stare until the muscles of his back tensed and she sat back on the bed.

"Let me see if I've got this straight. You don't know the price of milk, but you can drive like your last name is Earnhardt, throw a punch like you grew up in Southie, and now it turns out that you're some sort of ninja sharpshooter, too? Okay, Zane Grey Ellison, what other superpowers have you been keeping from me?"

He clicked off the television and turned back to her.

"It's just my life, Patience. I honestly don't know what else might be useful. I was a ranked polo player in High School. I can order dinner at Fugakyu in Japanese or at L'Espalier in French. I'm conversational in neither language, but my father doesn't know that because I've been faking it for years by pinching lines from Anime and the BBC's multilingual programs. The upside to that experiment is that he now finds me far more disturbing in Japanese and French than he ever has in English, so he rarely pushes me to speak either in public. I'm also a master at hiding the fact that when I told people what to do at any of the three banks he had me nominally in charge of throughout college, I was perfectly aware that they'd agree with me for as long as I was in the room, and then do things the correct way once I'd left."

Patience was quiet for a moment, letting his words settle.

"You faked being fluent in Japanese and French?"

"Not quite." He smiled. "Conversational was the best I could pull off. It's actually not an easy feat to accomplish. Learning the languages would have been a lot less effort in the end."

"Then why didn't you?"

"Because I have a complicated relationship with my father and because my language instructor was the easiest of my tutors to bribe. I ended up with ninety minutes to myself three afternoons a week, Monsieur Schwartzman ended up with a shiny new Harley, and Rutherford ended up reevaluating the importance of those summer internships he'd been devising for me at the Tokyo headquarters. It was a win all around."

She shook her head at the busy motel bedspread.

"But you put in all that effort and you have nothing real to take away from it. I'd love to be able to speak French or Japanese."

"I would too, as a matter of fact."

"Well, I don't believe those are the only things you can do well. Tell me about something you excel at that your father wouldn't know anything about."

He considered her question for a moment and then he smiled. "I am actually conversational in Spanish and I know how to mask the flavor of ipecac syrup in food."

"There," she said. "You see?"

"I also know how to refrain from pissing off the kitchen staff at my father's club. Hold on a minute, Patience. I think I need to give Mason another call."

The second-in-command of Rutherford Ellison's private security force stood in their motel room doorway with a black leather case in his hand. Zane glanced past him as the agent stepped inside.

"This is just us, right, Mason? No one's caught wind of what you're up to tonight?"

Mason raised an eyebrow at him. "Do all your requests for assistance come with insults now, Zane?"

Zane just grinned back and the agent shook his head. Then he shook Zane's hand and nodded at Patience as he set the case on the foot of the bed. "If this little adventure gets me into hot water with Ed or your father, it's going to be your ass."

"Has it ever been any other way between us?"

Mason shrugged noncommittedly. He looked around the room with an air of mild surprise, but he wasn't quite able to hide the spark in his eyes as he pulled a small box from the case. Zane reached for it, but the agent held a hand up between them. "Do you absolutely guarantee me that a prank is all this is? You're not in any trouble?"

Zane punched him on the shoulder and grabbed the box.

"If I was in trouble, Mason, I'd go to Ed. You know how this works. You're the guy I come to when I need to cause a little trouble. Joey's been begging for his comeuppance for far too many years, and with the election looming, I figure there's no time like the present. So help me, if I have to smile and introduce that guy to people I respect as 'U.S. Senator Joey Forsyth,' my head is going to come clean off. We just need some help shaking things up, and there's no one in the world better for that than you."

The agent drew his arms across his chest and narrowed his eyes at his protectee. "I don't deny that Joey Forsyth is a Grade A douchebag, Zane, but what have I told you about blowing smoke up my ass?"

Zane just shrugged. "You've told me never to do it. I'm not blowing smoke, Mason. I'm providing Patience with a little context, seeing as how you're dressed like Elliot Ness at two o'clock in the morning. Jeez, man, you could have thrown on a cardigan or something. This isn't my father's house."

"Maybe not, Zane, but like it or not, you're still an Ellison. The usual standards of conduct apply."

Zane shook his head, but he didn't say anything more about that. Patience, on the other hand, had been staring throughout the exchange with her mouth agape.

"Wow." They turned back as she retreated to a chair in the far corner of the room. "This is the one you said has the wild streak, Zane? He looks stiff enough to snap in two if you hit him at the right angle. No offense intended, Sir. You weren't joking when you said these guys were serious, were you?"

Mason didn't appear offended and Zane just nodded. "It requires a certain degree of formality to work for my family, Patience. This is who these guys are. They don't wear jeans on Fridays and they don't screw around in the break room between shifts. Yes, they're serious. They're also dedicated and extremely skilled."

"So, helping us pull a prank on a state senator would be considered acceptable behavior?"

"No." He grinned. "It definitely would not."

When he turned back again, Mason was staring down at him with his shoulders back and his jaw set for interrogation. He most certainly did appear offended now.

"What?"

"We have a break room?"

"Oh that." Zane shrugged. "Sorry, man, I thought you knew. It's that room off the kitchen Steve commandeered for his arcade games a few years back."

"You're referring to the locked room with the NO ENTRY sign on the door?"

"That's the one. You can't go in there unless you want to get into a stink with Steve about it, but, technically, it's all yours." They stared at each other for a moment, and then Zane laughed at the agent.

"Give it up, Mason. You've never taken a break in your life. You're just mad because there's something about the house you didn't know and because Steve's a weasel. Well, Steve has always been a weasel and that's never going to change. So what's with the attitude? That suppressed inner hellion of yours not getting enough exercise since I left town?"

Mason looked to the wall, but the corners of his mouth turned up slightly. "Just make sure everything's cleaned up when you're finished, and that your father's name stays out of it." He cocked his head back toward Patience. "I gather this is the patient?"

Zane nodded and she sat up straight as Mason pulled a rolled-up leather pouch from the case and turned toward her.

"I'm sorry," she said. "I'm the what?"

"Just hold still, please." He knelt down and pulled the hair back from her contusion without any further introduction. "Not bad," he said, pressing a finger gingerly at its edges. She winced and he eased up. Then he touched a particularly tender spot and she punched him in the chest.

He smiled and stood up again. "That is a perfectly respectable goose egg, Miss Kelleher. I don't think it'll require stitches, but you shouldn't feel at all ashamed about showing it around."

"Thank you?"

"You're welcome."

She looked back at Zane, but he raised a hand to the questions in her eyes. Mason removed an ophthalmoscope from the pouch and she pushed the instrument away. "What the hell is going on here, Zane? I thought you said this guy was with your father's security force."

"He is. Mason is also a doctor. This is important, Patience. Cooperate, please."

The agent leaned in, causing her eyes to water as the beam of light slid across. "I was finishing up my rotation in emergency medicine at Massachusetts General Hospital when Ed O'Brien recruited me to come work for my current employer. It seemed like a good fit at the time. I was getting pretty bored."

Patience closed her eyes and pushed his hand back again. "You were getting bored practicing emergency medicine at Mass General?"

"Little bit."

"So, you're a real doctor?"

"I'm a real doctor. Did you vomit after you hit your head?"

"No, I didn't. Pardon me, Mason, but how old are you?"

"I'm twenty-nine years old. Do you still feel dizzy at all?"

"Not in the slightest. And you've been working for the Ellisons for how long now?"

"Just over four years."

"Zane!"

"I know." He sighed. "Trust me, Patience, I've seen the transcripts. Just try not to over think it, okay?"

The agent set his ophthalmoscope down with a smile and pulled out his stethoscope. "I graduated from high school at fifteen. There wasn't much to do where I grew up, so I was ready to move on. I completed Columbia pre-med in three years, then spent four more at Harvard Medical School. After that, I did a year of residency in Chicago, followed by the two-year fellowship at Mass General. And now, I work for the Ellisons. Breathe deeply, please."

Patience breathed in and out a few times, and then he listened to her heart. Finally, he stood up and pulled Zane toward the door by the elbow.

"I'm a lot more comfortable getting a scan whenever there's been loss of consciousness. It's a standard precaution. Why is it, exactly, that you haven't taken her to the hospital?"

"I'm on the lam," Patience said.

Zane shook his head at her and turned back to the agent. "It's about the mission, Mason, and nothing more. It's time sensitive and we're trying to avoid leaving a trail, as I'm sure you can appreciate, but, if you think she's in any danger, screw that. I'll take her in right now."

"I'm not going to any hospital, Zane. You can just forget about that."

"She's also a little resistant, but if you say it's important, that won't be an issue."

Mason considered him for a moment, and then he returned to the bed and set his pouch down next to the case. "Her breathing and circulation seem fine. Her pupils are focused and responsive. May I assume that this is her usual mental state?"

"Hey!"

"Yep."

He rubbed his chin as he turned back to stare at her. "Honestly, I think she's fine, although she really ought to take it easy for a day or two. I'm going to write you a list of things to watch out for." He stepped over to the desk and grabbed a pad of motel stationery. "If you notice her exhibiting any of these symptoms, no matter how briefly, you take her straight to the nearest emergency room. No questions, Zane, and no exceptions. Then, you have me paged."

He ripped the page from the pad and passed it over. Zane read it carefully. "Increased irritability's going to be a tough one for me to measure."

"No exceptions," Mason repeated. "Give me your word right now or I'm calling for an ambulance." Zane nodded and the agent lifted the box from the table. "Okay then, let me show you how the bug works."

They huddled beside the television with their heads together and Patience stepped forward to stand beside the bed. She looked down into the case, stunned by what he'd been able to come up with in the dead of night, with only a few hours' notice. The IDs she was comfortable enough with—assuming that people who supplied that sort of thing were accustomed to working the occasional odd shift—and the surveillance equipment she was on the fence about. But the whistle and the set of track clothes with the tags still on them were another thing altogether. She'd probably have found Mason less intimidating if he'd delivered them a cache of weapons or a doctored up photo of Forsyth making an obscene gesture at the Pope.

She really didn't know what to think about the capped syringe of phenobarbital and the medical supply issue bottle of syrup of ipecac.

"Pardon me, Mason?"

The agent and Zane both looked up again from the bug.

"If you wanted to kill me right now, from all the way over there, and you couldn't shoot me with your gun for some reason, would you be able to do that?"

The agent shrugged. "Sure."

"How?"

He lifted the complimentary wine opener from the desk, flipped it open, and whipped it at her. The corkscrew whizzed past her jugular, missing it by mere centimeters, and embedded itself in the wall behind her. Patience stared at it for a moment and then returned her attention to the case.

"Okay then. Thanks."

"Anytime."

A flash of brilliance, tucked beneath the track pants, captured her attention. She reached down and withdrew a cacophony of mismatched beads and baubles, completed by an enormous purple plastic medallion in the shape of a fat-petaled daisy, and turned back to stare at the agent. The garish necklace was a masterpiece, no question. It was also a hell of a thing to come up with at two o'clock in the morning, no matter who his connections were.

"Pardon me, Mason?"

He looked back again and winked at the treasure. "My niece made that for me when I was appointed Second. As far as attaching that picture you requested is concerned, though, you two are on your own. I'm sorry, Zane, but a man's got to know where to draw the line."

Zane just shrugged and switched on the bug's receiver. He smiled as the red light illuminated in his hand.

"Fair enough. Did you have any trouble with my other request?"

"Right, sorry." Mason reached into his coat pocket and withdrew a couple of shiny new iPhones. "They're untraceable and untrackable. Try not to let them out of your possession, okay? Ed's not eager to share our toys with the world."

Patience dove at him and tore one of the phones from the startled agent's hand. Then she dropped to the carpet and burst into tears. Mason pointed to the list of symptoms he'd written out, but Zane just shook his head.

"She's been stranded all day with a phone that's got Joey stuck as the ringtone," he explained. "It's been kind of an emotional time for her."

CHAPTER FIFTEEN

Zane straightened his Celtics cap and dropped the whistle around his neck.

"What do you think?"

Patience looked him over carefully. To her, he looked just like an heir to the Ellison Empire dressed in an inexpensive track suit and nonregulation ball cap, but they'd been through a lot together over the past few days, so she figured that was just her. Anyway, she wasn't in the best of moods, so her judgment was likely clouded. The lump on her head throbbed like bad house music, and The Biz had remained silent since their argument on the highway. Communications from Him were maddening enough; His desertion was damn near destabilizing.

She pulled on a smile and lifted Zane's cap to smooth down his Brylcreemed hair. Then she handed him the tray of pancakes they'd picked up from the diner around the corner and plopped the jug of maple syrup on top.

"You're perfect."

She pulled the necklace from her pocket and placed it carefully in his hand, adjusting the medallion so the picture of a younger Forsyth they'd glued to the front faced outward.

"Go easy on it, if you can. I'm not convinced that epoxy is completely dry, and even the senator would probably realize that something's amiss if his necklace broke open over breakfast and a bug popped out into his juice."

Zane winked and she traded her new phone for his. "In case He notices something and decides it's worth ending His silent treatment over."

He smiled back with maddening unconcern. She watched as he disappeared around the corner of the building, on his way toward the tour bus idling next to Rockwell's Porsche at the far end of the playground, before she slipped back through the yard's rear gate. She crossed the street to a stretch of curb sheltered by an abandoned RV and pulled the receiver from her pocket. Then she raised her binoculars to watch for signs of trouble as the Styrofoam squeaked in time with Zane's footsteps.

He called out a greeting and it came through, loud and clear.

"I'm sorry, Sir." The responding voice had the authoritative tone of a seasoned security professional. "The senator isn't seeing anyone before the assembly."

"Oh no," Zane replied. "We don't want to disturb him. The kids are sure looking forward to his talk this morning, though, and they wanted to welcome him. A group of the middle-schoolers came in early to cook him up a batch of their special pancakes. They won second place in a pancake cooking contest last year, and the recipe even made it into a charity cookbook. They're pretty proud of that. They thought the senator might appreciate a taste."

"That was very thoughtful of them, Sir."

"They're a good group. One of the younger girls spent most of yesterday afternoon stringing up this necklace for him as well. We were hoping that maybe you could pass it on to one of his staff with the breakfast, and see that he gets it?"

"May I see your employee ID, please?"

The microphone thumped and crackled against the trays as Zane pulled the badge from his neck. The silence that followed seemed interminable. Patience's imaginings of what might happen if the guard detected the forgery—or if he called inside for Rockwell—grew more creative the longer she waited, and none of them were good. She lowered the binoculars and touched her fingers to her coat pocket over her gun. This separation felt even worse than Zane's agonizing test drive with the troopers, somehow, and she was beginning to question whether she had it in her to give a damn at this level. The worrying was too stressful. It made her ribs ache.

"Thank you," the guard said, and she exhaled at last. "Driver's license, please?"

Zane whistled and juggled the containers as he reached into his pocket. "You folks sure are serious about security. I had no idea how much went into guarding a state senator."

"This senator is special, Sir. His campaign demands more than most."

"Oh sure! Because of his music career, I'll bet. Well, that makes sense."

The guard didn't respond. Patience pursed her lips as he ruffled through his list of approved personnel, then startled for her gun again as the clipboard struck the security podium with a bang.

"Thank you, Coach Byrd. I'll have an aide take the breakfast in to Senator Forsyth, but why don't you have the little girl give him the necklace at the assembly? The senator likes that sort of thing."

"We've tried." Zane laughed. "She's developed a serious case of the shies this morning, and nothing will break her of them. I think some of the boys may have given her a bit of guff about the purple flower, and it probably hasn't helped that a few of the women on staff were big time Boi II Boi fans, back in the day. They've kind of got the kids all worked up about his visit. It was all I could to do to convince her to let me pass it on, after all her hard work. I suppose this sort of thing happens to him a lot."

There was a trace of a smile in the guard's voice. "Hazard of the job.

All right, Coach Byrd, you can hand me the necklace. Please pass the senator's thanks along to the little girl."

Patience turned her eyes to the sky as Zane's sneakers squeaked on the blacktop and faded into the distance. The guard radioed inside for an aide and then Zane appeared in the flesh at the corner of the building. He flashed her a thumbs-up, but she just looked away.

"Are you sure you couldn't have dragged that out any longer? Christ, Zane, I was waiting every second for that guard to pull out his .44 Magnum and write us an unhappy ending to this drama."

He smiled and stepped up onto the curb beside her. "I'd say it was a .38, judging by the bulge. Relax, Patience, the man could not have been more hospitable."

"Laugh all you want, but don't expect me to join in. I get my fill of quips from the Home Office." He reached for her arm and she pulled away. "Look, I don't know a better way to do this than to just be straight with you, so I'm sorry if it seems abrupt. I think it's a bad idea for us to have our attention divided right now. We need to stay focused on Forsyth and SolarTech."

The grin slid from his face as he considered her seriously for the first time since his pilgrimage to the bus. "Stopping Joey has had me pretty thoroughly engrossed since we met, Patience. What else were you looking to clear off our plates?"

"I think we need to break up."

His confusion dissolved at that and he laughed aloud. "Well, I can honestly report that this is the first time I've ever found out I had a girlfriend by getting kicked to the curb. I get that you don't typically go about things in the traditional fashion, though, so I don't mind. You're a really hard girl to read, Patience; this information is useful. It's good to know where we stand."

She raised the binoculars and turned away, as irritated by the glint in his eye as she was by his refusal to understand her. "We don't stand anywhere, Zane. As impossible as it may be for you to comprehend, you did just get dumped. It's nice to see you're having fun, though."

He grabbed her hand and the glasses fell back against her chest. "I'm doing something real here, Patience, something I could build an entire religion around. What happens today could help save the world, or I could wind up causing more harm than good and just praying for someone like your crazy uncle to charge in and clean up my mess. But, no matter what, I know some things about myself now that I didn't know before, and they're game changing. I'm not giving up until we're done or I'm dead—not on this, and not on you. I'm over-tired, under-caffeinated, and I'm in love with a girl who's got such a crazy perspective about life that everything I've just said sounds reasonable by comparison. So, yes, Patience, you bet your ass I'm having fun."

She pushed him away and tried to focus on the club, but it quaked inside the glasses and made her head throb. She gave up and thrust them back at him.

"Don't talk like that."

"I'm just telling you what I know. I'm not trying to freak you out."

"You've been freaking me out since the moment we met, Wayne. This isn't about that. I can't do what I need to while I'm preoccupied by what's happening with you or by the secrets you and The Biz are keeping from me. Forsyth and Rockwell are just a rec center away, and God only knows where my uncle is. This isn't a game we're playing. This is serious."

"You bet your ass it is."

Something in the tone of his voice made the hairs on her arms stand on end. He turned away and raised the binoculars. She did her best to ignore him, but her heart was carrying on in her chest like she'd stolen its wallet or something.

"What was it The Biz said to you by the side of the road last night?"

"I told you, it was nothing. It was personal, Patience, that's all."

She looked down again, listening to the muffled crackles through the receiver. "You could build an entire religion around this?"

"Yes."

"But, you wouldn't, right?"

"Right."

He smiled again with his focus steady on his surveillance, and she pulled her hair back from her face. He lowered the binoculars and brushed a stray lock of pink behind her ear. He seemed about to say something when they were interrupted by a click from behind.

"Make another move, son, and it'll be your last."

Zane spun back and Patience kicked her boot heel into the curb behind her.

"Damn it, Uncle John!"

The soldier kept his rifle trained on Zane, ignoring their guns as he stepped into the street with a dismayed look on his face. "I could have been the whole of Forsyth's security force, for all either one of you would have noticed. Hell, kid, I could have been that Rockwell corpse who knocked your lights out last night. Am I the only one still itching for his gizzards over that? You have to stay vigilant at all times. Don't ever let me sneak up on you again!"

"Oh, for crying out loud."

"We're at war, Pax!"

"We are not at war, Uncle John. We are provoking peace."

He lowered his rifle with a menacing stare at Zane, then dropped to sit on the curb before Patience and nudged her revolver aside. "I don't doubt for a second that you believe that, kid. You've always insisted upon good will and harmony, even when you had to battle every last person in the house to get it. I've always loved that about you, but it's not a sound foundation to build a world view on—not when everybody else is firing bullets at it. I'm sorry, I know that's a hard truth, but it's the truth, nonetheless." He lifted his rifle and poked Zane in the shoulder. "We called her our little pit bull of peace when she was just a tyke."

"Is that right?"

Zane was moving subtly behind the soldier, searching for his best angle. He lunged and John slapped a hand around his arm. He pulled the syringe from his fist and glanced down at the label. He just shook his head and released Zane with a sigh.

"I understand, kid." He turned back to Patience. "You've got a mission of your own. You had to try." He snapped the needle off the syringe and squirted a few ccs into his mouth. "Phenobarb's not a bad way to come down a notch during a hectic stint, if you want to know the truth."

Patience's eyes remained fixed on the transmitter. "Hush."

"I'm really not angry with you, Pax. There are some lessons they don't teach you in—"

"Hush!"

She held the transmitter up as Forsyth's voice crackled through, loud and nasally and demanding pancakes. Rockwell had confiscated them, it seemed, on the grounds that their strongest polling demographic was with women, ages thirty-five to fifty, and he'd detected a slight thickening at the senator's waistline since the start of the campaign.

"That bastard!" Patience was offended in some tangled solidarity with Forsyth. "Where does he get off?"

"The children made that breakfast especially for me," the senator persisted. "I can't disappoint them. Give me those fucking pancakes, Alex. I have to eat them for the sake of the children!"

Rockwell sent the aides scurrying and returned his attention to his candidate and lifelong friend. "The children will not be disappointed in the slightest, Joey, because you will lie to them."

The conversation felt like the dawning of crow's feet in Patience's anguished face and Zane pressed his palms to his eyes. Not a word was mentioned about the events at Rockwell's house the previous evening or about Forsyth's sudden change of heart about becoming a U. S. senator. His only real concern that morning seemed to hinge upon his breakfast.

Zane rubbed the back of his neck and paced the length of the RV, listening as Rockwell cursed Forsyth for hurling his yogurt to the floor. "He has to eat those pancakes," he pleaded to no one in particular. "Come on, Alex, you sadistic fuck. Don't screw this up for everyone."

"Why are we all fired up about what the senator eats?"

Patience looked up to her uncle, her brow nearly as tense as Zane's.

"Ipecac." She nodded. "It's in the maple syrup."

John stared back at them for a moment, his expression an even mix of surprise and horror. Then a smile slid onto his face and he laughed out loud.

"And you two don't approve of the way I do business? Jeez, Pax, I just want to kill the man, but you kids play dirty! Hell, I might even let him live through the assembly now, just to see how this turns out."

The clock ticked on toward show time and a compromise was reached at last—one pancake for the senator. Disapproval dripped from Rockwell's voice as he warned him, in the most hypercritical terms imaginable, to go easy on the butter and syrup.

"Control freak," Patience muttered.

"Plan wrecker," Zane added.

"Do you think it'll be enough?"

"I don't know," he said. "I really just don't know."

The racket clamoring through the receiver devolved into something resembling the backseat of a family station wagon about eight hours into a drive to the grandparents' house. The current squabble seemed centered around the senator's intransigence about wearing his new "trophy" onto the stage. Rockwell was strenuously opposed, and he delivered the nastiest blows of each round, denigrating the necklace and the senator himself. He even went so far as to insinuate that such a juvenile indulgence might pose a threat to Forsyth's physical welfare should their SolarTech benefactors catch wind of his foolishness and be displeased. Forsyth was entrenched, however, and he took the match in the end through stubborn, scrappy endurance. He doggedly remained in a snit until it was past time for him to take the stage before one-hundred-fifty rapt, school-aged children, their former-Boi II Boi-groupie mentors, and the gathering throng of media and Rockwell was left with no choice but to relent. He thrust the necklace at his sulking candidate, accompanied by a stern warning that he shouldn't form any ideas about wearing it to Milton later that morning—at which point Forsyth inquired whether Rockwell thought he was an idiot, and Rockwell declined to answer.

John nodded back at them and started toward the building. Patience glanced to the sky and then shook her head at Zane.

"What the hell am I supposed to do?" she whispered. "I can't shoot my uncle, and God only knows what would happen if we tried to tackle him here, with Rockwell and all those children nearby. I will never understand what The Biz was hoping to accomplish by sending him here."

Zane checked his gun and stepped into the street. "I think we just have to stay with him. I don't like the idea of taking him inside any more than you do, but incapacitating him obviously didn't work. Keeping an eye on him seems our only option now."

They started after him and Patience looked down at the phone again. The screen was as empty as it had been since His last message on the highway. She'd been telling The Biz to get lost for weeks, but

He'd waited until they actually had some need of Him before He'd turned His tail and run.

John pointed up to a second-floor window as they approached. "I checked the perimeter when I arrived, and our best bet is to shimmy up that downspout and push in through the administration office. That's the point of entry with the most tree cover, and the locks up there are a snap to force. It's a bit of a climb, but I'll help you, Pax. I do need you two to be prepared for something, though, on account of your particular sensitivities. There were a couple of folks working up there when I arrived. It may be necessary to subdue some stragglers, so I need you both to stay cool and trust that I'll always do everything possible to avoid causing undue harm to a non-target."

He stopped talking as he realized they were no longer with him. He turned to discover them ten feet back, glaring from a door beside the loading dock.

"We're not scaling up anybody's anything, Uncle John. Zane and I have been here since four this morning. We secured an entry hours ago, and it won't involve terrorizing any innocent people. What's wrong with you?"

She pointed to the door beside the loading dock and John shook his head.

"It's double-deadbolted. We could force it, or shoot our way through if need be, but we'll run a lower risk of setting off bedlam prematurely if we save all shooting for the main event."

"It's not deadbolted. We turned the locks around while the fire department had the exits disabled so the senator's guys could check the building. And what the hell are you doing climbing up a nonprofit organization's downspout? Do you have any idea how expensive those things are to replace?"

John stared back at her in amazement. Then he grabbed her and pulled her to the ground behind a wooden bin filled with basketballs.

A couple of guards came around the corner as he grabbed Zane's jersey and dragged him down behind them. The men passed and John jumped up. He brushed the tar from his hands before pulling Patience to her feet.

"Well, kid, I've got to hand it to you—your planning here today is about as convoluted and overly thought out as anything I've ever heard in my life. Are you telling me that you two broke into this building once undetected, and instead of staying put until show time, you spent God knows how much time screwing around with the locks, just so you could break back out again and risk getting busted three times instead of once?"

Patience pulled the phone from her pocket and bit her lower lip. Her uncle had received a heads up about the guards, but the screen remained dark. She shoved her hair behind her ear and turned back. "We had no choice, Uncle John. We still had work to do out here. Anyway, we needed a man on surveillance."

He pulled the door open with a shake of his head. "In ten years on the job, I've never once needed a man on surveillance. I work for the Good Lord God, Himself, kid. That's all the surveillance I need."

She shrugged and stepped onto the dock as a tentative smatter of applause erupted overhead, like raindrops on a plastic roof. "You've never had to guard against what we were watching out for this morning."

A voice shouted into a microphone and she turned toward the stairs.

"Okay, kid, I'll bite. You already knew where the senator and his goons were stashed. What else out here was so dangerous that it compelled you to increase your risk of capture threefold?"

She didn't look back at him.

"You, of course."

CHAPTER SIXTEEN

Patience pulled back on the grate of the hot air register in the tiny art supply room as Zane held both hands beneath to catch it. John reached down as it broke free of the wall and took the time-damaged iron skeleton easily in one hand and set it on the floor before the racks of dog-eared paper and brightly colored tempera paints. They all leaned in with their faces close to the dusty hole they'd created in the wall, where a second register aligned with it on the other side and afforded them an excellent view of the gym.

Forsyth was already on stage, peppering his speech with awkward, outdated slang as he impressed upon the audience how delighted he'd been to receive their invitation to come down from Boston and speak with them. Patience leaned in for a better view of the men surrounding the stage, searching for some sign of Rockwell.

John reached for his rifle and rose up onto one knee behind them. Patience glared in disbelief as the black steel barrel snaked alongside her and came to rest against the bottom edge of their spyhole. She grabbed it and jerked back hard with both hands, knocking her uncle off balance.

Zane leapt to his feet and reached for the closest thing at hand as Patience fought to keep John from lifting the weapon again. He tore the lid from a bottle and reached into the melee for the rifle, then yanked up and sent John and Patience tumbling back. A bright orange stream of paint burbled over the barrel and trigger assembly, splattering a fair amount onto the three of them as well.

John tossed his niece aside and pulled the ghastly-looking rifle from Zane's grasp. He poked him in the chest with it, striking a glistening orange gash across his jersey.

"So help me, son, I am at the end of my rope with you. The second we're back in the open air, you and me are gonna—"

Zane pushed the weapon away as Patience clapped a hand over her uncle's mouth. John pulled her hand from his face and reached into his coat for his revolver. Zane yanked his own out, but the SCUD just cursed at the orange streaks gumming up his slide and trigger.

"These are two good weapons your friend has just destroyed, Pax. They've seen me through a lot. I didn't mind the trick with the phenobarb, because I understood where it was coming from, but this is hitting below the belt."

She wiped her hands on her jeans. "It's hardly the thing I'm most ashamed of at the moment."

"Criminy, kid. I wasn't going to shoot the man here in the gym. But you've got to be on your guard for anything, at all times. When your target is in view, and he's surrounded by a whole load of artillery himself, that is not the time to start destroying your weapons."

Patience was unmoved. "You pulled out your rifle where children were present, so now you no longer possess a rifle where children are present. It's simple cause and effect, Uncle John. It doesn't get much more basic than that."

She turned back, choosing to ignore her uncle's apostolic grumbling and Zane's opportunistic needling at the newly unarmed man. As long as they kept the volume low and refrained from further physical confrontation, they could fend for themselves. She still hadn't located Rockwell, and the senator's attempts to connect with the young people of Brockton were growing stranger and harder to follow.

She was distracted from her search by some quiet activity at the back of the gym. She nudged Zane and pointed toward a couple of serious-looking suits who'd just entered through the rear doors. They stood alongside the wall and scrutinized Forsyth's performance with cool detachment. One was larger and younger than the other, and even from their distance, it was easy to note his deference toward the older man, but that was where their dissimilarities ended. They stood in identical postures, with expressions that were identically rigid, and Forsyth's sobs about his pancreas struck Patience as somewhat less absurd suddenly, as she stared at them. These were not your eco-friendly solar power enthusiasts, building panels to charge their home-built hybrid vegetable-oil cars and their hydroponic systems. The unblinking severity of their attention to the senator seemed to lower the temperature in the gym ten degrees.

"SolarTech."

Zane nodded and pointed back toward the stage. Rockwell was in the shadows at the back with his arm in a sling, watching over the men as they watched over Forsyth. Patience felt a conflicted sense of relief at the sight of him. His expression was as aloof and self-important as ever, and apart from the sling, he appeared visibly unaltered by his encounter with Zane's bullet. The damage seemed hardly unforgivable.

John nudged her shoulder and cocked his head toward the suits. "Who are the party fun guys?"

She just shook her head without looking back. "If your omniscient PA system hasn't filled you in, Uncle John, I guess it's not for you to know."

"Maybe not, kid. But it's for me to find out."

The noise from the bleachers was increasing in volume and variability as the kids seemed united by their confusion. They looked askance at Forsyth and at one another whenever he mentioned the fine pancake breakfast he'd enjoyed that morning or his abiding love for pancakes in general. They stared out the windows and up at the clocks on the scoreboards until a few of the older boys nodded a silent pact at one another, bumped fists, and climbed down to the gymnasium floor. They encircled their coach, who was standing at the wall beside the register, and demanded to know when basketball was going to start.

The tallest of the boys pointed up toward the stage and voiced their complaint, a little more loudly than he'd intended perhaps. Or perhaps not.

"You said that he asked to come here and talk with us, Chris, not the other way round. This is whack. We got our team in the finals and he's up there jawing about his breakfast, with a picture of himself on his chest. What the hell, man?"

"We'll keep the doors open late tonight," Chris whispered. He glanced back at the reporters and leaned in closer to the boys. "We'll get all the games in, okay, Maleek? This is a really good opportunity to raise awareness about the center, and maybe a little support. Come on, man. Help us out for an hour or so, would you?"

Maleek stared back at his coach and then he dropped his eyes to the boards. "Okay," he said. "Yeah, okay."

He motioned halfheartedly to the others and they slunk back to the bleachers. Patience turned to Zane, but his phone was in hand and he was tapping something onto the screen. He hit send and looked up again.

"That should keep them on budget for the current year, anyway. I'll have my accountants look deeper into the situation when I'm a little less covered in paint."

Patience was overcome. She grabbed him by the front of his jersey and kissed him. John cursed and nudged at them with his boot, but she ignored him. Forsyth said the word "confrabasticalation," and she ignored him as well. A couple of the kids asked their mentors if the guy on the stage used to be a member of New Kids on the Block, but Patience ignored them all. It wasn't until Zane seemed in danger of losing consciousness that she released him at last.

"Sorry."

He shook his head clear and pulled himself back together. "I suppose I'm just going to have to get used to it, aren't I? The breakup, however, is off."

Patience didn't respond to that. John snuck a sideways glare at Zane and turned back to the senator. He'd finished his speech at last and was ready for questions from the audience. The fidgeting ceased and the gum stopped popping, as the gym turned still as a stickup. The kids sat with their faces down until Maleek tapped one of his buddies and nodded to the stage. The boy lowered his head over his knees and pretended not to notice Maleek's stares, but then he dropped his shoulders and stood up with a hand in the air.

"Excuse me, Sir. Do you like basketball?"

"Basketball?" Forsyth scratched his ear and glanced over to Rockwell. "You bet I do! I mean, go Celts! Right, guys?"

The kid glared down at Maleek, who just shrugged and settled back on his bench.

"Right," he said. "Okay, then. Thanks."

The gym was quiet again, except for the occasional cough and some idle kicking at the benches. Maleek nodded to the boy at his other side, but he just sank lower and shook his head. A few seconds later, he, too, was starting to his feet when his dignity was spared by a fifth-grade girl several rows below. She stood up tentatively with her hand raised halfway.

"Excuse me, Sir. I have a question. Some of the boys on Chess Challenge were saying that you used to be a singer on YouTube, or something. That's not true, is it?"

Forsyth smiled from the podium. No need to look to Rockwell for this one. He pointed at her like his finger was a loaded .357 and cocked its hammer with his thumb.

"You bet it's true, darlin'. But back in my day, music didn't come from YouTube or the iTunes. It came from something called MTV. Now, I'm not looking to embarrass anybody, but I happen to know that there are some good folks right here in this very room who know me at least as well from my days as a successful R&B performer as they do from my work as a humble public servant."

Patience pressed her lips together and looked back at Zane. "R&B?"

"Try not to overthink it."

The young girl was still standing when she turned back, and she appeared more confused now than before. "But you don't do that anymore, right? Because the guys on Chess Challenge said that you were probably going to try to do a concert or something today, and I told them no way."

Forsyth adjusted his necklace with a wink, and then his smile turned dangerous. The room stilled until the air itself seemed afraid to stir. "I appreciate that, darlin'. I truly do. Normally, I'd be delighted to perform for an attractive, enthusiastic audience such as this, but this is a serious discussion we're having here this morning. This discussion is about the obstacles facing you young people and what I can do to turn those obstacles into challenges once I'm elected to the United States Senate next Tuesday. As much as I'd love to, I really shouldn't distract us from the weightiness of our topic."

The room relaxed at last and the girl sat back down on the bench. Forsyth became very still for a moment, and then he lowered himself over the podium. He gripped its sides with his head bent above the pages of his speech, and a strange expression passed over his face. Then his muscles constricted and he appeared to be holding his breath. Zane grabbed Patience by the hand and they awaited the finale in horrible anticipation.

The SolarTech Industries executives appeared equally alert and intrigued by what was happening with their candidate. Forsyth stayed low for another few moments and then he exhaled and wiped a bead of sweat from his hairline. He straightened his posture, nodded to no one, and flashed a big, white smile in the direction of the cameras before returning his attention to the crowd.

"What's your name, sweetheart?"

The girl who'd asked the question hugged her backpack to her chest and glanced furtively around the gym. She was hoping, it seemed, that he'd moved on to someone else while she'd been daydreaming, but this flirtation with optimism was belied by a hint of fatalism in her eyes that Patience found deplorable in a child her age. Her head lowered and her shoulders raised, like a tortoise attempting to retreat into its shell, as she looked back up at the senator.

"Jasmine?"

He winked again and pulled the microphone free of its stand.

"Well, Jasmine, let me tell you something about Joey Forsyth." He performed a modified kick-ball-change, clapped once, and turned a hip forward as he pointed directly at the mortified ten-year-old. "Joey Forsyth could never refuse a request from one of his constituents, particularly from such a pretty little future voter as yourself. So hey, kids, what do you say we liven this place up a bit, after all? And Jasmine, sweetheart, this one's for you."

The crowd turned to stare as she hid her face in her hands and refused to look up again. Forsyth pulled once on the mic cord and stepped out from behind the podium.

"There's one song I cowrote a few years back that I think might be appropriate to our discussion here this morning. Kids, I want you all to go home today and remind your parents that Senator Joey Forsyth is doing it 'Again and Again for You, Baby.' I think they'll understand."

He raised an arm and began to croon in a way that niggled at

Patience's brain for a moment. Then she gasped and clapped her hands over her ears.

"Oh, my God!" she whispered. "This song has the word *plunged* repeatedly in its refrain, and *not* in any home maintenance sort of context. What the hell is he trying to do to these poor children?"

Senator Forsyth didn't appear to be the slightest bit concerned about what he was doing to those poor children. He performed his demented little heart out, a cappella, complete with all the spins, and *OH!s*, and hip thrusts of his younger days. Rockwell stepped from the shadows and stood beside the stage, his face taut as he stared across the gym at the men by the rear door. He mobilized his people to surround Forsyth, and they applauded with fervor and gusto as the senator finished his song at last. The crowd clapped along uncertainly until Rockwell stepped up and took control of the microphone. He raised Forsyth's hand into the air.

"Your next representative to the United States Senate, ladies and gentlemen, Massachusetts State Senator Joseph M. Forsyth! He will do it, and he will do it again and again, for you!"

Forsyth appeared drawn and somewhat shaky as Rockwell dug his fingers into his coat sleeve. They waved once more to the crowd, and then he turned his candidate toward the exit and escorted him from the stage under the stark scrutiny of the SolarTech executives. They disappeared into a sea of suits, and then the rear door of the gymnasium clicked shut and the executives were gone as well.

Zane shook his head at Patience as he sat up on the art room floor. "He didn't blow."

"We'll think of something else."

"He didn't blow."

John nodded as they got themselves together, and then he turned without a word and punched Zane in the face. Zane's revolver flew from his hand as he sailed across the floor and Patience dove for it.

John plucked it easily from her fingers and turned back to Zane, setting a size-sixteen boot down on his chest.

"That's for the guns. And this is your final warning to watch it with my niece. I'm not going to tell you again."

He looked up at Patience then, who was standing before him with her own gun drawn, and he shook his head. He took that from her as well, reset the safety, and dropped it into his pocket. Then he kissed her on the forehead as Zane scrambled back onto his feet.

"You're a good girl, Pax. I'd recommend keeping your bias against bloodshed as privileged information, though, if you're going to be pointing guns at people. Now, I'm sorry about this. I was actually sort of rooting for you this time, but I think we both know what I've gotta do. Don't think of it as a failing on your part. For a novice SCUD, you're doing all right. Your planning's a tad convoluted, and there's still a lot of learning ahead of you, but that's to be expected. Now, go and get some rest while I finish up here. I'll see you on the other side."

He strung his orange-streaked rifle over his shoulder and turned toward the door, and something unexpected crept into Patience's gut. She was terrified of what he'd do out there on his own, but his leaving stung her in new ways that caught her off guard. She might have even asked him to stay, if she'd still had her gun.

Her pocket chimed and Zane grabbed the phone. He tossed it to her and picked up a three-legged plaster of Paris badger from a shelf in the corner. Then he dove at John and smashed it over the soldier's head.

"I guess I might have thought of that myself," he said to the window as the giant toppled to their feet. "Thank You."

Patience just glared down at the screen. "Where the hell have You been?"

WE WILL TALK LATR

THER IS WRK 2 DO NOW

"Do You have any idea what's been going on around here? Christ, Biz! We're making this up as we go along, and You're the one who started it. How could You just disappear on us like that?"

I SED LATR!

She held the phone up to show Zane, but he just shook his head and knelt down to check her uncle's pulse. He slid a couple of painter's smocks beneath John's head and retrieved their guns from his coat pocket.

"You and The Biz are going to have to sort this out yourselves, Patience. Argue about it on the road."

"You're flaking out on me now too?"

"No, but I'm finally learning not to engage." He pointed down at John. "Any thoughts on what we should do about this situation?"

She shook her head at her beloved uncle, the Lord's assassin. "There's no room to bring him with us, obviously, but we can't just leave him here, where some unarmed person could stumble upon him. I guess we'll need to find a better place to hide him."

Zane scratched his head and the phone chimed in her hand.

SHPPNG/RECVNG LOOKD PRTTY CLUTTRD

Patience turned her face from the message. "So, You're speaking to me now?"

NO IM JST SAYNG

Forsyth's bus was still idling exhaust beside Rockwell's Porsche as they stepped back into the crisp fall air. Zane pulled the receiver from his track pants and switched it on.

"Let's hope Joey's still got his necklace nearby."

Forsyth did, in fact, still have his necklace nearby. From the sound of it, it seemed he might actually still be wearing it, so they had no trouble hearing Rockwell berate him for what he'd considered a less than inspired performance of Boi II Boi's highest charting single. They also had no trouble hearing Forsyth complain about his stomach or Rockwell's wave of curtly dismissive vitriol, followed by his instruction to the senator that he get himself together by the time they reached Milton. Then the bus door opened with a bang and Rockwell stormed off to pick up some Maalox for his bellyaching candidate.

The doors snapped shut and Forsyth told the driver to take off. The brakes squealed and the sound became distorted as they pulled toward the playground exit. Forsyth turned his attention to one of his aides as his voice started breaking up.

"Go get me those pancakes off the bar," was the last thing they heard him say. "And don't be stingy with the syrup."

CHAPTER SEVENTEEN

Zane was trying his damnedest not to engage in the argument beside him. Patience had the phone close to her face, glaring as though she could set it afire by heat of her eyes alone. He glanced over once and returned his attention immediately to the road. He didn't look entirely convinced that she couldn't.

"It was bad enough having Forsyth and Rockwell and those two SolarTech freaks all together in that gym with those kids. The whole building could have exploded from the sheer malevolence in the air. We've been killing ourselves, trying to accomplish what You've asked us to do, and You just bailed on us with my crazy uncle on the scene, setting up target practice! What the hell was that?"

I GAVE U A TIME-OUT

Her jaw dropped and she looked up at Zane. He shook his head and kept his attention forward. "I told you, Patience, I won't be involved. I've been zapped once already, thanks."

"My point exactly!"

"No."

She tossed the phone onto the dash and glowered out the window. "He's got all the time in the world for emoticons and ridiculous jokes, so long as everything's under control. But, the second things start to get a little hectic, we're on our own. The Big Guy is out of here."

SIGH

"He just texted me a sigh!"

Zane sighed himself and the phone chimed again.

WEN U SEE 2 SETS OF FOOTPRNTS IN THE SAND U NO I WALK B-SIDE U

WEN U SEE 1 SET OF FOOTPRNTS IN THE SAND THT IS WEN I CARRY U!

She took it back from the dash and stared down a moment, her eyes filling with tears born of indescribable emotion. Then she blinked them away and glared up at the sky. "That isn't even Yours! That poem was on the walls of half the houses I babysat for as a kid. Jesus, Biz, if You're going to steal Your material, why can't You at least steal it from the Bible like everybody else? You're not even trying!"

ITS A NICE POEM

"I can pick it up at the car wash, stamped on an air freshener!"

GOLDN RULES NOT MINE EITHR BUT I LIKE THT ONE 2

SUE ME

"Do You think I can't find a lawyer arrogant enough to try?"

R U DONE???

Zane took the phone from her hand and tossed it back into the console. "I'm about to give you both a time-out. My basic theology's been through enough for one day, thank you. Patience, what are you doing? All you ever do is bicker with Him, and He just bickers back. The two of you are seriously starting to screw with my head."

"Well, your head should be safe from now on, Zane, because I'm done. As far as I'm concerned, I have no need to speak to Him at all."

"You've said so about a thousand times, but when I ask you why, I get twenty minutes on the atrocities of text speak or railing about His invasion into your personal space. I'm going to ask you a serious question now, and I'd appreciate an honest and thoughtful answer for once. What the hell is wrong with you?"

She stared down at the orange paint trapped in the corners of her fingernails. Then she answered him before she'd even decided what she'd say. "I just feel more comfortable fighting with Him than I do talking to Him."

"Why?"

"Because I don't understand Him. I don't understood who He is, or if He's real, or what role He's supposed to play in my life. Those things have never been clear to me the way they seem to be for some people. His presence here confuses me, and things that confuse me make me angry. When something makes me angry, I fight it until I win, and then I feel better."

He was quiet for a moment. "You know something? I think I can actually sort of understand that."

"Well, that makes one of us."

CHAPTER EIGHTEEN

It was not for the faint of heart. They hid in the shadows behind a display case at the back of the town hall and watched through their hands as the good people of Milton, Massachusetts jumped back in dismay and the good members of the local press rushed forward. Forsyth was doubled over at the front of the hall, white-faced and quaking, as he vomited his breakfast onto the floor with astonishing velocity. The expulsion was so violent, and so protracted, it was nearly two full minutes before Rockwell could get anywhere near him, during which time he'd been caught by the cameras crying that he didn't want to kill the world, and then he soiled himself.

"Wow."

Patience studied Rockwell's face, transfixed by the daggers of disgust in his eyes as he stared down at his ailing candidate. He looked up again to the SolarTech executives across the room, and then he turned to two of Forsyth's aides and directed them to lift the sobbing, heaving senator from the floor and carry him back to the bus.

"That was effective."

Zane nodded back.

"More so than I'd predicted."

The cameras kept filming the mess around the podium and the people fleeing the hall, some of whom had been sitting quite close to the senator and bore the stains of their misfortune on their clothing and stricken faces. Zane appeared just a little bit stricken himself, because he was nice that way, but his unease lessened after a minute or so and then he smiled.

"The senator is a man of his word, if nothing else. Joey sure did do it, and he did it again and again for us."

CHAPTER NINETEEN

Patience opened her apartment door, and then she turned back to warn Zane that they were still out of luck in regard to his morning coffee. He just took her face in his hands and kissed her before any such nonlife-threatening concerns could be addressed. The phone slipped from her fingers and he caught it in mid-air, then kicked the still broken door shut behind them.

"Wait."

He pulled back with a trace of concern in his eyes. It disappeared as she grabbed the edges of his sweatshirt and stripped him of it, then wrapped the phone up inside. She led him to the bedroom and buried the bundle in the darkest recesses of her closet. He shook his head as she turned back.

"Seriously, Patience, you must understand by now that it's never been the phone that's communicating with you."

"Of course I do, Zane." They fell together onto the tangle of sheets as their fingers got to work ridding each other of unwanted clothing. "But nothing in the world would kill this mood like an emoticon-riddled message from The Biz, and I really don't want this mood to be killed."

There was no arguing the validity of her point, and Zane seemed in no mood to argue, anyway. Patience had already forgotten what she was saying by the time his lips touched hers. Zane Grey Ellison made love to her that night with all the drive and heroism of a man who'd just saved the world from destruction, and Patience Abigail Kelleher responded to him in kind.

It wasn't until the next morning that Patience realized she was in trouble. It had taken most of the night to satisfy the thing that had grown up between them, feeding on their angst and adrenaline until it had swelled into a state of epic overload during their fight against God and the Apocalypse, their futility and fear, and too many goddamn guns all around for either of their tastes. The time finally came, however, when Zane could focus his attention where he wanted it most, and that was on Patience. He didn't seem to be in any hurry as he whispered the sorts of things a girl charged with saving the world would probably consider to be dangerous distractions, but to a girl just released from duty, they were pretty nice things to hear.

She pushed the hair back from his eyes and he looked down at her, and that was that. Patience was done for. She didn't try to pretend that things were any less complicated between them; she simply acknowledged that there was nothing left to be done about it. Zane had uncovered all her secrets in a single night, and curiously, she felt better now that they were known.

There was a strange lack of heaviness in her chest as the sunlight warmed her skin through the window. A surge of relief rose up so suddenly inside her that it might actually have felt good to burst into tears. The thing she'd dreaded for so long had come and gone, and the world hadn't come to an end. Neither, for that matter, had she. Patience Kelleher was just beginning.

Zane smiled back at her and then he slipped from the bed. She watched in self-conscious silence as he crossed over to her paint-chipped bookcase and poked through her books and keepsakes. He grinned down at a photo of her at age eight, sticking her tongue out at a birthday party clown, and then he plucked her fuchsia-furred teddy bear from atop a stack of paperbacks and came back to lay beside her. The bear had retained a remarkable degree of vibrancy for a dye-job achieved via felt-tip marker, and its right leg was attached by a large bolt and nut encased in a swath of pink felt designed to protect the delicate skin of its ardent and obstinate young companion. Zane shook his head and held it up to her.

"I can't conceive of a person going to such pains to fix a toy that could simply have been replaced."

Patience clutched her heart in horror and took the bear from his hand. "Frank promised me that hip-replacement patients always returned from surgery stronger than they'd been before. I think he may have taken some liberties with my six-year-old gullibility there, but Kool-Aid did seem to be a more resilient bear when all was said and done."

Zane raised an eyebrow at her. "Frank did this?"

She smiled back. "My screams must have been heard for a mile. You'd have thought it was me who'd lost the leg."

"How did it happen?"

"Tragic miscalculation with a parachute I'd invented from plastic bags and a bungee cord. I was so sure it would work, because I'd seen it on TV. I was such a mess when poor Kool-Aid went splat. Mom could barely get me into the car. She drove straight to the pub with me screaming the whole way and Frank took it from there. That was a pretty hard day for my mother."

"I'd say it was a hard day for Kool-Aid as well." Zane paused. "This seems an unexpected side of Frank."

She laughed. "I think he was mostly just relieved that I'd let Kool-Aid take the first jump. I was a pretty exuberant kid."

Zane took the bear back and twirled a bit of pink thread around the bolt. "I've never had a man threaten to toss me from his establishment for talking too much," he said. "Actually, I've never had anyone threaten to toss me out of anywhere. That was sort of nice, if you want to know the truth. It meant a lot to me."

Patience grinned and settled back. "Frank once bounced the governor and his staff during a campaign meet-and-greet because they were getting on his nerves. As long as you're respectful and you don't cause any trouble, he really doesn't care what your name is, if he even knows it at all."

"Not even if your name is The Biz?"

"Ah," she conceded. "No, that would be altogether different. Irish Catholic and all that. The Biz would never be tossed from the pub, no matter how insufferable He became, and Frank would make my life a living hell if he ever found out what's been going on." She paused and glanced toward the closet door. "Do you think He'll let me live a normal life, now that this is over?"

"What's normal?"

She shrugged. "I'm probably the last person on Earth qualified to answer that question, except perhaps for you. It might be kind of nice to find out, though."

He reached across her to set the bear on the nightstand.

"What I think, Patience, is that there's a pretty good chance that He's up there right now, complaining to anyone who'll listen about the novice waitress SCUD who got Him to promise not to smite her, and then made Him regret that promise almost every hour of every day thereafter."

She suppressed a smile and turned her face to the sheets. "I don't recall anything from my Sunday School lessons about Moses getting hit by an abundance of OMGs and LOLs, Zane. He was goading me."

"Moses appears in the writings of several religions, with mountains of text attributed to him." Zane nodded. "And I've yet to come across a single occurrence of Text Speak in any of them. That said, I'm not sure I'd go up against him when it comes to the assignment of unreasonable tasks. There are those who'd argue that Moses' entire journey with The Biz was one giant WTF."

She pressed a finger to his lips. "Fine." She sighed. "Moses wins."

"I do agree that He's likely been goading you, however. I keep coming back to what you said about fighting the things that confuse you until you feel better. You're really not His every day, garden variety adherent, and I suspect that He's on to you there. He's probably just been doing what He felt was necessary to keep you in the game."

She untangled herself from his arms and sat up. "How pissed off do you think He is?"

Zane just chuckled. "I think He knew what He was getting into. It's over, though, Patience. What's the harm in asking Him that now?"

"I've actually been thinking about checking out some new wireless carriers. There's got to be a phone out there somewhere that can't receive text messages."

He hit her with the pillow and she lay back.

"While we're on the subject of supernatural wrath, how do you think it's going to pan out when your phenobarb-loving uncle finally catches up with me?"

Patience sighed and shook her head. "I haven't seen John in a decade, Zane. The man I knew before he signed on to whack people for the Lord couldn't have hurt a fly, so it's obvious that he's changed a bit. You might want to exercise caution whenever faced with the business end of his rifle for a while."

"I think that's probably sound advice."

They were jolted from the bed by a room-shuddering thud that sent them scrambling for their clothes and their guns. They dashed to the living room and dove behind the couch as the door flew back on its hinges.

"Is it Rockwell?"

Zane peered around the couch at the enormous pair of boots stalking toward them. "Worse," he whispered back. "I think we're about to get the answer to my question."

"Damn it!"

Patience jumped up and pointed her gun at her uncle. Zane stood before her and stretched an arm between them, but she stepped around it with her lip quivering angrily.

"The landlord just had that door fixed a few hours ago, Uncle John, and it was hell trying to explain what happened the first time! Do you even know how to knock?"

"Hello, Pax. Glad to see you're still alive."

John gave her a kiss on the top of her head and punched Zane in the jaw with the full force of his might. He fell back into the wall as Patience screamed. For a moment, it seemed he might right himself, but then he listed and stumbled to the floor.

Patience dropped beside him with a glare up at her uncle.

"That's done." John nodded. "And well deserved, as I'm sure you'll both agree. Look, kid, I just stopped by to check that you were okay before moving on, and to make sure that Rockwell corpse wasn't pulling any funny business. Everything seems to be sewn up now, but I know how sensitive you are about killing and such. My conscience wouldn't let me go until I saw you."

She turned away from the lump forming on Zane's jaw and gaped up at her uncle. "What are you talking about? We just made the senator sick and he handled the rest on his own. He'll be all right in a day or two, as long as he doesn't show his face at the country club anytime soon."

John shook his head. "Pax, if you're going to serve the Lord, you've gotta stay better informed. It's a topsy-turvy world out there." He paused and looked away. "What have you done with It now? Did you grind It up again, or drown It in acid?"

She colored slightly. "I just gave It the night off. It's been a stressful week, and we thought—"

He held his hand up. "I don't want to hear anything more. You go let the phone out of whatever you've got it stashed in while I get Romeo, here, some ice for his face."

Patience looked sideways at her uncle. That light space inside her was increasing in density as she rose slowly from the floor. It swelled to full-blown dread as she reached her bedroom. An ice cube tray cracked in the kitchen and she pulled the closet door open to the thwopping of cubes into a plastic bag, followed by the muffled chime of a message alert.

She reached to the bottom of the clothes hamper and relieved Zane's sweatshirt of the phone. A single message awaited on the screen. It was a picture of the headline from that morning's *Globe*.

Massachusetts State Senator Joseph M. Forsyth, 42, Dead After Sudden Illness.

CHAPTER TWENTY

She heard them calling from somewhere far away, but couldn't respond. She lay on the floor, locked in a ball with the phone trapped between her hands as Zane brushed the hair from her face and John shook her again.

"You didn't do this, Pax."

She couldn't understand what he meant. Her trembling turned to shuddering as the phone chimed again. Finally, John pushed Zane back and lifted her from the rug. He carried her into the bathroom and dropped her into the tub. Then he pulled her hands apart, removed the phone, and turned on the shower.

The blast of cold water hit her face and she threw her arms over her head. Zane shoved past her uncle and jumped into the tub beside her. She turned her face to his chest and cried into his drenched T-shirt.

"We didn't do this," he said again and again.

John turned off the water and leaned against the sink. He dropped his head to his hand as she choked on the last of her tears and Zane turned her face to his.

"I don't understand."

"It's what we've been trying to tell you for the past ten minutes," John said. "You didn't kill the senator. It was his mad corpse of a campaign manager." He held the phone up to show her the screen. The Biz had texted a single word.

ROCKWELL

She shook her head and he set it back down.

"That doesn't make sense. Joey Forsyth has been his meal ticket for over twenty-five years. If they're really as scared of these SolarTech guys as he suggested, wouldn't keeping the senator alive and finding a way to rehabilitate his image before Tuesday be their only hope? Rockwell is nothing to SolarTech without a candidate. Why would he kill him?"

"I don't know," John said. "Autopsy hasn't been performed yet, and for the moment, everybody's taking it on faith that he was overcome by some acute illness after what happened at the town hall yesterday. All we know for sure is that we had a problem, and for whatever reason, Rockwell has decided to solve it for us. So, I guess that's it for me, kid. I've got to pack it up now and move on to the next catastrophe. But, I can't go until I know you're okay."

"I'm not okay!" Patience shouted. "Nothing is okay. Forsyth may have been an egomaniacal moron, but he was still a human being. Rockwell would never have killed him if he thought he could still get some use out of him, but I guess we took care of that. What Joey Forsyth needed was a good spanking and a job where he couldn't do any harm. He didn't need to die, for Christ's sake."

John just shook his head at her. He looked tired. "Human nature is a funny, fucked-up kind of a thing. It veers off in unexpected directions. If you try to follow too close behind it, it won't be long before you find yourself heading straight for the edge of a cliff with no time to hit the brakes. You've gotta step off a bit. You can't save the world without considering it from a whole world perspective. What you're doing right now is humanizing the enemy, and you can't ever win that way."

She stood up and turned to him with water dripping over her face.

"I thought you said we'd already won. Rockwell has solved our problem, and the world is now safe to fuck itself up all over again. Kudos to us, Uncle John."

He took her by the shoulders and pulled her from the tub.

"I've just turned the hose on the person I cherish most in this world, after she got her heart stomped on by her own beliefs. Nobody's won here, kid. It was a mean trick of the Lord's, letting you run crazy without the proper guidance or preparation, but that's my beef with Him. Looking at your face right now, there's only one thing in the world I know for certain. Nobody's won."

Zane stepped between them and nodded up at the SCUD. "What do we do now?"

John just shook his head. "Nothing. What needed doing is done. I'll admit that I'm a little uncomfortable about the lack of apparent reason to how this all went down, but I learned a long time ago not to get caught up in the whys and wherefores of a job. Senator Joey Forsyth is no longer a threat to the world, and there's always more work to be done. So, I'm going to go have my own little heart-to-heart with God, and then it'll be off to the next place He needs me to be."

Patience grabbed him by the arm and he smiled back indulgently. "You can't just leave, Uncle John. Rockwell can't get away with this. We have to do something... We have to tell the police what we know."

He shook his head and laid a hand on her shoulder. "What will you tell them, Pax? That you know the senator didn't die of natural causes because God told you so in a text message that no one else can see? Or that you kidnapped the man and his campaign manager at gunpoint, shot one of them in the arm, and then fed the dead man a load of ipecac the morning before he kicked? Men have been killing men for as long as they've been on the Earth. I'm sorry, but this is outside of our jurisdiction."

Patience shook his hand from her shoulder.

"I agree," Zane said. "There's no way this ends well if we go to the police. I'm sorry, Patience, but I'm with John on this one."

Her uncle leaned in and turned her face back to his. "And if this Rockwell corpse ever threatens a pink hair on your head again, I'm going to kill him dead. There won't be anything that you, or God, or all the SCUDs on Earth can do to stop me, you can be certain of that." He turned to Zane then. "Same goes for you, rich boy. You watch yourself."

Patience waved toward the door. "Just go."

He rubbed her wet head and turned away. She stood where she was until his heavy footsteps paused at her newly rebroken door and then she yelled his name and ran back into the living room. She found him waiting for her before the threshold.

"How can I reach you?"

"I've got your number," he said. "It won't be so long this time, kid, I promise. And if you ever need me, I'll know it."

She looked away. "I needed you for ten years."

"Nah," he said. "You really didn't."

And then he was gone.

CHAPTER TWENTY-ONE

It was all so horribly clear.

"How did we miss this?"

They stood together before the television, staring down at Rockwell's sad and serious face. The campaign manager fought back his threatening tears with the perfect notes of courage and vulnerability. He appeared the very picture of a man determined to honor his late friend's legacy with professional decorum, despite his personal grief, and the sling restraining his injured arm only heightened his heroic effect. Patience looked up at Zane as his right hand tightened into a fist and the spindly fingers of horror wound their way up to her throat.

"How could we possibly have missed that this would be his plan?"

He shook his head, his jaw twitching as Rockwell described the fearlessness of Forsyth's final days, and how he'd refused to allow a grueling illness to deter him from reaching out to the good people of Massachusetts. He went on to describe how he, Alexander Rockwell, would live out the rest of his years with the knowledge that his great friend and mentor had been more gravely ill than he'd let on, and that he'd succumbed to the senator's wishes to be allowed to continue with his busy campaign schedule.

"The Commonwealth of Massachusetts lost a champion last night." Rockwell's voice broke eloquently. "More importantly, the Commonwealth lost a friend. Senator Joey Forsyth was devoted to the state he served for nearly four years, so much so that he never left it, despite his enormous success in the entertainment industry. Long after most who'd achieved what he had would have moved on to lives at the beach and red carpet events, Senator Forsyth made the choice to roll up his sleeves and go to work for the people of Massachusetts. He was determined to give back to those who'd so embraced him all his life and to make sure their interests were represented on Beacon Hill with tenacity and vigor. And until the moment of his death, Senator Forsyth was determined to take their fight all the way to Washington, D.C."

There was a smattering of applause and Rockwell fell silent. He nodded once to the cameras and looked down.

"It's with a heavy heart this afternoon that I respond to the party's request that I continue in the senator's place for the remainder of this campaign. It will be my sad privilege to fill his seat, should he be elected to the United States Senate this coming Tuesday, until a special election can he held to determine the seat's permanent fate. And I will make this promise to you, his friends and constituents, right here and now: I will represent your interests with every ounce of the passion that Senator Joey Forsyth would have. When you go to the polls this Tuesday, I hope you'll show this great man, this great friend of Massachusetts, your appreciation for the fight he took up on your behalf. It was a fight he ultimately gave his life for. Please thank him with your vote. I thank you very much for listening, and God bless."

Patience looked up at Zane as Rockwell took questions from the reporters. "What do we do now?"

He was saved the trouble of responding by a rapping at the door. She opened it to find a courier in the hall. She signed for the envelope and frowned at its plain, printed label.

"It's for you," she said. "Delivered here, with no return address."

"I don't like the sound of that."

He ripped it open and removed a letter and a small stack of photographs. He stood very still as he read, with scarcely a glance at the pictures, until the page crumpled in his hand and he sat down on the floor. He pressed his fists to his forehead and the photos scattered over his knees and around his feet.

"What is it?"

She knelt beside him and he looked up. His eyes were terrible.

"It's me, Patience. I fucked up." She reached for a couple of the pictures as he pressed a hand over his eyes. "Alex has everything. We're no safer now than we were before the town hall meeting, except that Alex isn't as stupid as Joey was, and I'm about to be removed from the equation entirely."

She stood up with the pictures in hand and a sick feeling in her gut. The shots had been pulled from what was clearly a security camera mounted to the Forsyth campaign's tour bus. They were stills of Zane, chatting with the security guard, while carrying a brightly colored plastic necklace, a take-out container, and a generous jug of maple syrup.

Her vision blurred for a moment. "How could we not have known about this?" She looked down at him again, but he was folded over his knees with his face in his hands. "The Biz must have known about those cameras, Zane. This doesn't make sense. How could He not have...?" She looked toward the window, and then her heart broke. "I was in a time-out."

He looked up, uncomprehending. She just shook her head and pointed to the letter. His shoulders dropped as he held it up.

"Alex knows about the ipecac. The bug too. He's got everything. Joey died of extreme dehydration and gastrointestinal distress, followed by respiratory failure. The only traceable substance they've found in his system is ipecac. For the moment, they're ruling his death an accident, because it's been confirmed by his camp that he'd been known to fool around with some questionable weight control methods, but Alex has what's left of the syrup I sent in. He's giving me until six o'clock tonight to convince my father to cozy up or he's taking everything to the feds, along with his harrowing account of our past three days together. I have to get in front of this, Patience. I have to go in and tell them everything I know."

Her mind went into lockdown. "That's out of the question."

"Patience, please."

She charged past him, collecting her coat and the weapons. Zane tried to follow, but she wouldn't stop moving. Finally, he grabbed her by the arm and pulled her back to face him.

"I have to go right now. I've got just a handful of hours before Alex's deadline, and if I wait for them to come to me, I'll have no credibility whatsoever."

She pulled her arm back. "So help me, Zane, if you do this, I will make your life a living hell. You'll barely even know you're in federal prison, that's how miserable you'll be."

He took her by the hand to stop her from turning away. "I'm sorry, Patience, but I'm in love with you. Ten years is not enough. I need to go."

She pulled away and thrust the phone into his hand. "Don't be an ass, Zane. You need to call your father."

He stepped back with his hands in the air, forcing her to catch the phone again. "Not on your life."

The lines of her face tightened, but she didn't back down. "I'm sorry, Zane, but I'm in love with you, too. Ten years isn't nearly enough. Especially if I only get to see you on visiting days. We need more than six hours to contain this, and appeasing Rockwell is the only sure way of buying us the time we need. Please call him."

"Patience, listen to me. You cannot begin to imagine what involving Rutherford in this would unleash."

She kept her gaze and the phone steady. "Will it be worse than what's going to be unleashed once you've surrendered to the feds for poisoning a senatorial candidate?" He dropped his face to his hand. "We were introduced by God, Zane. Do you really think He'd have gone to the trouble if you were meant to spend our last days before the election detained and interrogated for something Alexander Rockwell did? Does that make any sense to you?" He didn't respond, so she pressed her lips together and turned toward the window. "Does it make any sense to You?"

The Biz seemed disinclined to step into this one. She shot the sky a look. "Because our way will not be easy, right? Well, maybe if You'd quit making it harder than it has to be, we'd all be surprised by what could happen. With just a little more guidance and a lot less interference, this might become slightly less impossible and we might actually manage to get the job done. But You wouldn't want that, would You? That would totally blow the point You're trying to make."

LOOK IM DOING MY BEST 2 HELP U

BUT U R IMPOSSIBLE!

"Gah!"

"Patience?"

She turned back with her hands on her hips. "I'm sorry, Zane, but I'm not doing this without you. If you cop out on me now, I'm through. I realize that probably sounds manipulative, and maybe it is, but enough is enough. I'm one hundred percent serious this time." His mouth fell open and she looked away. Then her expression softened a little. "I'll try harder with the phone, okay? I'll be less antagonistic and I'll let It finish Its thoughts without cutting It off or throwing It into traffic. You have my word on that. Please call your father."

He crushed the letter into a ball and hurled it at the window. Then he dropped to the couch and slumped over his knees. "My God, Patience! You go through the first four stages of grief in one fell swoop when you're not getting what you want, don't you? I mean, *bam!*"

She didn't respond. He looked up again and held out a hand for the phone.

"I don't call my father. I request an appointment. I can usually jump the line, though, if it's important."

"Will we have to buy me clothes for this?"

"Yes."

"Super."

CHAPTER TWENTY-TWO

Patience ignored the estate completely. The main house was as elegant as Forsyth's was ostentatious, and it could fit the whole of Rockwell's into a single wing. The grounds were larger than any of the parks in Allston and they were intimately manicured. She was in no mood to be intimidated by such wealth, however. If anything, she was put off by its subtle insinuation that she should be.

"What do I need to know?"

She smoothed her hair down with a glance in the rearview mirror as Zane cut the engine and leaned back. She was still a little irritated by his refusal to let her to have the pink stripped out before their appointment with his father, adhering to some code or standard about her personal identity that she didn't have time for or care much about, considering the circumstances. He'd even gone so far as to drive past Government Center at one point during the argument, with the implied threat of turning himself in if she changed who she was at the time he needed most for her to be herself, so he'd won that one. But she was irritated nonetheless.

He shook his head and turned his attention back toward the entrance of the house. He looked a little pale.

"I can't begin to imagine how to answer that, Patience. I'm sorry."

Her irritation dissolved at the sight of his expression. She'd managed, in her fervor to keep him out of prison, to ignore how hard a thing it was that he was doing, but there was no ignoring it now. She was fairly certain she was right about this, but that didn't prevent her from hating everything about it.

He reached a hand to her collar and straightened it over her blouse. "In the past, when I've introduced girls to Rutherford, I've recommended that they say as little as possible. But somehow, I don't think that advice will get us very far today. Just do what seems right at the time, and know that I'll have your back. That's the best I can offer."

She tugged at his hand and he looked up at her. "Your father is not a bigger man than you are, Zane. He never has been."

He shrugged back with a tired smile. "Try not to say things like that in front of him, if you can help it, or in front of his security detail. There hasn't been a good threat on Rutherford's life in months, so they're probably getting pretty itchy for a fight."

"And what I just said could be perceived as a threat?"

"If you framed it right."

Rutherford paused in the hallway, and then the muscles of his face set as he continued toward his office door. He scarcely glanced at her black Italian suit and distressingly expensive heels, yet from his expression it was clear that, apart from the singular feature of her attire, the girl on the bench outside his office was entirely unacceptable. Zane had outdone himself.

He nodded to his son and turned toward the door.

"Zane, your car sounds a bit rough. You're not having it serviced by some neighborhood mechanic, I hope. You must have a man flown in from France."

"Yes, Sir, I know. It's nice to see you, Father. You're looking well."

"Come in."

The agent outside his office opened the door and stepped aside.

Rutherford pointed to a couple of chairs before his desk as the door closed again behind them.

"Is she pregnant?"

"What?"

"Twins." Patience held up two fingers as Zane paused in the middle of the room to stare at his father. "One is his and one is yours. It's all terribly complicated, Mr. Ellison, but the paternity suit will be fantastic."

"I see." Rutherford Ellison looked long at her. She glanced at the chairs he'd indicated and he nodded, then turned back to his son. "What's this really about?"

Zane sat down next to Patience and brought his hands together.

"I need you to publicly endorse Joey Forsyth's candidacy to the U.S. Senate."

A line of red traveled from Rutherford's collar up into his neck. "Joey Forsyth is dead, Zane."

"Yes, Sir. I know."

"Joey Forsyth was a wad of gum I could never scrape off the bottom of my shoe, thanks to my business entanglements with his father. That pissant Alexander Rockwell is nothing more to me than a decades-long nuisance. He's called my office twice a week since Joey took up his unfortunate interest in politics, and it's been twice a day since the start of this blasted Senate campaign. I'm alarmed to find you here, now, advocating for these men. Explain yourself."

Patience glanced at Zane once, then looked back at his father. "I'm blackmailing him."

"No," Zane said. "She's not. Settle in, Rutherford. I'm about to do something I don't believe I've done in twenty-five years of living under your roof. I'm going to tell you the truth."

Rutherford Ellison's face turned to stone as he stared back at his youngest son. A chill descended through the room and Patience reached for Zane's hand.

"Zane, maybe I should—"

"Thank you, Patience." He settled back in his chair, appearing oddly at ease, suddenly. "It's quite all right. I've got this."

Rutherford's eyes were ablaze as he grabbed the phone from his desk and instructed his secretary to get Alexander Rockwell on the line. Apart from the inexplicable detail of The Biz and His ominous prediction, Zane had left nothing to his father's inference. He'd barely settled back to stare his incredulity at his son when the secretary rang through with the call.

"I understand from my son that he supports my endorsement of the Joseph Forsyth campaign. I don't consider that sort of thing without meeting a man face-to-face, Alexander. Come to my office at four o'clock this afternoon and we'll discuss it."

He hung up without any form of goodbye or, near as they could tell, even waiting for Rockwell's response. Rutherford stared at a framed picture on his desk for a moment and then back up at Zane.

"You can go."

Zane smiled down at his fingernails. "I'd love to, Sir, but I hadn't counted on you inviting the man over for coffee. Alex is dangerous and pretty desperate right now. We're not leaving you here alone with him."

Rutherford picked the phone up again and instructed his secretary to send the agent outside his door into the office.

Zane laughed and held a hand up. "Don't trouble yourself, Sir. You win. It's been a pleasure as always, Rutherford. I'm very sorry about the mess."

Rutherford just grunted in response. Zane took Patience by the arm and turned her toward the door. The mogul was scribbling something onto a pad behind them, but the writing stopped as Zane reached for the knob and the pen dropped back onto the desk.

"Did you really shoot the prick?"

Zane paused and turned back to his father. "Yes, Sir. I really shot the prick."

"Good."

They hid the car out of sight from the road up to the main house and slipped back to the edge of the grounds. Zane kept watch for Rockwell's Porsche as Patience hid behind the stone wall and changed from her "acceptable" clothes into something a little more service-able.

"Shouldn't we just try to cut him off now, before he even gets to the house?"

He shook his head. "Not on my father's property, I can't risk it. We need to get him alone and as far from here as possible. Rutherford may not be the warmest man on the planet, Patience, but this is a hell of a thing I've just laid at his doorstep."

"I know," she said, as she laced up her boots. "I'm sorry."

He just turned back to the road with a shrug. "It is what it is, I suppose." The phone chimed and he nodded. "Here we go."

They crouched low as the black 911 sped past and screamed up to the gates of the estate, revving its engine impatiently at security. The gates opened at last and Rockwell gunned it up to the main house. He paced erratically until the door opened and he pushed his way past a housekeeper.

Patience and Zane stood idly by, kicking at pebbles in the dirt at the side of the road and not saying much to each other. The inactivity felt strange after the labyrinths they'd been forced to navigate at warp speeds over the past few days. They were still getting accustomed to being in love as well, which was a whole other thing of its own. Zane looked up finally and seemed about to say something, but he was interrupted by another chime.

Patience checked the message and turned back to him. "Oh, no."

They sprinted back to the car as a rumbling arose in the distance. The Hummer blew past them and smashed through the estate's gates. Two of Rutherford's guards sprang from the booth and fired after it. The bullets just bounced off the armored vehicle as Zane cornered onto the driveway and overtook the guards. John screeched to a halt and jumped out, armed with a rifle larger than the one he'd had before. Zane pinned the Hummer in and burst through the open door of the estate. They followed the sounds of shouting back to Rutherford's office.

The agent at the door was unconscious on the floor outside and John was moving in fast on Rockwell. The campaign manager had lost his sling, and John appeared blind to the gun he was holding to the still-seated mogul's head. Zane dove at the SCUD as the rifle discharged, sending the round into the wall above Rutherford's chair, and John tossed him back. He righted himself and lined up another shot.

"Uncle John, no! That man is Zane's father."

A throng of black-suited agents raced into the hall from both directions. John backed off just long enough to kick the office door shut and lock it, and then he was right back at the center of the room with his rifle ready. The agents lost no time starting to break the door in until Rutherford slammed a fist down on his desk.

"Stop!"

Everyone in the room turned back to stare at him. The banging ceased and there was a moment's silence in the hall. Rutherford looked up at his youngest son and then turned back to the door.

"This is a family matter!" he shouted. "Go away now, please."

"I'm sorry, Mr. Ellison," an agent's voice replied, "but, you know we can't do that."

"I want you gone from the hall immediately. If I have to tell you again, you'll all be fired. Now, get out."

The pause of approximately one second was a testament to their respect for Rutherford's authority.

Then the agent spoke again. "Break it down."

John kept his aim locked on Rockwell as he reached into his bag for a canister. He pulled the pin with his teeth and backed up to the door again. He punched the butt of his rifle into it several times.

"Don't trouble yourself, Sir. No bodyguard worth a damn is going to leave his charge unprotected in a room with shots fired, and I'd be willing to bet those men of yours are worth a good sight more than a damn."

He shoved his arm through the splintered hole in the door and tossed the canister into the air, smiling as a couple of the agents grabbed hold of him and tried to wrestle the arm back on his elbow. There was a hollow-sounding plunk on the marble tiles, followed by a dull pop and a hiss.

They let go and fell back, retreating from the gas. He caught one of them by the wrist and held tight as the agent's body turned slack. Then he pulled the crisply tailored arm back through the hole to plug it. It hung at the center of the door like some macabre showpiece in the workroom of a taxidermist who'd lost it.

John nodded back at his niece's horror-stricken face.

"They'll be fine, Pax, after a nice, restful nap. Try not to breathe too deep, though, if you can help it."

He stepped back toward the desk and looked down at Rutherford Ellison, never lowering his rifle. "I'm very sorry about this, Sir. This corpse has got to be stopped, I assure you, but I promise to do the very best I can for you while taking him down."

A shot rang out and the rifle flew from John's grip. Zane lowered his gun and retrieved the weapon from the floor as John gaped down at the bloody streak across the back of his right hand. He turned to look at the slug in the wall behind him as blood trickled between his fingers.

"Did you not hear Patience tell you that this man is my father?"

John pressed the fingers of his good hand over his wound and narrowed his eyes at Zane. "So help me, rich boy, you and me are going to have a real go-'round when this is through."

"Name the time and the place, SCUD."

"Excuse me." Rutherford pointed to the gun at his head. "Do you think we might move this along, Zane?"

"Sorry."

"Staying on task has never been your strong suit."

Rockwell smiled and pointed to the desk. Zane reset the safety on his revolver and lay it down. He looked at Rutherford for a moment and then he set the rifle down beside it.

"You too, Pink."

Patience smiled coolly at him and relinquished her weapon. Rutherford leaned back as he watched the performance, making it clear to everyone present that he was as unimpressed with the gun at his head as he was with the man who was holding it.

"I've had about enough of this, Alexander, and I wouldn't count on those fumes keeping my men down for very long. You've got thirty seconds to tell me what it is you want me to do. In thirty-one, you're going to have to confront how successful you think you'll be once you've pulled that trigger."

Rockwell shook his head and waved them all toward the coat closet. "We'll talk about it in the car."

John sneered up from his injured hand. "You're going to need a lot more than what you've got to get me in there," he spat. "And you'll keep your mitts off my niece altogether, you sissy, sociopathic fuck."

Zane sighed and punched him in the jaw. The SCUD went down and Zane turned back to Patience as he shook out his hand. "Your uncle is really getting to be a lot of work."

She turned her eyes to the ceiling for a moment and then she helped Zane drag John to the closet. They wedged him in sideways with his legs up along the wall, leaving just enough room for them to squeeze in with him. It wasn't an easy fit, but it was what it was.

Rockwell pulled Rutherford up from his chair and the older man turned away, ignoring Rockwell's repeated yanking at his arm as he snatched an earnings report from his desk and flipped it over. He grabbed a pen and scratched a note across it in large black letters, slapped it to the back of his chair, and drove the blade of an onyx-handled letter opener through its center.

ED-

<u>*NO POLICE*</u>

-RCE

Rockwell smiled as he lifted John's bag from the floor and waved goodbye. Zane looked up at his father as the door slammed between them, and then something thudded to the rug, followed by a pop.

"For the love of God, Zane!" Rutherford shouted. "Don't do anything stupid."

The sound of breaking glass was the last thing they remembered as Rockwell disappeared with Rutherford Ellison and their guns.

CHAPTER TWENTY-THREE

Patience tore north up Route 3 with her uncle tied to the passenger seat of the Hummer, as the sun played hide-and-seek with the trees and overpasses at the corners of her eyes. She was miles behind Zane, who was a good forty minutes behind Rockwell and his father, but doing everything in the Bugatti's power to close the distance. She glanced down at the phone in John's hand, which she'd tethered to the armrest so he could hold it for her, and then she glanced up at the man himself.

He looked a bit worse for wear. She'd bandaged his right hand quickly as Zane shattered his father's gun case and pulled a couple of handguns from the racks, and then she'd bound it to the roll bar in order to keep it elevated. He'd anesthetized the wound (and himself) with a fair amount of Rutherford's Johnnie Walker Blue.

John had been the first in the house to come to, and to his credit, he'd stuck around after punching his way through the closet door and roused them with a few blasts of seltzer from Rutherford's office bar—only to find himself subdued by Zane for the second time that hour. The deed and its result had earned him a few drops of goodwill in the sea of mistrust between Patience and her uncle, and she loved him very much, but she was beginning to wish she loved him just a little bit less.

He grunted and shifted in the seat, and she grabbed his hand as the phone dipped from view. She was keeping an eye on the live feed

The Biz was streaming from Beacon Hill. The footage of Rutherford and Rockwell on the State House steps was helpful in many ways, and Patience was trying to be conscientious about acknowledging that from time to time. She also made a concerted effort to let Him finish His thoughts without cutting Him off at the power button, regardless of how she felt about what He had to say. She didn't trust herself to broach the subject of the time-out at all, or the photographs Rockwell had captured of Zane, or even her anxiety over the fact that Zane had just drawn blood again (regardless of how little choice John had left him in the matter). She was trying very hard to honor her promise to try harder with The Biz, so she pushed the thoughts that provoked her from her mind. The result, thus far, had been a marked decrease in His emoticon reliance since they'd left Hyannis, and He hadn't LOLed at her once. Her uncle's inebriated interjections notwithstanding, the drive north had been relatively noncombative.

John shifted again and Patience took the phone from his hand. The cameras on Beacon Hill pulled to a close-up of Rutherford's face and Patience raised the volume. The mogul was nothing if not convincing, as he voiced his support for the late Joseph M. Forsyth as the next representative from the Commonwealth of Massachusetts to the United States Senate. Only the most astute of mental health professionals or his late wife could have picked up on the meaning behind the glance he shot Rockwell as they stood together beneath the gold dome.

Patience shook her head and nudged her uncle to take the phone again. "He doesn't even look scared."

"He's pissed." Zane's voice cut through the speaker. "Everything appears fine on the surface, but inside, he's ready to take someone's head off. It's a look I know well."

John snorted. "I'll bet you do."

"What's that?"

"Uncle John says thank you," Patience yelled back. "How far are you now?"

"About five minutes out. And, Patience, I'm not going to wait for any traffic lights, if you know what I mean."

She nodded. "Do what you have to do. Uncle John will take care of any bail that's needed. He says it's the least he can do after everything that's happened." John grunted and she pointed a finger at him. "Just sit there and be drunk."

"I'm coming off the highway," Zane broke in. "I'm going to hang up now."

She frowned at the phone. "Please be careful."

There was no response for a moment. "Back at'cha."

He hung up and her gut tightened. She looked over at her uncle. "I can't stand this. I made him do it, and now I can't even be there with him. It would be one thing if I could at least see what was happening, but the not knowing is something I don't think I can ever be good at, Uncle John. I'm just not built for this."

The scene from the State House gave way to a split screen, and a live traffic copter feed materialized beside it. The cameras seemed fixated on a red Bugatti screaming around Leverett Circle. It wove between a couple of cars and slid up onto Staniford Street.

Patience realized her mouth was open and she shut it. She hadn't a clue how to respond to an answered prayer she hadn't even thought to make.

UR WELCOME

She nodded and pushed the hair back from her eyes. It almost made her wish she believed in Him—believed the way her uncle did, or even Zane, who'd accepted His intrusion into their lives with less strife than she experienced upon finding a new receptionist at her dentist's office.

A smiley appeared on the phone's screen and disappeared again as the press conference moved on to questions and Zane was only occasionally driving on the correct side of the road.

John's attention drifted to the phone with an inebriated nod. "I don't much like the guy, Pax, but I've gotta give credit where it's due. The kid can drive."

"Yes, he can. He can shoot too, as you discovered tonight, and he knows how to handle himself with his fists. These are all things that speak to your heart, Uncle John. If you two would just stop knocking each other out for two damn minutes, you might actually discover that you have a lot in common. And, I'd think you'd want to, if only because he's important to me. Zane really came through when The Biz showed up out of the blue. I didn't take that very well."

He lowered his face toward his lap. "No, I don't imagine you did. I'm real sorry about that, Pax. I should have prepared you better."

"You didn't prepare me at all."

"I know I didn't. I meant to, though, honest to God. I always just figured I'd have more time. You were such a little thing when I left, and you're really not much bigger than that now. It's too soon for you to be facing these sorts of responsibilities."

She reached over and smacked him on the shoulder.

"I'm twenty-three years old, for crying out loud. Joan of Arc had found God, led an army, kicked England's ass, and been dead for four years already by the time she was my age. I thought you and The Biz had this communication thing down. Didn't He warn you that this was coming?"

He studied his bandaged hand in silence for a moment. "It's a topic we've been going around about for a while. It appears that my extensions ran out before I realized. I really am sorry."

Patience needed to scream, but there were so many things to scream at once, and he'd begun speaking again before she figured out where to start.

"I think it was about twenty minutes after my call came that I realized yours would too, someday. It's not uncommon to find SCUD clusters in families, and there are things I've always been able to figure out about the world that you seemed to have been born just knowing. I think that's what makes you so cranky most of the time. You're too sensitive to have everyone's number the way you do. So, I was hoping He'd hold off a little longer, see if you'd toughen up a bit more with age. I am sorry I wasn't here for you, though. I honestly didn't think He'd call you if I wasn't around to see you through it. I had my grandfather, Joe, when my time came, and you were supposed to have me. That's how it's supposed to work."

Patience wiped an arm across her eyes, irritated by the tears that had sprung up without warning and furious with her uncle.

"Great-grandpa Joe was like us? Do you have any idea what my mother's been through all these years? First her grandfather went 'round the bend, then her uncle, and finally you? She's always kept a worried eye on me, as well, no matter how hard I tried to hide the similarities between us. Do you have any idea what I've been through, worrying about the exact same thing? How could you have kept this from us?"

He turned his face back to the window. "The job doesn't come with a manual, kid. Or worse, it comes with thousands of them, and every last one of them contradicts all the others. Hell, I've been writing a book for you for a decade, but I'll be damned if I'll ever let you see it. Your way is different from mine. Your way is harder. The world is more complicated than it used to be, and maybe the harder way is better now. But, I'm just not a *harder* kind of guy. I'm a *finish the job* kind of guy. I've forged my own path, but I'm starting to get that it's not a path you can follow. You've got to carve out your own."

She turned her blurry eyes away as the phone chimed. She took it from his hand and pressed down on the accelerator. "Damn it! They're leaving."

She punched in Zane's number and watched him on the screen as he tore up Cambridge and onto Tremont. The phone rang until it went to voicemail and Patience hit her hands against the wheel.

"He can't hear me over the engine."

She put the pedal to the floor.

CHAPTER TWENTY-FOUR

They slammed to a halt behind the Bugatti and Patience jumped from the truck. She sprinted up the State House steps and found Zane about halfway up, slumped against the bannister. She didn't like the looks of him.

"They're gone," he said. "I missed them."

"I know." She pulled him up and turned to the street. "Let's go get him back."

He just stared back with a disconnected expression, as though she was speaking a language he didn't understand. "They're gone, Patience. Don't you understand what's happened? I think I may have just killed my father."

She gave him a prod and turned toward the street. It was a struggle not to point out that his claim to the blame for Rutherford's predicament was pretty thin as long as she, John, and The Biz were in the picture, but she kept her mouth shut. Zane tended to respond negatively to recriminations against her or The Biz, and they really didn't have time for that particular conversation. The look on his face alone was almost more than she could bear.

"Alexander Rockwell hasn't angled for your father's attention all these years just to throw it away now. He's much too valuable an asset. Rockwell is going to keep him polished up and camera-ready, so he can parade him around at every available opportunity. You know

I'm right about this. He's got years of begging to make up for." He hesitated and she turned back to face him. "Will you please stop screwing around, Zane? Let's go fuck up Rockwell's world."

His face set then and he nodded. He fell into step beside her, and she felt some of his fight return as they approached the bricks. Then her phone chimed.

Six black BMW twin-turbo SUVs careened up Park Street and Patience spun toward the truck. Zane reached for her arm and shook his head. The vehicles cornered and skidded onto Beacon, scattering tourists as they slammed to a stop around the Bugatti and the Hummer. The passenger door of the lead car opened and a lone agent stepped out. He approached them with an even stride and uttered a single word as he continued past.

"Zane."

Zane glanced at her, and then he turned to follow the agent. Patience just watched them for a moment, too stunned to move, and then she looked back to the vehicles. The windows were all heavily tinted, but she could taste the firepower.

"I don't know what to do."

SUMTIMES THTS A SIGNL 2 DO NUTHNG

"It feels bad to do nothing."

I KNOW

She slipped down to the Hummer and stood beside her uncle. He grinned back at her through the open window. "Now, these are some guys I could party with. I may not have given them their due back at the house."

"Uncle John, I'm scared."

He leaned closer and looked up into her eyes as some of the inebriation fell from his face.

"Untie me then, kid, and I'll make your fears go away."

She frowned and glanced back at the cars, idling in formation around them. Their presence seemed charged with an assurance of authority over the Hummer and its occupants. Patience turned back and kissed her uncle on the forehead. "That's a very disturbing offer, Uncle John, but I'll probably always love you a little bit for making it."

"Anytime," he said. Then his face turned serious. "Listen, Pax, about our earlier conversation, I do need you to understand how sorry I am that you were alone when God came for you. I'm sorrier about that than I know how to be."

She turned her eyes up to Zane with the agent. "I wasn't alone."

"No, but you weren't with the one who'd sworn to be there. I really thought it would buy you some more time if I stayed away. Now that that's off the table, I won't duck out on you again. You might wish that I would half the time, but I won't."

She didn't respond for a few moments. Zane's exchange was growing tense, heated on his side, clipped and managerial on the agent's. Zane pointed to the Hummer and then he shook his head as the agent turned to stare down at them. Patience looked back to her uncle.

"I don't think you were supposed to be with me, Uncle John. For what it's worth, I think The Biz was in control of that decision, and I think He was right. If you'd showed up here, all fired up and ready to show me the job as you know it, I'd have split so fast your beard would have burst into flames. I don't think you ducked out on me. I think you were pulled off the job."

His eyes lowered for a moment. "I can't say for certain, kid, but I'm pretty sure that makes me feel worse."

She just sighed. She was pissed as hell at him, and trying very hard not to give in to any compassion she might also be feeling.

"He's sent you here now, though, and maybe I'll actually figure out what that's about before all is said and done. You've changed a lot since you left, and you really are driving me up the wall, but I seem to feel better when you're around for some reason. Don't get me wrong, I feel worse in lots of ways, as well, but there's a part of me that breathes easier when you're here. I'm sure it's some weakness of character I need to work on."

"Likely."

"Or it could be a strength I don't understand yet. So you can let yourself off the hook for not being here at the beginning, but only for that. I'm still really unhappy with you about many, many other things."

She turned away as Zane's conversation broke down and he started toward them. He and the agent paused about ten feet from the Hummer and he nodded.

"This is Ed," he said as she approached. "He's here to help."

Patience turned her eyes to the bricks. So this was Ed O'Brien, the agent everyone always went to and no one ever wanted to disappoint. He was nothing at all like she'd imagined him. She'd pictured an older version of Mason, broad-shouldered and strong-jawed, but with a slightly weathered appearance to suggest experience and command respect. In the flesh, Ed O'Brien was pale-skinned and slender. His features were angular, and his inflexible posture did nothing to enhance a lackluster physique. His expression was all business and his hair was meticulously combed. He seemed about as contrary to the invincible super-agent as anything Patience could imagine. Until he turned his attention to her, that is. Once she found herself the object of his scrutiny, his dominance over her airspace forced her back a half step.

She glanced over to Zane for help, but Ed recaptured her attention with a look.

"I'm in a hurry, Miss Kelleher, so let's skip to the ground rules. From this moment forward, whenever anything occurs that involves Rutherford Ellison, or any member of the Ellison family, I am your first call. In fact, I'm your only call. Zane knows this. It's been drilled into his head since he was a small child, but he's somehow managed to let procedure slip his mind these past few days. I believe you've been a factor in that lapse, so why don't you help him out now by telling me everything you know."

She searched Zane's face for some clue as to what she should or shouldn't say, but his expression was inscrutable. "Zane and I been together this whole time, Mr. O'Brien. What he's told you is exactly what I know."

The agent leaned closer and her shoulders drew together. He smelled of Clive Christian and authority. "I'm not playing games, Miss Kelleher. Rutherford Ellison has been taken, and I intend to get him back now. You can talk to me here, or we can talk in the car, but I'm not going to waste any more time being polite. Do you understand what I'm saying to you?"

She was determined to hold her ground, but Zane took her by the arm and pulled her back another step. "It's okay, Patience. Ed doesn't work with the police. His only job is to protect my family from anything that threatens it, up to and including the police, if need be. I've already told him about the ipecac, about the abductions, and shooting Rockwell, all of it. He's been with my family since I was eight years old. You don't have to protect me from him."

She exhaled. "You've told him about the phone?" she whispered.

The shake of his head was little more than a flinch, but she caught it. Ed caught it as well and looked away for a moment. His expression was almost weary when he turned back to Zane.

"What's this about a phone?"

Zane paused and lowered his eyes. "I think I may have left my cell behind when we went after Alex the other night. It was the night the troopers showed up, the night I shot him. I'm not certain it's there, but I haven't been able to find it since. I've picked up a new one, but it would place me at the house if he's got it."

Patience was impressed by his quickness, and a little surprised by his cunning.

Lines deepened in the agent's face. "No one is placing you anywhere, Zane. What else have you left out?"

"Nothing that I can think of. The phone just slipped my mind in light of more dramatic events."

Ed paused and looked past him into the distance. "You do understand that your father's life is in jeopardy, don't you, Zane?"

He returned his attention to his charge and Zane nodded. "I do, Ed. I'm the one who put it there."

The agent was silent for a moment. Then his brow lowered behind his sunglasses and his expression tempered from steel-lined to merely stoic. "Alexander Rockwell is the one who put it there. You know better than to take responsibility for the actions of a psychopath. Your mistake was not coming to me the second you knew you had trouble on your hands. That's plenty to answer for without lifting additional blame from Alexander Rockwell."

He turned back to Patience and she shook her head.

"Other than the missing phone, I really can't think of anything other than what Zane's just mentioned. Do you really want to hear it all again?"

He stared at her for a moment, and then he turned toward the vehicles. Patience remained where she was, unclear whether she'd been dismissed or if she was still on the hook, until Zane took her by the arm again.

"If anything else that's 'slipped your mind' comes back to you or your girlfriend, Zane, you tell me about it immediately. Now, I'd like to meet the man who crashed through the gates of the estate this afternoon and gassed eight of my men."

Patience sighed and pointed to the Hummer. Ed paused at the sight of the SCUD's predicament, but John just smiled and waved a couple of blood-stained fingers from the roll bar. "How's it going, G-man?"

"I'm not a federal officer, Sir. Zane, why is this man tied up? I thought you said he was with you."

"He is. We've had to rein him in a little as a safety precaution, but John's after Alex, just like we are."

"Did Alexander Rockwell shoot him?"

"No," Zane said. "That was me."

Ed turned back to him and Patience stepped forward.

"He's my uncle," she volunteered.

John just winked back at her. He appeared to be feeling a little better, now that they were back in his comfort zone, with the potential for physical confrontation on the horizon and no time to explore their feelings. He glanced appreciatively at the bulge under the agent's coat.

"You know how it is with families sometimes, G-man."

Ed didn't respond to that. He was starting to look sorry that he'd come over.

"Sir," he said. "Do you have anything to add?"

John leaned his head out the window and nodded up at the agent. "You bet I do. If you happen to catch up with this Rockwell corpse before me, please be sure to shoot the sorry bastard many times in the head."

Ed turned away and started back toward the lead car. "I think that may be the first sane thing anyone's said to me today."

Zane turned to the Bugatti, and then both men paused as they reached for their doors. Ed looked back to his protectee.

"Go home, Zane, and stay out of sight. Your new detail will do their best to remain unobtrusive, as long as you lay low."

Zane turned back and leveled his gaze at the chief of security.

"I'm sorry, Ed. You know I can't do that."

The agent's face remained impassive, his eyes shielded like the windows of the cars surrounding them.

"No, I don't suppose you can."

He lifted his cuff to his lips, and the doors of the car next to Zane's opened. Two agents stepped out.

"Your independence is on hold for the moment, son. Collins and Polaski will give you a lift back to Hyannis."

The agent closest to him reached for his arm and Zane dove into the Bugatti. Patience stared after him for a moment, and then she jumped into the Hummer and threw it into reverse. She hit the gas and took out the passenger side headlight of the rear-most SUV, crumpling half its front bumper as she made room for Zane. He pulled back within centimeters of the Hummer and the lead car gunned its engine, then thought better of filling the space between them as the Bugatti roared and peeled up onto the wide, low-bricked sidewalk below the gold dome. It blew around the black armored convoy, leaving a plume of smoke in its trail as it dropped back onto Beacon Street with Zane's detail in pursuit. The SUV cut abruptly right as the Bugatti flipped a one eighty at Joy Street and came back up onto the bricks next to Ed.

The Bugatti's passenger-side window lowered as Zane's detail pulled up and the agents jumped out. The chief of security held a hand up and they paused.

"What are you doing?!" Zane shouted across his snarling vehicle. "This is a waste of time and manpower that ought to be dedicated to finding Rutherford. Collins and Polaski are good men, and neither of them responds well to failure. You're setting them up for a long and frustrating night."

"Frustration is character building." The agent nodded. "It inspires creativity. I appreciate your concern, son, but they'll be fine."

"Come on, Ed. You're throwing two of your best men at a token gesture. If you were serious about this, you'd have put Mason on it."

The agent's eye twitched. "Mason's not available to you right now, and I couldn't be more serious." He glanced at his driver as his window rose again. "Let's go."

Zane yelled his name into the glass and nothing happened for a moment. Then it lowered once more and Ed looked back out with paternal indulgence.

"How did you know where to find me?"

The chief of security removed his sunglasses and smiled for the first time since arriving on the Hill. "You don't really think your father had a two million dollar car built for you without installing a GPS in it, do you, Zane? Rutherford may not be the most hands-on father in the world, but he does like to keep tabs on where his children are."

CHAPTER TWENTY-FIVE

The battalion of armored SUVs was gone as quickly as it'd appeared. Five cars sped off, each in a different direction, on the hunt for Rockwell and his precious hostage, as the sixth idled on the sidewalk behind the Bugatti. The Hummer lurched up onto the bricks next to Zane and Patience leaned out to pass him her phone.

He lifted a hand as she started to speak and gestured back to his agents.

"Go home, Patience. I don't have much time to explain, but this has just become a whole other thing. These guys get paid a lot of money to do what they do, and they're extremely serious about it. They have to protect me, no matter what happens, and that's exactly what they'll do—but the opposite can be said for you and your crazy ass of an uncle. If they think for one second that you're interfering with their efforts to recover my father, forget about protecting you, they will shoot you themselves. Rutherford is their only objective now. Nothing I can do or say will stop them from doing whatever it takes to get him back."

She folded her arms across the window. "The feeling's pretty mutual at this point. If I think they're interfering with our efforts to recover your father, Zane, or preventing us from stopping Rockwell, I'll just loosen John's ties. He's stopped them once today. He can do it again if need be."

"Damn it, Patience! This isn't a joke."

"I couldn't be more serious."

She held the phone out and refused to pull it back until he'd taken it. The screen was illuminated with a map of central Massachusetts. A route to a small town outside Worcester was highlighted, which ended at a big red arrow pointing to an annex of the FORSYTH FOR U.S. SENATE campaign headquarters.

"I think the décor's probably a little WB Mason for your father's tastes, and the building looks pretty rustic. We should probably get up there. Would you pass me your phone, please?"

He stared back, uncomprehending. She reached across and tapped him on the shoulder.

"What?"

"I need your phone."

He passed it over and she rolled her window up halfway.

"Avoid getting wrapped up in the emoticons thing if you can help it. If you do get stuck, though, just remember that He usually caves after a few tries and tells you what it is, so it's quickest and least labor intensive to just toss out random thoughts and keep moving. I'd also be careful about bringing up religious figures, regardless of their persuasion. It'll end the game fast enough, but you'll find yourself stuck in a history lesson that probably won't be what you're expecting. Of course, I don't have degrees in religion and philosophy from Harvard, so maybe that one's a judgment call."

"Damn it, Patience!" He thrust the phone through the window. "Take this back. I realize that you're not going to honor my request that you go home, so there's no way I'm letting you be separated from It."

"Oh, for crying out loud!" She leaned back slightly, confident that a guy as nice as Zane would never hurl the Lord's iPhone at her. "I thought you understood that it's never been the phone that's communicating with me. That one does seem to get better reception, though." She reached for the gearshift, and then paused and looked back again. "There's one last thing, Zane, and it's kind of a biggie. He hates call waiting. If you take a call while He's trying to tell you something, be prepared for some serious attitude when you click back."

"Patience!"

She threw the Hummer into gear. "Go with God, Zane."

She flipped a wide U-turn around him onto Beacon as the Bugatti remained on the bricks. Then it boomed and shot past her with the BMW in pursuit. Patience smiled as she watched them round onto Park. The driver Ed put on Zane was clearly no slouch behind the wheel. Character-building exercises of this nature were probably rare occurrences for him. It felt almost as though she was moving backwards as she turned in their wake and started toward the highway.

Zane's phone rang a few minutes after she'd made it onto the Pike and she grabbed it from John's hand.

"That was dirty pool, what you did back there." His voice cut in. "I didn't think we played that way."

"Sometimes we do." She smiled. "But never unless it's absolutely necessary. Where are you now? What's happening?"

He sighed aloud, and Patience realized that she knew exactly what the expression on his face was at that moment. It wasn't a happy expression, but it made her feel good to know that she could do that.

"I'm about three miles past the ABC tolls," he said. "There's some construction past Framingham, from what I understand. I'll work around it, but you may be slowed up for a bit. In other news, Alex has been playing his Tom Jones boxed set for my father, in an attempt to make some sort of peace, and that's not going very well. Precisely who is most in danger of being shot right now is anybody's guess. If Rutherford manages to get his hands on a weapon, we may have to find something else to do tonight."

She set the phone back down in her uncle's hand. "Where's your detail?"

"They've just cleared the tolls. They're doing pretty well, considering. Collins is a good driver." He paused for a moment, and then his voice lowered an octave. "Listen, Patience, I've called Ed with Rutherford's location, so please be ready."

The smile set in her face and she looked over at John. He seemed more interested in arguing with the headlights of oncoming cars than worrying about Zane or his agents just then.

"I guess you really meant it when you said that you trust this guy."

"He taught me how to ride a bike."

"Okay."

"He also taught me how to drive. Ed taught me how to shoot a gun and how to throw a punch. He's the only person my father's ever considered competent enough to teach me anything substantial, and the only person Rutherford's ever approved of who I could stand to have around. I don't recall him ever admitting to being off duty when I've needed anything, either, no matter what the hour. I can't keep him in the dark about this, not now that he's involved. Anyway, he'd already picked me up on the GPS and was doubling back to the Pike when I called, so it wouldn't have done much good to try. His driver knows what to do with an M-class X5. He won't catch me, but he won't stay too far behind."

"Was he angry?"

Zane paused again. "Ed doesn't get angry. Ed solves problems. He did want to know where I was getting my information from, though, and it's safe to say that he was less than impressed with my response."

"What did you tell him?"

"That you're psychic. It didn't go over very well. I'm confident, however, that telling him God's been sending Intel to your iPhone would have just pained him more."

Patience glanced over at her uncle. He appeared to be sleeping off some of the Johnny Walker Blue at last.

"How is that going...between you and my phone?"

Zane paused.

"It's a little awkward, to be honest with you. He seems particularly hot to hear about a shoplifting incident from when I was twelve. I didn't even steal anything, Patience. It was my brother, Steve, and his crew. I was just the wheelman. I'm trying to focus on the road here, and I swear to you, His memory is longer than Rutherford's. Is this what it's like for you all the time?"

"No," she said. "He's easing you into it. The real fun comes later."

"I'm so sorry."

"I'm starting not to mind it so much. Just drive and keep the phone close, okay?"

There was a pause at the other end. "But do you really think He cares about some minor incident from the summer before eighth grade? Because that's a lot of pressure, considering the magnitude of the fuck-up I could be driving into as we speak, not to mention the colossal potential of the fuck-ups still to come."

She shot a stern look at the sky. "He's screwing with you, Zane. Honestly, I'm a little embarrassed for the both of you if this is the best He could come up with. I thought you said you were a hellraiser."

"I said I was rebellious," he replied, "and a blight on my father's peace of mind. Those things are easy enough to accomplish without breaking any laws or risking anyone's safety. I was difficult, Patience. I wasn't destructive."

She sighed and shook her head at the phone. "He's definitely screwing with you. Don't worry about it."

"Okay," he said. "I'll see you in Rutland."

"See you in Rutland."

CHAPTER TWENTY-SIX

Patience lay on the horn, startling her uncle awake as the Toyota in front of them fled the Hummer's path. It wasn't enough. None of it was enough, and the fact that there didn't seem to be anything more she could do certainly didn't guide her thoughts toward more productive trains of thought. Even if they did everything right—if Rutherford was home safe again and the world was relieved of Solar-Tech and Rockwell's political aspirations forever—it still wouldn't get Zane off the hook. After everything they'd been through and all that had happened, they still had no proof that it had been Rockwell, and not Zane, who'd killed Joey Forsyth.

She shoved her hair back and flashed her headlights at a Mercedes. John stretched a finger from his ties to touch her on the arm.

"I'm real sorry, kid. It was a nasty bit of luck about those cameras on that bus. A paranoid mind is a tough thing to keep ahead of, but if you feel inclined to make a quick stop over to Wellesley on our way past, I could help you torch the corpse's house. Maybe those disks would be burned up in the—"

Patience looked back at her uncle. "What did you say?"

"Oh, come on now, Pax. He's not even at home."

"Not that." She pulled left and flipped a U-turn through an emergency access break in the highway. A couple of cars flew past and she pressed hard on the accelerator. "We have to get back to Brookline."

"Brookline? That's a ways out of our way."

"I know that."

She felt like Zane as she came off at their exit, gunning it around parked cars and running lights at speeds she had no business driving, except that, unlike Zane, she spent the entire drive crouched low in her seat, wincing and apologizing to the cars she cut off and the horn blasts that greeted her at every intersection. John sat back and watched with interest as the world whizzed past them. Finally, they raced up Forsyth's gold-lined driveway and jolted to a stop. He smiled at her with a nod.

"Never been so glad to be drunk in my life."

She threw the truck into neutral and stomped on the emergency brake.

"It's a Hummer, Uncle John. I'm required to drive like an asshole."

"Touché, kid."

She turned to him then, and her face was serious.

"I can't untie you. I realize that this could get sticky if anyone happens along while I'm inside, but I'll just have to work as quickly as I can. I'm sorry."

He shrugged back at her as best he could in his tethered condition. "You worry too much, Pax. If your conscience really is giving you the business, though, you could make amends by bringing back something interesting from the senator's bar."

She just shook her head and jumped down from the truck. Zane's phone chimed halfway up the walk and she froze.

UR PROBLY GONNA WNT THE CODE 2 THE ALARM

UNLESS A VISIT FROM BROOKLINES FINEST IS PART OF THE MAS-TR PLAN?

She stared at the text for a moment.

"You're here?"

I M EVRYWHER

"Yes, I understand that. It's just that You've been pretty persnickety about Your phones until now, and I was under the impression that You were with Zane tonight."

HELLO? OMNISCIENT!

"I understand that, too. But, You've been so... You know what? You're right, it's my mistake. And, yes, that code would be very helpful. Thank You."

He texted her a sigh, and then He texted her the code.

69 0-0-0 69

Patience closed her eyes and sighed right back at Him. "I have got to stop these people." Then she ran up to the mansion and punched the code into the keypad. The light blinked once and then it changed from red to green.

Then she kicked in the door.

Locating the concealed control room was a challenge, but she found the right mirror at last with a little help from The Biz. She stepped inside as the door swung forward, praying that Rockwell hadn't discovered the senator's secret first.

The screens were still alight with the eerie stillness of the rooms they watched over. Patience touched a button below the lifeless living room and held her breath as the tray slid open to reveal a disc. She closed it again and hit play. She skipped forward through the first few hours and then she hit pause.

"Oh, my God."

She pressed button after button, her eyes darting between the monitors as she took in as much as she could in what little time she could spare. The footage from the kitchen was particularly fascinating. She stepped closer to the monitors, transfixed by the scenes from the very last hours the discs captured before they'd run out of

space—not so very long after their owner had run out of space—
and then she hit the eject buttons and nodded to the ceiling.

She slipped from the room and ran back to the truck without
missing a single turn.

CHAPTER TWENTY-SEVEN

Patience helped herself to a Glock from the back of the Hummer and looked up at her uncle before locking him inside. Then she turned down the alley toward the entrance of the makeshift campaign headquarters and slipped behind one of the parked BMWs to shield herself from view of the office. The windows were papered over with posters of the wide-smiling senator, occluding her view of what was happening inside. She tucked the gun into her coat pocket and turned toward the door, but Zane's phone stopped her from stepping out from behind the vehicle.

NO GUD! TRY THE PZZA PLCE NXT DOOR

THRU THE BCK

She steadied herself against the bumper and nodded, then slipped back up the alley toward the adjacent pizzeria. The rear door was propped open by a large tin of tomato paste, presumably by the delivery man who was now arguing into his cell phone beside the dumpsters. Patience ducked into the shadows and glanced down at the phone. She felt some trepidation about her next request.

"I can't call inside, Biz. It's too risky. I might escalate a situation already in progress, and maybe wind up getting Zane or Rutherford hurt. I was wondering if You could keep an eye on that situation for me, and get word to Zane about what I found at Forsyth's, should an opportune moment arise?"

He kept her waiting a beat before He chimed back.

R U ASKNG 4 MY HELP?

She tightened her grip and fixed her eyes on the deliveryman's back.

"Yes." She nodded. "I am asking for Your help."

WULD I HAVE 2 CHNGE OUT OF MY SCKS & SNDLES FRST?

She smiled tightly and let her eyes fall closed a moment. "I'm sure whatever You're wearing will be fine."

She slid the phone into her pocket before He could respond further and crept behind the driver. She slipped through the door and turned onto the dilapidated basement staircase just inside, hurrying down past the canned goods and fifty-pound bags of flour. She worked her way through the dim light from the open door above, heading straight for the trap door in the floor by the furnace. As she reached down for the handle of her target, the lights flickered overhead. They came on with a buzz, and the staircase shuddered beneath the weight of a heavy footstep.

Patience dove beneath some shelves behind the furnace, knocking her boot into its rear panel as she pulled into a ball. The creaking stopped and the basement turned silent. She could feel him listening in the hairs of her skin. She tried to quiet her breathing as he restarted his descent, moving more slowly this time, and he paused again at the bottom.

"Hello?"

The voice was deep and wary.

"Freddie! You down here?"

She pressed her face to her knees as he wandered the basement, checking the office space and opening the walk-in refrigerator's door. Then he turned back and started toward the furnace. He paused so close to her that Patience could smell the flour and cooking oil on his clothes.

"Son of a bitch."

She opened her eyes as a meaty arm in a white chef's coat stretched above her.

"Hey, Freddie!" he hollered. "The rats are back!"

He pulled a tin of olives and a plastic tub of oregano from a shelf and turned away. She lay still and silent until the basement was dark again and his footsteps shook the floor overhead. She heard him discussing the rats with someone she presumed to be Freddie and sat up at last. She wiped the sweat back from her temple and felt around on the floor for the handle of the door. She pulled it back on its hinges and stepped down onto a second staircase. She wasn't eager to find out how Freddie dealt with a rat.

The building's shared sub-basement housed a tangle of pipes running overhead and underfoot, carrying the sewage and drainage systems for all the adjoined businesses. Patience worked her way across with the aid of the light from the phone's display, and an occasional prompt from The Biz. She smacked her forehead once against a low-hanging pipe and swallowed back a curse as she fell onto a stretch of the sewage system. The phone chimed softly.

SORRY

She nodded and pulled herself up. She didn't stop moving until her hand came down on the banister of the campaign office's basement staircase. She grabbed ahold without hesitation and climbed up into the unknown.

Voices greeted her ascent to the main floor. Ed O'Brien was explaining to Rockwell that he'd better lower his weapon or he was bound to spring a leak. They had all the time in the world, and it was a simple fact that Rockwell's arm was going to seize up on him at some point. The moment that happened, *bang.* Ed wasn't going to tell him again. Patience kept low and listened for the campaign manager's vitriolic response. She wasn't kept waiting long. She followed his voice to the end of a hallway and stopped before the door of the headquarters' central office.

She caught a hint of Rutherford's cologne as she approached the open office doorway, followed by a blast of his disdain. "Good God, Ed, this has gone long past tiresome. Would one of you just shoot the prick, so we can be done with it?"

For what was possibly the first time in his life, Rutherford Ellison gave an order that was met by no response. The room was silent, until the only one who dared chimed in. Patience held her breath as the phone rattled away on the other side of the wall, then took advantage of the distraction to slip across the doorway. She crouched low beside the frame, finally able to get a glimpse of the action.

Rockwell and Rutherford stood a few feet to her left with Rockwell's back to the wall. He held his hostage in front of him as a shield. Zane was about ten feet before them, surrounded by Ed and his men. He grinned up from the phone and held it over Ed's shoulder, allowing Rockwell to get a look.

"Well, imagine that!" He winked. "It's a message from God." He held Rockwell's stare and the coolness in his eyes belied the smile on his face. "You really are a demented son of a bitch, aren't you, Alex?" He glanced at his protectors and then resumed his command over Rockwell's attention. "Joey died from tetrodotoxin poising, Ed. He fed him pufferfish. It's deadlier than a heart attack and won't be detected in an autopsy unless they know to look."

Rockwell's voice was like the sound an ice pick makes when it breaks a block in two. "Who was that on the phone, Zane?"

"I've just told you who it was, Alex. And I've got everything, how you prepared the nastiest parts of the fish into that soup you fed to Joey, through those hours you spent dancing around his living room to your Tom Jones CDs while he lay watching you from the couch, conscious and aware of what his best friend had just done to him, but paralyzed from head to toe by the poison. The moment of his death was particularly moving, when you drank a toast from the good senator's bar and then called your SolarTech friends from that throwaway cell before placing your anguished nine-one-one call from Joey's landline. It's over now, Alex. Let Rutherford go and let's end this. Joey was a pain in the ass, and he sure as hell wasn't worth the trouble either of us has been through on his account these past few days. Why don't we both just stay out of prison together, now? How does that sound?"

Rockwell's eyes were fixed on the phone as his face turned to stone. He spoke slowly and more deliberately still. "I won't ask you again, Zane. Who was that on the goddamn phone?"

"I won't tell you again, Alex. It was God, so you might want to watch it with the goddamn language. And please try to pay closer attention to this next part, if you can, because it's my favorite. The whole ugly scene at Joey's place was recorded for posterity at twenty-four frames per second." He winked. "And I've got it all right here."

He waved the phone again.

Rockwell's grip tightened on Rutherford's arm, but then he relaxed and spat out a clipped little laugh. "You see, Zane, this has always been your problem. You never know when to stop. You almost had something there, but you took it too far, and now I know you're bluffing. There is no way you've got footage of anything you've just described, so back off, sport. You're about thirty seconds from a premature inheritance as it is."

Zane shrugged and leaned across the top of Ed's arm. "The clips of you dancing are a little rough to watch, if you want my honest opinion. You never did have Joey's sense of rhythm, did you?"

Rockwell took a step forward to lean in and Patience lunged while his balance was off-center. She knocked him aside and the mogul was ensconced behind a wall of suits and weaponry before she'd even hit the floor. Ed turned his gun on Rockwell and Patience's world turned very still. Then Zane broke from the agents in slow motion as Rockwell spun back in a burst of action and grabbed her up from the tiles. She punched him in the jaw and his head flew back, but he held her tight in front of him as Zane dove between them and the line of fire, spinning back to face Ed with his arms out.

The skin around the agent's eyes tightened. "Step aside, Zane. Please don't make me do this the hard way."

Zane shook his head at his hired guardian and turned an exasperated glare back to Rockwell. "Don't be an idiot, Alex. These men won't spare Patience if it'll prevent them from cutting down your murderous ass, but they won't have a choice if it's me. I'm standing right here, you deranged dumbfuck. Use your head for one damned minute, and let her go."

Patience's disgust at being captured by Rockwell turned to horror as she registered what Zane was saying. She tried to shove him toward the agents, but couldn't reach, so she kicked him.

"Ow."

Rutherford pushed toward his son, but the agents pulled him back. "For the love of God, Zane! Don't be a damned fool."

Zane didn't respond to his father. His eyes were fixed on Ed. The agent wouldn't turn his sights or his gun from Rockwell, looking for that one clear shot.

"Ed?"

"Don't do this, Zane. Please, son, just step back. We'll do everything we can for her once you and your father are safe."

Zane held the phone up and turned it back over Patience's shoulder. A tiny Rockwell continued his dance around the screen. The campaign manager flushed a deep crimson and turned the gun on Zane at last.

"Was that so hard?" Zane pushed Patience aside. "Christ, Alex, get it together. I can't do everything for you."

Patience felt as though she was trapped underwater, staring back at him from the center of the room. The air turned heavy and everything slowed down around her. She hardly noticed as Mason broke rank and grabbed her by the arm. He pulled her back behind him as Rockwell relieved Zane of his revolver and the phone.

"What the hell is wrong with you people?" she cried. "You've got about a thousand guns on the measly psychopath. Can't one of you get a shot at him?"

Zane smiled past the agents' shoulders. She glared back in return. "If they'd had a shot, they'd have taken it, Patience. They're not the only ones who know what they're doing, here. Come on, you know this is right. So it's time to get creative again." There was something so different about him now. He looked easier in his skin than he had since they'd first heard that Forsyth was dead. Since before then, really. Zane seemed more at ease then he had since he'd pulled the trigger on Rockwell.

"Our way is harder." He nodded. "It is what it is."

Rockwell kept his back to the wall as he pulled Zane toward the door and Rutherford fought past his men at last.

"Goddamn it, Zane! What have you done?"

The mogul remained free of the sea of worsted wool just long enough to catch his son's eyes. Zane nodded back, his apology set in his face.

"What needed doing, Dad," he said. "I'm sorry for all the trouble today."

"Don't do this!"

Rockwell looked past the agents into the sharp, dark stare of Rutherford Ellison. "If I see even one car I don't like in the rearview mirror, your son is dead. Keep your men back, Ellison, do you understand me?"

The mogul nodded, ashen-faced and looking every one of his sixty-eight years for the first time in his life.

"That goes double for Pink." Rockwell flipped the latch of the office door behind him and tapped Zane on the shoulder with his gun. "You're driving."

Zane shrugged. Then he turned to Patience as Rockwell pulled him back through the door. "This is right," he repeated. "Just do what has to be done, and for the love of God, try not to piss these men off." Then he winked and mimicked her uncle's gruffer voice. "I'll see you on the other side."

The door slammed shut and the agents ran forward. They ripped the posters from the windows, but Rockwell was too intimate with the paranoid mind to leave himself so exposed. He used Zane as a shield as he backed into the Bugatti and climbed over the console, pulling his latest Ellison hostage into the car behind him. Zane waved to Patience as he settled into his seat. Then he looked up at his father and then at Ed, and his door slammed shut.

Patience didn't even realize Mason still had a hold of her until the Bugatti ignited and sped off down the street. She pulled her arm back and he released it, appearing surprised by that realization as well. She turned away, her mind empty of productive thought until Rutherford Ellison looked at her with an expression that seemed a fair representation of how she felt inside.

She turned to stare back at the agents all around her, on the move in a flurry of action, with the sole exception of the chief. He still stood at the window and stared down the street with a vacant expression on his face.

And then Ed O'Brien, the agent who never got angry, punched his fist through the double-paned glass of the campaign office door.

CHAPTER TWENTY-EIGHT

Ed stood in the center of the room, menacing her with his stare as he held his mangled hand in the air between them. He'd allowed Mason to stitch up the worst of the cuts and splint it as he grilled her, but that was the extent of the intervention he'd submitted to, and it was now swollen to the point that it resembled an inflated surgical glove. Beyond keeping it elevated, however, he appeared entirely disinterested in it. Ed's attention was focused only on finding Zane. His uninjured hand stood sentry at his revolver, and his jaw twitched on occasion. Patience stared back through eyes equally set and narrow. They were two people united by a rigidity of purpose and mutual frustration, and they were each determined to move on despite the other.

"I will ask you for the last time, Miss Kelleher, where are you and Zane getting your information?"

She turned her face back to the crowd of capable men, suspended in action as their boss wasted their time and Zane's. She could appreciate his attempts to wear her down, but she had no patience left for his process.

"And I will tell you for the last time, Mr. O'Brien, you're not getting an answer to that question. Just trust that it's reliable, and consider it a gift, because that's all I'm telling you tonight. Now, for the love of God, can we please move on?"

Ed pulled his gun. Mason stepped between them, but he cut him off with a look. "What I trust, Miss Kelleher, is that your interference has just put Zane's life in danger, and that I'm going to make sure it doesn't happen again. Those are the only things I trust tonight."

Rutherford Ellison pushed between his two highest ranking agents and pulled Patience from their reach. His grip on her forearms was awkward and abrupt, but it wasn't an aggressive maneuver. It was beseeching.

"Young lady, do you care for my son?"

She pulled her arms free of his grasp, more comfortable suddenly, under the threat of Ed's gun than the plea in the tycoon's eyes.

"I love him, Sir. And I need to go now."

He nodded and his face returned to a more recognizable version of Rutherford Ellison. "I'm coming with you."

He turned and pulled her toward the rear exit as Ed stepped in front of his employer. Rutherford raised a hand and stepped around him.

"Nothing happens to this girl while Zane is missing, Ed, do you understand me? I don't give a rat's ass whether she's getting her information from God, or from the goddamned Twitter. She knows things and that's all that matters. I want my son back right now. Let's go."

"I'm sorry, Sir. I can't let you do that."

Rutherford pushed past him again, following as Patience burst into the alley. She looked up at her snoozing hulk of an uncle and choked on the cold air stinging her skin and eyes. The sight of John in the Hummer made her want to cry from some strange and unexpected surge of relief.

Zane's father reached for her arm as they approached the truck.

"I don't know how to address you."

She turned back, startled by the strange plaintiveness of his remark. "My name is Patience, Mr. Ellison. Please call me that. How would you address me if I was any other girl Zane brought home?"

"I would address you as 'Miss Kelleher.' But, something tells me that would irritate you."

She just stared and he released her arm.

"It would," she said. "And something tells me that you'd mean for it to. I don't mind that sort of thing from Dick Tracy back there, because he's obligated by the job to have a stick up his ass. But from you, it's condescension disguised as courtesy, and that's a hard thing for a polite person to complain about without coming across like an ass. Of course, I'm often not a polite person in situations like this, so sooner or later we'd wind up with angst and drama, when all Zane was trying to do was introduce his girlfriend to his father." She slapped her uncle on the shoulder and pulled the Hummer's door open. "You're welcome to ride with us if you can make it past your guards, Sir, but this man who nearly got you killed this afternoon is my uncle. He's the same man who's going to help me get Zane back now. It's up to you, but I really think you'd feel more comfortable with your own men."

Ed's good hand came down on Rutherford's arm. "Please come with me now, Sir. It's time to go."

Rutherford stared back at Patience, then allowed himself to be pulled back toward the awaiting SUVs. She jumped into the driver's seat and thrust the key into the ignition, catching a glimpse in the rearview mirror of Rutherford Ellison's haunted expression as she threw the truck into first. She cursed under her breath as a stream of passing cars forced her to a stop at the mouth of the alley. She needed to get out of there. She could only fight on so many fronts.

A sharp bang came down on the Hummer's roof and the rear door flew open. A figure dove inside and slammed the door shut behind it.

"Go."

Rutherford slapped his palms against the back door locks, turning back as his agents tried every door. Then one raised an elbow to the glass at the seat next to his.

"Go!"

Patience went. A dozen men in dark suits ran behind the Hummer as she cut into traffic. A sedan skidded to a halt behind her and they scattered, then turned as one and sprinted back toward their vehicles with their radios and guns in hand.

John appeared both sober and relieved to see her. Patience reached a hand to his face and turned it to hers. He caught the fury in her eyes and set all questions aside but one.

"What do you need, kid?"

She pulled her hand back and held it up for him to see. "They won't stop shaking, Uncle John. I think I need you to drive now, but that would mean I'd have to trust you. I don't know what to do. Alexander Rockwell's taken Zane and I'm useless. I think I might finally be ready to consider that grenade launcher, though."

"Kid," he interrupted, "are you gonna cut me loose and let me take over? Because I'm suddenly feeling like maybe I'm not the parent of most concern in this carpool group, and that's sort of freaking me out."

She pulled Rockwell's Buck knife from her coat and slid it beneath the knots at the armrest. Then a vision of John, with his rifle raised in Rutherford's office, flashed before her and she slammed her fist against the truck's door.

"Was it something I said?"

She looked up to Rutherford's reflection in the mirror. His gaze was fixed on the traffic outside and his expression was unreadable. John touched a finger to her hand and said nothing more. Then the phone chimed.

CUT HIM LOOSE

She reached over again and sliced his left arm free. John took the blade from her hand and cut his right from the roll bar, then shook the blood back into them with a grin.

"That's better, kid. Now, let's get this show on the road."

He stretched a long arm across her and pulled the seat release back. Patience screamed and clung to the wheel as it whipped back and he jumped in behind her. He reached around her for control of the wheel and jammed his feet up under hers and onto the pedals. Patience scrambled over the console to the passenger seat and lay back, gasping for air as she pushed the hair from her face. Then she caught Rutherford's reflection again. He seemed hardly to have noticed the histrionics at the front of the truck. She closed her eyes and swallowed back some of the adrenaline.

"Are you sure you'll be able to do this, Uncle John?"

"What, you mean this?" He grinned and lifted his bandaged hand from the steering wheel. "I've had worse mosquito bites. Don't you worry about me."

"No, I meant will you be able to do this without killing anyone?"

He was quiet too long and Patience's gut turned to lead. She covered her face with her hands and turned away. "Oh, Jesus, what have I done?" She grabbed the phone from her lap. "I sure as hell hope You're more confident about this than Your SCUD seems to be."

It chimed back immediately.

PT ON UR SEAT BLT

A pain shot through her like a drill bit, and then she heard another chime.

AND WULD U PLS TRY 2 HAVE SUM FAITH?

"No!" She glared up toward the sky. "What I need, Biz, is information. You said to untie him, so I assumed that You were confident that he'd come around. But he hasn't come around to a damn thing, has he? This is like the 'time-out' all over again."

There was no response to that.

"How can You expect me to have faith when we just keep chasing our tails? Even You don't seem to know what's going on most of the time, and You're the freaking omniscient One!"

OMNISCIENCE IS NOT THE ANITDOTE 2 FREE WILL

HUMAN NATURE IS FLUID & SELF-CONTRADICTRY

ITS A NUISANCE, TBH

Y DO U THNK I NEED UR HELP?

She dumped the phone back onto the console. Rutherford was now staring down at John's cache of weapons, appearing to have noticed it for the first time.

"Miss Kelle—" He paused. "That conversation you were having just now, was it about my son? Please tell me who you were arguing with."

She turned her eyes down from the mirror. "I was arguing with a madman, Mr. Ellison. I'm sorry, but I can't tell you anything more than that. Do you think you'll be able to handle that?"

He looked down at the weapons again, then glanced up to the man who'd nearly brought about his demise just a few hours before. "Are you going to get my son back?"

"You bet your ass we are," John said.

Patience turned back to look Rutherford in the eyes. "We're going to get Zane back."

"That's the only thing I need to know."

Rutherford was starting to look a little ill as John followed the directions in his head, darting around the traffic at over a hundred miles per hour while Patience followed along on Zane's phone. He seemed to be holding his own, though, and he didn't complain. He lifted his face from his hands after a span of shared silence and tapped Patience on the shoulder.

"Those videos Zane says he has of Alexander killing Joey Forsyth, are they real?"

She nodded and kept her eyes forward. "Yes, Mr. Ellison. They're very real."

"Do you know who sent them to him?" She didn't respond to that. "Have you seen them?"

She turned back, finally, and nodded again. "Those videos are Alexander Rockwell's worst nightmare. They're also what guarantee us that he'll keep Zane alive. He can't kill him without knowing who's got them or how widely they might be distributed. They're Zane's lifeline, Sir, and he and Rockwell both know it."

The mogul never turned his eyes from the traffic as it fell back from the speeding Hummer.

"He can hurt Zane though, can't he?"

She turned forward again and nodded a final time. It was the only thought she'd been able to maintain with any consistency since Zane had disappeared. It was like a punch to the gut, hearing it spoken aloud.

Rutherford nodded back. "Thank you for your candor."

She turned to face him again. "Zane never wanted you involved in this, Sir. It's important that you understand that. I was desperate to keep him out of prison, so I played dirty to get him to come to you today, even though he was innocent of every charge he was being threatened with. If I'm certain of anything in the world right now, it's that he'll regret what happened at your office this afternoon for the rest of his life."

Rutherford shifted his gaze past her. "Well, that makes two of us. Zane has always had difficulty thinking for himself. It's a shortcoming that doesn't seem to have improved at all since he's left Hyannis."

"I'm quite certain the opposite is true."

His laugh sounded like a beaten down version of what it had been a few short hours before. "Are you, indeed? Well, let's take a look at it. Within a month of exercising his independence, Zane has turned his back on the security protocols that have effectively protected him his entire life. He's concocted a scheme to abduct a sitting state senator, one who happens also now to be dead, and he's destroyed my social and political credibility. Apparently, that wasn't rebellion enough for him, however. He's now insisted upon being taken hostage by a delusional sociopath with a Tom Jones fixation. And all this occurred promptly upon his falling under the influence of a common, pink-haired Allston barmaid."

Patience caught her uncle's wrist before his hand reached Rutherford's throat. She held it fast and met Zane's father's eyes.

"Most of what you've just said is accurate, Mr. Ellison, regardless of the fact that it isn't true. Zane wouldn't be mixed up in this if he hadn't met me. That's correct. But everything he's done, he's done for very good and very serious reasons. Few people will ever understand how deeply in debt they already are to him, and that's probably the way it should be. But if you could do me just one favor tonight, I would ask that it be this: Back the hell off your son."

The silence came down around them like snow from an overburdened roof. Patience released her uncle's arm and looked down to the phone for more directions. It was Rutherford who broke their stalemate at last. His voice was quiet, but not soft.

"Thank you for telling me how it was that Zane came to see me today," he said. "It does help to know."

She closed her eyes and fought the tears she didn't have the time or tolerance for. She nodded and looked away again.

"I don't enjoy being afraid for the people I love," he continued. "I understand that I'm not very good at it."

She could feel her uncle watching her. He reached a hand out and mussed up her hair. Then he pressed down on the gas. She didn't look back at him.

"Just drive."

CHAPTER TWENTY-NINE

They pulled up on Washington Street, where the X5s had doubled in number and created an ominous-looking herd that dominated the street outside O'Malley's. Rutherford jumped out, in defiance of security protocol, and the rest of the doors opened quickly in unison. Twenty-four of his best agents stepped down and stood beside their vehicles.

Ed approached his renegade employer as Patience and John joined him on the sidewalk. The agent's stoic reserve was strained by a terse determination.

"Mr. Ellison, Sir, what are we doing here? We've tracked Zane to a—"

Rutherford raised a hand and turned toward the pub. "Not here, Ed. Inside."

The muscles of the chief's jaw twitched, but he gestured to his men. Patience entered first and waved to Frank. He glanced up and nodded his usual greeting. Then his jaw dropped at the sight of her long-missing uncle, shadowed by Rutherford Ellison and his army of men in dark suits with wires tucked behind their ears. She pointed toward the function room at the back and didn't wait for his response. His expression turned from alarm to anguish as he shoved his way through the agents, pushing Rutherford aside as he fought his way toward his goddaughter.

A few of the men drew their guns, but Frank just waved them off like gnats. Rutherford shook his head at Ed and the agents reholstered their weapons as the barkeep grabbed John by the shoulders and drew him into a fierce hug. He pushed him back again with equal force and smacked him soundly on the head.

"John Patrick Flaherty. My God, man! Your sister's been half out of her mind these past ten years. Where the hell have you been?"

John grinned at his lifelong friend and clapped him on the arm. "How goes it, Frank? I understand that you've been doing what you can to keep my niece out of trouble. That's a thankless job, but I thank you nonetheless."

Frank glanced at her as a pained expression slid across his face. "You can keep your thanks for that one. This past week alone, she's pulled a stunt that terrorized a block of Comm Ave, she's run half the local frats back to the White Horse Tavern, for Christ's sake, and it took her all of five minutes to drive a priest from the church. I think that last one might be a personal best, but I'll have to check my notes."

"I did what?"

Frank crossed his arms and turned to face her. "Father Rick was in again last night, sporting a three-piece suit and a blonde on his arm. It seems the good father's got an MBA and an uncle with a brokerage firm. He's trading his life of servitude for the opportunity to make friends and influence people. He bought a round of drinks for the pub and drank a toast in your honor, my dear. The Church has groomed another stockbroker, after a five-minute conversation with you."

She shrank back, at a rare loss for words, but Frank was having none of that. "I'm sorry to hear that," she said at last. "He seemed like a decent priest, although in retrospect, I guess his competitive streak was a little intense."

Frank's face was nearly crimson now. "What in God's name is going on here, Patience Abigail, and exactly how many guns have you just brought into my pub?"

John stepped forward, but she shook her head and looked back to her godfather. "It's about Zane," she said. "We just need a few minutes where we can get our act together. Alexander Rockwell is having our places watched, and this was the best location I could think of, that I was certain he wouldn't know about."

Frank's eyes flew up as his mouth dropped open. "What's a con man like Alexander Rockwell got to do with you, Patience?"

"It's an extremely long story."

"Then you'd better get into the storytelling mood."

Rutherford Ellison stepped between them. "Mr. O'Malley, do you know who I am?"

Frank paused. "There's not a man in the country who doesn't know who you are, Mr. Ellison. What's that got to do with my goddaughter?"

"Zane is my son. Alexander has taken him, and every second that passes is a second that he remains at the mercy of a madman with no conscience. All we're asking for is a few minutes here alone, so we can make some arrangements and get on the same page. I'd consider myself in your debt, Sir. Of course, I'd be happy to pay whatever you feel is appropriate for the inconvenience."

Frank leaned against a table. He raised a hand to his eyes after glancing down at Patience. "I don't charge family for things, Mr. Ellison, and my convenience is not the problem here. The problem, if I'm understanding this situation, is that you people appear to be handling it on your own. You need to call the police, Sir. Right now."

Patience touched her godfather on the shirt sleeve. "Rockwell's already killed one man, Frank. If he gets too twitchy, he could kill Zane as well. These men are better trained for this sort of thing than the police are. Please, Frank, we can't let him kill Zane." Her breath caught. "I love him."

Frank's head fell back and he groaned aloud. "Well, this is one for the books, my dear. You can have the room, but you won't be with these men when they leave. You're staying here with me tonight, and you're not setting a foot outside the pub until I'm one hundred percent convinced that Alexander Rockwell is no longer a threat to you or to anybody else. Do you understand me?"

She shook her head. John pulled out his revolver and tapped it against the handle of his rifle.

"Patience is covered, Frank, my hand to God. I'll see that she comes out of this safe."

"Your word has become more than a little suspect over the past decade, John Patrick. Patience stays here. The rest of you can do what you need to for Zane, and feel free to give Mr. Rockwell a jab in the gizzards from me as well. Your son's a nice kid, Mr. Ellison. I like him more than most."

He fought his way to the door and then turned back to his god-daughter. "And just so there's no misunderstanding, Patience, I'm about to go offer each of the BC Eagles at the bar a semester's worth of free beer to guard that rear exit. Unless you're willing to let these men shoot their way through a bunch of college football players, I recommend that you come out through the front when you're done here."

The door banged shut and he was gone. Patience crossed her arms as John gave her shoulder a squeeze.

"I didn't notice The Biz chiming in with any bright ideas for diffusing that one."

The message tone itself sounded defensive.

WHT DO U WNT FROM ME?

HES UR GODFATHR!

Ed stepped past them and turned to his employer. "Mr. Ellison, Sir, why are we in Allston? Zane is ten miles west of here."

John nodded at the agent. "Wellesley. They're back at Rockwell's stronghold. The problem, G-man, is that the major exits are all being watched, and there's a sweet little welcoming party awaiting us on

Cliff Road. He's got a whole lot of muscle around him now, courtesy of SolarTech's never-ending cash flow, and he's putting it to good use. Now, I love a castle-storming as much as the next man, but it's gonna take something a little more finessed to get your boy out safe before I lasso Mr. Rockwell's entrails to a rocket and blast the corpse back to hell where he belongs."

Patience punched him in the gut as Ed turned away. He stood silently for a moment with a hand to his ear, then spun back and removed the chiming phone from her hand. He hit the touch screen a few times and cursed at its vacant display.

"Miss Kelleher, I've just received satellite confirmation of a suspicious congregation assembled on Cliff Road. I've also received confirmation of increased activity around Alexander Rockwell's residence. So, I will ask you once again, where are you people getting your information?"

They stared at one another as the tension in the room grew palpable. Ed took her by the arm and she pulled back. They shouted in unison.

"You've got satellite?!"

"Where are you getting your Intel?!"

John grabbed the agent to the twig-snap threat of hammers cocking all around them. "Rockefeller!" he hollered. "Get your man off my niece or I'm taking his head off!"

Rutherford just looked at Ed and he released her arm. John nodded at the chief and brushed down his lapels as the mogul dropped into a folding chair.

"Get it together, all of you. Ed, I've already told you that I don't care about that now. You're working together tonight, and the next person to waste a second of my son's freedom with senseless arguing, I will shoot him myself. Am I clear? I want my son back, goddamn it."

"Yes, Sir."

Rutherford turned his attention back to Patience.

"Let's finish this now, please. What do you need from my men?"

Four of the agents held Frank against the bar as several more kept the crowd contained. Frank just stared past them to the doorway, where Rutherford Ellison stood, flanked by two of his men.

"This is a hell of a way to repay a favor, Sir."

Rutherford nodded as the agents turned him back to the waiting SUVs. Patience broke from her uncle's grip and squeezed between the suits. She threw her arms around her godfather's neck.

"You knew I'd never let these men get into it with a bunch of college kids, Frank. They're not screwing around. What else could I do?"

"You could go home and spend some time with your mother for the first time in a month. You could go out to the movies with a friend. You could sit your arse down on that stool until Zane is safe, like we agreed. You could be anywhere but where you're going, doing anything but what you've got planned. That's what else you could do."

She gave him a squeeze and her uncle reached between the agents to pull her back by the coat sleeve. Frank called to her again as John turned her toward the door.

"Understand this, Patience Abigail. If I have to explain to your mother tonight that you've been hurt or worse, doing something this reckless, and that I failed to prevent you from going, neither one of us will ever recover from it. I won't forgive you for that, and the not forgiving you is what's going to kill me the most."

Her eyes dropped to the floor. "I know that, Frank. I never want to kill you at all, I promise. It's going to be okay."

John squeezed her shoulder and nodded to her godfather. "She's a lot scrappier than you'd ever believe, Frank. I can't explain it, but this is the way it's meant to be, and Patience will be with me every second. Nothing's going to happen to her tonight that doesn't happen to me first."

Frank leveled his eyes at the SCUD until John looked away. "So help me, John Flaherty, if Patience doesn't come out of this alive and unharmed, you'd better just go back to being dead. Because, if you fail, I will make your life such hell, you'll be begging for the grave."

John turned Patience toward the door again. "I'll see to it, Frank. I give you my word."

The agents released the barkeep once Patience was safely entombed in the Hummer. He followed them out to the sidewalk as his happily scandalized patrons spilled out behind, and picked the fight up again. Ed and his men turned back and Patience looked to John. He stepped back down from the truck to referee.

She sat there, barricaded from the muffled chaos beyond and alone for the first time since the madness had begun. She couldn't bear the sight of her godfather surrounded by all those men—though he was giving as good as he got—so she turned her face from the action and reached for the phone with mechanical determination.

"Okay, Biz, You win. I'm asking. Why am I here? If You'd just sent Uncle John in at the start, this would have been over days ago and You'd both be on to other things by now. All I've done is slow You down and complicate things to the point where I question whether the world can survive my intervention." She paused. "I question whether Zane can now as well."

PATIENCE U NEED 2 HVE FAITH

FAITH N ZANE, FAITH N URSELF

Her chest tightened around her heart. "What I need is information. Why won't You tell me if he's okay? You had no trouble showing me the code to Forsyth's security system, or beaming me pictures of Zane driving miles off in the distance. I can't understand why You won't just tell me the one thing in the world I really need to know."

The Biz did not respond right away.

"You know what? Forget about it. It's obvious that my instincts about communicating with You have been right all along. I retract my question. I retract them both."

I SMPLY SUGGESTD THT U TRUST URSELF

"Joey Forsyth is dead. Rockwell is doing God only knows what to Zane as we speak, and we're just sitting here, wasting time, while my godfather takes on two-dozen men armed with Rugers. All Frank's done my entire life is watch out for me and call me on my shit. He doesn't deserve this kind of anguish and aggravation. So pardon me if I'm having trouble figuring out which of my contributions so far are supposed to inspire this great faith in myself. On second thought, I unretract my question. Why *am* I here? What could You possibly want from me that You couldn't have gotten faster and more efficiently from Uncle John?"

There was a bang outside her window and her godfather was gone. John nodded to the door of the pub, and then started back as Ed resumed his rigid stoicism and the agents pushed through the excited crowd.

The phone chimed in response at last.

U DO WHT U DONT WNT 2 DO

U GO WHER U DONT WNT 2 BE

U LUV WHO U DONT WNT 2 KNOW

U DO NOT GIVE UP WEN ITS HARD

She caught her breath and her eyes filled with tears. "There's too much at stake here, and I have no idea what I'm doing. You need someone better for this. You need someone real. I don't understand what You're doing with me."

I M TIRED

She stared down at the words, uncomprehending, and the phone chimed again.

I M TIRED OF THE BLOOD

Her uncle pulled the Hummer's door open. The truck swayed as he dropped his weight into the seat and reached his keys toward the ignition. He paused midway and turned a critical eye to her.

"You okay, kid?"

She was quiet for a moment. "Uncle John, tell me about the last man you killed."

His keys hung suspended below the steering wheel as her request hung suspended between them.

"This is a real change of gears, Pax. I'm not sure I'm any more comfortable talking about violence with you than you are hearing about it." He lowered his arm and turned to her. "I go into every job prepared to do whatever's needed to get it done, nothing more and nothing less. What's brought this on?"

"I just really need to know." She stared down at the phone, straining for some glimpse or sign of her alleged faith and still coming away empty. She straightened and met his eyes. "Please answer me, Uncle John. When was your last kill?"

He sat back as the streetlamp above cast a translucent ring of light onto his hair. Then he nodded with a reserved expression. "Things happen, kid. Rifles jam. Renegades wind up ensnared in crocodile traps. Your boot slips on a discarded condom at the same moment the National Guard storms in and takes down the evil-eyed granny running the explosives factory from her nursing home's basement. It's not about numbers. What's important is that I'm willing to do whatever the Lord needs, and I'm always on my mark. You seem rattled after that exchange with Frank. Are you sure you're okay?"

She was quiet then. He waited. "I'm fine," she said. "Let's do this."

CHAPTER THIRTY

Ed smashed the window of the house next door to Rockwell's and flipped the back door's locks. "God help me, Miss Kelleher, if it takes me a year or more, I am going to find out how you knew the code to this security system."

She shrugged as he slid the glass aside and pushed the door open. She was already bored with the topic.

"Punk rock kid's got better Intel than I have after more years in the field than she's been alive," he grumbled as his men filed into the foyer. "Something's not right here."

Patience couldn't help but laugh at that remark. "Hell, Dick, I still haven't figured out how to upload pictures from my phone. I'm working exclusively off the knowledge and skills of others tonight. I wouldn't get too bent out of shape about it."

John snorted and the phone chirped. Patience quashed the call without a look. Communications with The Biz had become a bit awkward since their exchange outside the pub. He seemed hell-bent on building her confidence back up now, and more than a few of the motivational missives He'd sent during their drive along the back roads to Wellesley would unquestionably be classified as cheesy. It wasn't the ideal time for an emoticon-laden pep talk.

She looked up again and Ed and her uncle were both staring. She flipped a hand at them and turned toward the staircase. Ed stepped past with a shake of his head and she followed. John came up next, and then Rutherford stepped up with a couple of agents on his heels.

Rutherford's presence had been a sticking point during their discussions at the Pub. Ed wanted him as far from the action as possible, for strategic considerations as well as for his safety, and John agreed. But Rutherford was intractable. His chief of security had failed to come up with a secure place to send him that wasn't nixed by Patience and John, and Ed had become wary of sending him anywhere, anyway. Rutherford was now threatening to fire or shoot anyone who tried to prevent him from driving back to Wellesley on his own, and the discussion had gone on longer than they'd had time for. It concluded, finally, when Ed dropped his face to his hand and cursed the X5 for its lack of a proper trunk.

They reached the top of the stairs and Ed turned back to point a swollen index finger at Patience. "I want to be absolutely certain that we're clear about something. When we tell you that we won't jeopardize our objective here tonight by protecting you, that's not idle chatter. Furthermore, we will obliterate any obstacle in our path, regardless of how Zane might feel about the obstacle. Do you understand what I'm saying to you?"

She sighed and rolled her eyes at the agent. "You know, your shell's not too bad, Dick, but your speech chip seems a bit outdated. You might want to look into an upgrade or something."

He remained where he was until she crossed her arms and turned back to face him.

"I've known Zane since he was a small child, Miss Kelleher. I'm exceptionally fond of him. It would disappoint me to have to shoot his girlfriend over a misunderstanding that could have been avoided."

She laughed. "That would disappoint me as well. You know, I think you're actually starting to grow on me, in your tight-assed, I'm-on-duty sort of way. I appreciate your diligence in explaining this to

me for the fifth time, but I feel we're clear about the situation between us and I'd appreciate it if we could move on."

John raised an eyebrow, but she just pointed to the panel in the
ceiling above them. He reached up and slid it aside and pulled a rope
ladder down from the attic floor. Ed's eyes narrowed at the phone as
the SCUD climbed up into the ceiling. She stashed it in her pocket
and he grabbed onto a rung.

Patience climbed up behind him and watched as Ed dropped his
bag next to John's and got to work breaking the sealed dormer window
furthest from Rockwell's house. John joined him as the rest of the
men appeared, one-by-one, through the hole in the attic floor. She
spied Mason through the crowd, standing alone off to one side, and
looked back to ensure that Ed was still occupied before sliding over
to him.

"You screwed up," she said. "Back at the campaign office, when you
pulled me from the floor. You eliminated any chance that Rockwell
could take someone other than Zane when you did that. I believe
there are pretty strict rules against that sort of thing."

He barely glanced at her before returning his attention forward. "I
thought I instructed you to rest for a couple of days." He let the silence
hang for a moment before shrugging. "Zane had already eliminated
any chance of that, Miss Kelleher. Anyway, I was in the doghouse with
Ed long before we arrived at the campaign office. Aiding a protectee
and his girlfriend in a harebrained scheme to dose a state senator
with syrup of ipecac is the sort of thing he frowns upon as a general
rule. When that scheme ends with the abductions of not one, but
two of his protectees by a heavily armed psychotic, it tends to piss
him off to no end."

Patience turned to look him full in the face. "Who told Ed that you
helped us?"

"I did."

She groaned and he held a hand up. The gesture bore a remarkable resemblance to his superior's common habit. "I'm the one Zane comes to when he's looking to cause trouble, Miss Kelleher, because he knows I'm always good for it."

"Damn it, Mason! You're hardly six years older than me. Would you please stop calling me 'Miss Kelleher'? It creeps me out."

"Yes, ma'am. You two were able to lie to me about how damned idiotic and dangerous a thing it was you were involved in because Zane also knows I'll never dig too deep once I've heard what I need to. He's got my number. A large part of the reason he's in the situation he's in now is because he understands me as well as he does. If I'm in hot water with the boss, it's because I damn well ought to be."

"That's crap, Mason. We were going to do what we did whether you helped us out or not. We just wouldn't have done it as safely or effectively. If Ed's too pigheaded to understand that, then—"

"Ed's not pigheaded."

"Ed's not clear why you're standing around here talking to Miss Kelleher, Mason."

The agent nodded over Patience's head. She spun back and crossed her arms at the chief of security standing a few feet behind her with a grappling hook in hand.

"Look, Dick, Zane didn't come to you the other night because he couldn't. Having an army of agents come screaming down on the situation was precisely what we didn't need then. If that offends your ego, then I'm sorry, but that's just the way it is. Getting him back is the only thing that matters now, and you've benched your best agent. If you want to freeze Mason out or fire him tomorrow, then you can be an ass tomorrow. But for tonight, would you please just get over it and focus on Zane?"

Ed lowered the hook and stared past her. "Miss Kelleher, please don't make me shoot you."

She shook her head and turned back toward Mason. "Did you even bother to tell him that we lied to you?"

He looked away with no discernible change in expression. "Miss Kelleher, please don't make me shoot you."

She threw her hands up in frustration. "When Zane told me that you people were die-hard, he forgot to mention that you were also out of your goddamn minds. At this point, I just hope I won't have to shoot either one of you."

Ed turned back without another word and cleared the last teeth of glass from the window. He leaned out and swung the hook for a few revolutions with his non-injured hand, and then it thumped over-head as he released it onto the roof. There was a scratching, scraping sound as it caught hold, and he tugged at the line a few times before pulling himself back in with a nod to John and his men.

John nodded back. "Is that even your dominant hand?"

Ed didn't respond. He just returned to the bags and John nodded again. Patience hadn't seen her uncle impressed by much since he'd been home, but it was clear that he'd been impressed by that toss. It was equally clear that he was unimpressed, however, when Ed pulled a harness from his bag and turned back to the window. He stepped forward and grabbed the agent by the arm.

"Don't be an ass, G-man."

He grabbed Ed's arm and held the swollen hand between them and his men moved in like sharks to blood in the water. They pulled John back and pushed him aside, but he just shrugged at Ed with his arms crossed over his chest.

"That hand of yours looks like a round of ham crammed through a tin can. You've got about twelve broken bones right there, and even I'm not crazy enough to make an unsecured climb in that condition. Now, I'm sure any of these men can handle the job just fine, but unless you've got an expert climber on your force who's also tracked renegades through the Himalayas and up Mount McKinley, I say we nominate me for this task."

Mason stepped between them as Ed turned back to the window. No one spoke and no looks were passed, but a sense of disquiet had spread throughout the attic. The second-in-command took his boss by the arm and drew him a few steps away from the rest.

"You know better than this, Ed." He kept his voice low and refrained from looking at the hand in question. "There's good and fearless, and then there's reckless and tunnel-visioned. I've never known you not to recognize the difference. Mr. Flaherty is right. Anyone here can make the climb, and you damn well know it because you're the one who trained them. Pick a man, Ed. Anyone but you."

The chief looked up finally, and Mason stepped back. Ed pulled the harness from his shoulder and held it out. John grabbed it and bounded to the window with a glint in his eye. There was a brief pause in the action as he squeezed his body through the smallish frame, and then he swung out onto the rope. He hung suspended over the ground for a moment, and then Patience watched in awe as he began to climb, amazed by the raw artistry of his work when he was allowed to do what he loved without restraint. She hoped she'd get to see him in action on his own terms someday, without worrying about knocking him unconscious or tying him to anything.

The roof creaked overhead as his boots trudged up to the ridge. He released the hook and secured the rope to the chimney's base, and then he tied off the harness and lowered it down. He secured himself to the chimney as well and signaled for Ed, followed by Patience. He pulled them up as they scaled the wall, and then he called for Rutherford. Once the mogul and his agents were secure, Ed and John lay down on the shingles and peered at Rockwell's house. Men in dark clothing popped up all around them and John grinned back at the chief.

"It's starting to look like a fucking Mary Poppins chimney sweep routine up here."

Ed ignored the remark and pointed forward. They crawled, military style, to the ridge, and lay their bags down. Ed pulled out a pair of infrared goggles and studied Rockwell's lot.

"What have we got?"

He didn't respond at first. He stared down at the men assembled at the front and rear of the house and passed John another pair. "I count eight," he said. "I don't like it."

John ran a quick inventory of their situation and shook his head. "Those boys are pros by the looks of it. This Rockwell fellow is one paranoid corpse, and SolarTech appears to be accommodating his mania nicely." He glanced furtively back at his niece and lowered his voice. "It's your call, G-man. Plan B?"

Ed nodded and John reached for his rifle. He screwed a silencer to its barrel as the agent called for six of his best shots to come up from the rear. They lined the ridge beside them as Patience scurried up from behind. She grabbed her uncle's rifle and pulled it from his hands.

"What the hell are you doing? This isn't what we discussed."

Ed pulled her back down, but she held tight to the weapon. Her uncle removed the agent's hand from her collar and his niece's from the rifle. He pointed a warning finger at Ed and turned his attention to Patience.

"I'm sorry, kid, but we've had to rewrite the script a little, now that we've had a better look. Everyone here is committed to getting your friend back safe tonight, but it's time to accept that there's probably going to be a price we'll have to pay for him. I didn't mean to shock you. It seemed like you'd been catching up to the seriousness of what's happening here these past few hours."

"I have been." She turned back to Ed and her face became very still. "If you shoot any of those men down there, Dick, it'll be all over for

Zane. I know you're not about to let that happen. Now, you can bet against my Intel, if you're comfortable doing that after everything you've seen tonight, but you'd better be ready to make good on that promise to shoot me first."

Her uncle's face froze into a hundred unspoken words. "Pax, your Intel has told me nothing of the kind."

"Is it telling you anything to the contrary?" She pulled the phone from her pocket and set it on the shingles between them. "Do you really believe I could lie about a thing like this and get away with it? If you don't think you can pull off what we discussed at the pub, then come up with something else. Just make sure it doesn't involve killing anyone. And hurry up."

John and Ed both stared at her, and then John backed down from the ridge with a glance at the sky. He waved the agents back as well and reached for his bag.

"Plan A it is, then."

"What the hell is going on here, Mr. Flaherty?"

"I honestly couldn't tell you, G-man, but our best bet is to keep moving and not waste any more time arguing. We're back to plan A."

Ed wiped his brow with his injured hand and set his rifle beside him. He was silent for a moment, then turned back and grimaced at the phone. "You'd better be sure about this, Miss Kelleher. I don't care for this plan of yours. Particularly with Zane's life on the line."

She hoped the sickness in her gut didn't show in her face. "Let's say we did do it your way, Dick, and even one of your men missed his shot. Whose life would it be on the line then?"

"These men don't miss their shots."

The exiled second-in-command disregarded his chief's warning glance and crawled up from below. "Ed, if you're not sure about this, then why are we—"

"Because these two are the spookiest pair I've come across in over two decades on the job, Mason, and I was around for Steve's Scientology phase. The only thing that matters right now is Zane. Let's just do this and get the hell off this ridge."

John winked at Ed and they repositioned themselves at their stations. Collins and Polaski slid in to either side of them as the agents behind them removed the weapons from their cases. They loaded them up as the four adjusted and refocused their night vision goggles.

"You and Mr. Flaherty take the rear," Ed said to Collins as he reached for his weapon. "Polaski and I will handle the four in front."

Collins nodded and Ed curled his injured arm over the ridge. He jammed his rifle against his splint, steadying it with his shoulder as he slid his finger over the trigger. Then he turned very still as the others waited for their cue. He cursed his hand and pulled back again, removing his goggles.

"Mason."

His second-in-command took them without question and slid into Ed's vacated spot beside John. The SCUD just winked and turned back to the house.

"We need to do this fast and hard, champ, so be ready on the count. These two beside us will follow with the second round. One should suffice, but I'm not crazy about the distance or the open air."

Mason glanced back to Ed for confirmation and then nodded. "Yes, Sir."

Ed said "Go" into his sleeve and the ten agents remaining at the back of the roof dropped their lines and jumped out into the night. Then Ed counted back from three and John and Mason fired. Eight men on the ground panicked, crashing into one another as the gas canisters exploded and they reached for their guns and their radios. Ed said "Go" again and Collins and Polaski fired. The eight men collapsed into the clouds before a shot was fired or a button pushed.

Patience crawled up to her uncle as the ground team pulled down their masks and closed in on Rockwell's unconscious guards. She was nearly speechless from relief, but managed to locate the one word available to her as he knelt down to repack his bag.

"See?"

He shook his head. "What I see, Pax, is eight men who can wake up and cause God only knows what kind of trouble for us, as opposed to eight men who can't. That said, I think you understand what's at stake here at least as well as I do. I just hope you know what you're doing, that's all."

"Me, too."

He foisted his bag over his shoulder and a strange expression passed over his face. Patience tightened her stance as he gazed silently at her for a few moments. Then he stepped closer and reached out a heavy hand. He laid it on her head.

"I think I finally understand what's going on here, kid, what's maybe been going on from the start. No matter what happens, just know that I've got your back. This is the way He wants it now, so you're calling the shots. It's going to take some settling into, but that's to be expected. Now, let's go get your friend back and shut this Apocalypse down once and for all, because, Lord knows, it's been a long few days for everyone."

He released her and left her standing there alone, too stunned to move. She felt as though he'd thrown her into a pool of icy water and withdrawn the ladder. She heard him whistling as he trod down the roof with his weighty bag over his shoulder.

"What do you mean I'm calling the shots, Uncle John?" she cried. "Settling into what?"

CHAPTER THIRTY-ONE

Rockwell's unconscious guards were disarmed and immobilized in the carriage house, and Ed's men on the ground were moving in on the mansion. Patience was mesmerized by their stealth and precision as they surrounded the perimeter with their parabolic microphones and portable through-wall radar systems. Those men down there were the real thing. Ed and Mason were the real thing. Her Uncle John was the real thing. The Biz's words tripped around inside a mind under renovation, with her uncle's strange avowals interjecting wherever they saw fit. Nothing in the world made sense.

Ed and John knelt together a few feet away, listening as the ground team swept the house with the mic. Every so often, they'd pause and raise a hand in unison, causing Patience's mouth to run dry and her brain to freeze up. She struggled to keep herself focused and to refrain from ripping the headphones from their ears whenever they'd glance up with their expressions of grim concentration. Interrupting their work with her need to know wasn't going to help Zane. She had to stay on task.

Rutherford startled her with a tap on her shoulder. The sharp-shooting, steel-jawed mogul appeared to be trying his best to ignore the pair of agents now tracking his every move at Ed's command. He seemed reticent about speaking with her as well.

"Do you need something, Mr. Ellison?"

"We've been up here fifteen minutes," he said. "That's my son down there, Miss Kelle—" His face set as he caught himself. His fear was not well covered by the rigidity of his expression as he stared down at the side of Rockwell's house. "What I need is for someone to tell me what the hell is taking so long."

Patience glanced at her watch. "We've been up here twelve minutes, and I've changed my mind about how you should address me. I'd prefer it if you'd call me Miss Kelleher after all. You diminish your own dominance when you trip over yourself like that, trying to avoid pissing me off. It's as if you've stripped yourself of a superpower or something, and it's unsettling. We all need to be at our best tonight, Sir, and at the moment, you're not."

He was quiet for a moment, but then he looked back at her and something in his expression inspired just the faintest impulse to smack him. Patience was satisfied.

"You are a very strange young woman, Miss Kelleher."

"Yes, I know that."

"Well, now it's been fourteen minutes."

She sighed and looked away from him. "I'm aware of every second that passes, Mr. Ellison. If you'd like to help move things along, perhaps you could take it up with your men. Dick still insists on getting confirmation of everything my uncle or I tell him, or he's convinced he'll have to shoot us or some such nonsense. Beyond that, I'm afraid there's nothing more I can tell you."

He turned away, but then stopped again a few yards off and spun back on his heels. "You can tell me why my son left Hyannis. That's something more you can tell me."

Patience straightened, as taken aback by the humanity of his demand as by his condescension to demand it of her. He remained where he was and continued to stare down at the house.

"I'm painfully aware that Zane was never very happy at home, Miss

Kelleher. What I'd like to know is what, precisely, it was about his upbringing he found so unbearable that he now prefers a life of rat-infested squalor to the relative comforts of his family home."

Patience sighed. "He's not living in rat-infested squalor, Mr. Ellison. Allston is a solid, working-class neighborhood. I'm sure you employ lots of people who live in the area."

He didn't respond to that. She found his inappropriate, off-base bid for information touching, in a Rutherford Ellison sort of a way, so she pushed her hair back from her face and considered his question seriously.

"If you want my honest opinion, I'd say that Zane left Hyannis because he's a lot like you." Rutherford straightened and turned back at last. "You didn't want to do what your father did for a living any more than Zane wants to do what you do. You wanted to shoot guns and race cars, and to figure out what else might interest you before you settled into anything permanent, but you weren't given any choice about that, were you?"

He was silent again, so Patience turned her attention to her uncle and the agents' progress. Mason stood up next to Ed and pointed to a window at the first floor and she dug her toes into the soles of her boots.

"Did my son tell you this, or is it more wisdom from your mysterious source?"

"Zane told me this."

"Well, regardless of what I may or may not have wanted, I behaved like the adult that I was when I was Zane's age and faced up to my responsibilities. I'm sorry, Miss Kelleher, but the comparisons you're attempting to draw between his behavior and mine are lost on me."

She pressed her lips together and turned away again. Her exasperation made it difficult even to look at him. He cleared his throat at the dismissal and she turned back and punched him on the arm.

He appeared stunned by the action, staring down at the spot where she'd struck him as though he'd been stabbed. He raised a hand to fend off his advancing agents.

"Young lady, have you lost your mind? That's a quick and certain way of getting yourself shot."

She was too frustrated even to hear him. "You named the heirs to your imperial empire Steve McQueen and Zane Grey, Sir. If that wasn't a message to your father, I don't know what was. It certainly was one hell of a message to your sons."

"Good God, I'd say that's a reach."

"And when Zane started to rebel, did you send him off to one of those expensive schools where naughty children of the wealthy elite learn how to become nastier and more socially acceptable? No. You kept him home and let Dick teach him how to shoot clean and drive dirty. You may not like some of the choices he's made, and maybe deep down you've even resented him a little for having had the guts to make them, but you've always made damn sure he's had what he needed to do so. You've all but forced him to test his freedom. You may not be able to see it, and Zane may not be able to see it, but to someone looking in from the outside, it's pretty much Psych 101."

Rutherford was the first to break their stare this time. "Miss Kelleher, I believe you may be even more ridiculous a person than I'd imagined."

"Then I'm sure you'll be more cautious about asking for my opinion in the future."

Ed stepped past them to speak with Rutherford's detail and Patience grabbed his arm without thinking. "What did you hear down there? Can they see Zane on the radar? Please tell me what's happening in that house."

He wrenched his arm free and John pulled her back from the agent's withering stare. He drew her down the roof a few feet as Mason raised a grappling hook gun and fired over the treetops.

"The radar doesn't work that way, Pax. It can pinpoint the location of human presence, but it can't paint us a picture. Come on now, you can't get mired up in this stuff when you've got work to do. The best thing you can do for him right now is to stay focused on the job at hand and try to have a little faith."

It was more the way he said it than the echo of the words she'd heard from another source not a half hour before that sent the buzzing up her spine. She understood that something had changed since she'd last grabbed the muzzle of his rifle, but she was still in the dark as to what it was. His communications with The Biz seemed restored now, but his manner had changed—both toward Him, and toward her. She shook her head and he winked.

"Your part's coming up soon, kid, and you're the only one who can do it. Keep your head in the game, now, and don't waste any time trading shots with the suit patrol, okay?"

She exhaled and nodded. When she looked up again, Ed was staring back with a strange expression on his face. It appeared, for a moment, as though he had something he wanted to say, but then he looked away.

"Christ, Dick, either spit it out or take it someplace else. I've had my fill of people weirding out on me for one night."

He didn't respond to that, but her phone chimed in his place.

HE KEEPS FINDNG THNGS WHER U SAY THEY WILL B

HIS GADGTS R EXPNSIVE & HARD 2 COME BY

GO EASY ON THE GUY—HES ADJUSTING

"Well, he's going to have to step it up. But since You bring up people adjusting to things, would You care to shed any light on Uncle John's one hundred percent kill failure rate, or his bizarre and sudden pledge to cover my back from now on?"

The Biz, it seemed, had no comment.

CHAPTER THIRTY-TWO

Traversing a rope between two rooftops fell somewhere between dangerous and disastrously stupid, in Patience's opinion—particularly with one end secured solely by a grappling hook—but John assured them all that he'd survived far stupider feats in the past and no one felt in a position to doubt his word, particularly as time was short and their options were few.

Patience tried not to dwell on it, just as she tried not to dwell on what was happening in the house below or the sky above, or on the sweat that broke out at her hairline and palms whenever she moved too close to the ridge. She'd decided that John's advice was good. She needed to stay clear and focused, and that would be best accomplished if she avoided two things: thinking and looking down. A racing heart and slipping palms would do no one any good at go time.

The only unguarded entrance to Rockwell's mansion was a set of French doors opening out onto a terrace from the third-story master bedroom. The terrace, like the rest of the house, was made of stucco and impenetrable to the hook. Someone needed to get in from above and secure the line by hand. There was only one point of entry this could be accomplished from, and only one member of their party small enough to fit through any of Rockwell's tiny attic windows.

Ed checked the line a final time as Mason shot a second hook across for a backup. John stepped over to Patience as he refastened his harness.

"I'll get you over there safe, Pax. My hand to God, I will. Don't you worry about a thing."

"Damn it, Uncle John! Would you threaten to blow up the garden shed or something, just so I know you're still in there? You're really starting to freak me out."

He rubbed her head and turned to the ridge. She'd never wanted to kick a man so badly in her life. She grabbed a fistful of his jacket and pulled him back to face her.

"I don't know what you and The Biz have cooking at the moment, but if it involves the exchange of one person I love for another, there's going to be hell to pay. You two will spend the rest of eternity dodging my calls, and I've got unlimited minutes."

He laughed as Ed and Mason stepped up beside him. He sat down and Mason rechecked his emergency line before he lowered himself into the air.

"I'm not wired to be a martyr, kid," He called back. "I may be going through a slight period of modification at the moment, but let's not blow it out of proportion. You stay cool over here, and I'll see you on the other side."

He began traversing and she grew dizzy at the sight. Then her phone chimed and she glanced up. No one's attention moved from her uncle's endeavor, so she slipped down to a dormer window to check the message.

IT WAS NOT BECAUSE OF THE TIME-OUT

She paused, wondering if she'd misread Him.

"What are You talking about?"

IT WAS NOT BECAUSE OF THE TIME-OUT

Her mind locked up and her hands began to shake as she knelt there alone, squinting at the glowing screen. Did He not understand where she was? How could He do this to her now?

"Christ, Biz, I'm doing everything I can just to keep it together right now. Can't You maybe take a pill or something until Zane is safe? This would be a really bad time for us to get into another blowout."

FORSYTH WAS SECRETIVE ABOUT HIS SURVEILLANCE

ROCKWELL DIDN'T KNOW ABOUT THOSE CAMERAS ON THE BUS

She gripped the phone tighter, uncertain where this was going and unnerved by the understanding that she was about to find out.

UNTIL I NEEDED HIM TO

The world screeched to a halt around her. Ed disappeared. Rutherford disappeared. Even Uncle John, dangling one broken shingle from a nasty death, disappeared. All she could see was the traitor in her hand as it sprang to life again.

ONCE FORSYTH WAS DEAD, ROCKWELL FELT UNTOUCHABLE

BUT HIS BRAVADO WAS TENUOUS, UNSTABLE

HE WAS PARANOID, AND HE WAS OFF HIS LEASH

I COULD SEE NO WAY LEFT FOR YOU TO STOP HIM FROM AFAR

Patience's dizziness was growing and her nausea had developed an edge. It wasn't that what He was saying sounded wrong, exactly, but she couldn't understand what it meant. She certainly didn't understand what it meant for Zane, or for SolarTech, or the polar ice caps.

"Why didn't You just tell us that? Why did You have to trap Zane the way You did?"

I OFFERED YOU AN EASIER PATH BUT YOU LACKED FAITH IN MY JUDGMENT

YOU LACKED FAITH IN YOURSELF, EVEN AFTER I'D ASSURED YOU OF MINE

The phone slipped from her fingers as her gun tapped against the slate like an armored woodpecker hammering at an unyielding oak. She scraped her knuckles across the tar to save it from smashing against the shingles with the blocks of text burning her eyes.

"Anything that happens to Zane tonight is my fault."

He chimed back furiously.

SHOW ME WHERE I SAID THAT!
THOU SHALT NOT PUT WORDS INTO MY MOUTH!
YOU WILL ALWAYS HAVE HARD CHOICES TO MAKE
SO YOU MAKE THEM, AND WHEN THINGS GO WRONG
YOU LEARN WHAT YOU CAN AND GET BACK TO WORK!

She shook her head as her breath stung her throat. She'd made all the wrong choices. She'd been so self-righteous, and she hadn't learned a damn thing. And it was Zane who was paying now for her hubris.

WOULD YOU STOP LOOKING FOR THE SUBTEXT IN EVERYTHING I SAY?

She dragged a sleeve across her eyes and blinked down into the message.

"I'm sorry, what?"

STOP PICKING MY WORDS APART!
WE DON'T HAVE TIME AND IT'S ANNOYING!

They were quiet for a moment, and then the phone chimed again.

LOL! HOW MANY EONS HAVE I BEEN WANTNG TO SAY THAT TO YOU PEOPLE?

FELT GOOD TO GET THAT OFF MY CHEST! :)

She was trying to keep up, but He was texting her in circles now.

"So, wait a minute... Is this or is this not about the grenade launcher?"

THAT WAS ALMOST A WEEK AGO!

"Oh."

I TOLD YOU YOUR WAY WOULD NOT BE EASY
CAN'T WE AGREE THAT I WAS RIGHT AND MOVE ON?

She shook her head and looked up to the light of a plane overhead. "You know something, Biz? I haven't a clue as to what the hell we're even talking about here."

THAT'S BECAUSE YOU KEEP INTERRUPTING
I'M TRYNG TO EXPLAIN THAT YOU ARE HERE TO ACHIEVE SOME-THING

*YOU ARE NOT HERE TO ATONE FOR SOMETHING THAT YOU'VE
BROKEN*

She let her head fall back against the dormer and tried to quiet her
mind.

"Oh." She nodded, pressing her eyes closed. "That's actually..." Her
throat tightened and she looked down. She knew she'd say it badly
and she decided not to try. "Thank You, Biz." She turned back toward
the agents and paused again. There was still one thing she had to
ask, and His answer was what she feared most in the world.

"Why did Zane look as though he'd just won the game when Rockwell turned that gun on him tonight? Is this what You offered him
the other night beside the highway? Is Zane down there right now
earning Your forgiveness for taking that shot at Rockwell?"

The phone was silent for a moment. Then it chimed.

I TOLD HIM HE WAS ALREADY FORGIVEN

Her eyes fell low a moment. Of course He had. No pound of flesh
had been required of Zane, no bullying or bribing. He'd made a dangerous decision at a complicated moment, and it had been met with
understanding and absolution. It was everything he'd never had.

"And that's when he knew he was all in, no matter what it took?
And he knew I'd see it in his eyes if he tried to talk to me about it.
Christ, Biz, what the hell has he—?"

She caught herself and wiped a sleeve across her forehead. Then
she stood up and brushed her hands off on her jeans. "My part's coming
up pretty soon. Thank You for the talk."

The phone was quiet now. He'd said all that was needed for the
moment.

John was about two-thirds across when she rejoined Ed and Rutherford at the ridge. She hid her damp palms in her pockets, more

grateful than ever for The Biz's distraction, particularly when she noted the twitch at Ed's jawline. Every pass of her uncle's hands seemed a catastrophe in the making.

She turned her eyes down, but they flew up again as there was a stoic, collective straightening on the roof. The hook had shifted and John dropped a few feet as Patience swallowed a cry and Ed's attention turned brittle. The air was still as stone as the hook found new lodging and John began to settle. He resumed his journey, more slowly this time, and gained about ten more feet before the hook shifted again. He eased his emergency line through its clip, working steadily and calmly to pull the line taut, and then the hook broke free of the ridge.

Ed threw his arms around Patience, stifling her cries with his unbroken hand, as her uncle plummeted in a screaming trajectory toward the side of the house below them. John gripped the rope as he yanked on his emergency line, wrestling to get it pulled firm again. He pulled back with enough force, finally, and came to a stop about halfway between the houses, where he hung suspended between the lines, performing violent feats of acrobatics forty-five feet above the ground. Patience doubled over as Rutherford gripped her arm with his eyes still locked on her uncle. She watched through her hair as John did his thing up there and waited for the lines to settle.

"He's okay." Ed exhaled and drew her back to standing, then released her and stepped away. "He's okay."

The men on the ground spread out with their guns drawn as the men on the roof dropped into position to cover them, but there was no response from the house. Ed held his good hand to his forehead for a moment while Patience stood paralyzed beside him, watching as John lowered himself parallel to Rockwell's house and then scaled up the emergency line to the roof.

Rutherford finally let go of Patience's arm as her uncle threw his leg over the rain gutter. He stood up and pointed to Mason, with a piece of the emergency line in hand, and then he flashed them all a double thumbs up before grabbing the rope from his harness and retrieving the wayward hook. He crawled up the shingles to the chimney and Ed turned away. Patience just looked to the sky for a few minutes and tried not to think.

The only one present who seemed not to require a moment to recover from the incident was John, so he got to work on the zip line. Patience couldn't be certain at their distance, but it appeared that he might be whistling.

The chief of security stood at the ridge with his broken hand in the air and a hollow expression on his face. Rutherford Ellison, the ruler of his empire, hung back behind the men he employed and tried not to get in their way. Patience stared across the treetops at her uncle, with his head full of secrets and his heart full of storms. She was coming for Zane with a mismatched army of damaged heroes, but maybe that was right for the matter at hand. They were driven and adrift, and they were, each of them, not what they'd been when they'd awoken that morning.

CHAPTER THIRTY-THREE

Ed hooked his harness to the line and, without a word of farewell or final instruction, slid to the roof next door. He came down easily on the shingles and John pointed back to Patience.

Mason grabbed her and clipped her harness to the trolley, and then he lowered her into the air. She ignored the bitterness of the adrenaline and her slipping palms, hoping the agents wouldn't notice her trembling as she gripped the harness straps. Mason gave her a push and she squeezed her eyes shut. The world turned into a whirring rush of air and momentum, captured in a continuous loop, until it ended abruptly at an enormous pair of arms.

"You did good, Pax."

She glared at him as he set her down, then slapped his hands away. She unfastened the harness herself and unhooked it from the trolley.

"Don't speak to me."

He grinned back at her with a slight shrug. "That's fair, I suppose. It wasn't nearly as exciting as it looked though, kid. I promise. I had that emergency line for a reason. It's not as though I was totally unprepared for something like that to occur. Now, how are you doing? Still afraid of heights?"

She dropped the harness onto the shingles and shivered at the cold air passing over the skin of her neck. John pulled her hair back on one side and passed her the receiver to her new earpiece. She looked away as she fastened it into place.

"I can't be afraid tonight, now can I?"

He connected the cables and switched the unit on with a wink. "That's exactly right, kid. You can't be afraid tonight."

He started up toward the window and Patience looked down at Ed, crouched at the base of the chimney as he checked his weapons after the flight. He appeared serious about the task, and perturbed that it wasn't effortless. He didn't return the look, but she could tell that he was paying attention.

She tied her hair back and wished it didn't require so much effort just to breathe.

"Will you hold it against me if I cry?"

Ed paused for a moment with his eyes still fixed on his revolver. Then he glanced at John with a wry smile and raised his splinted hand into the air. "Will you hold it against me if I do?"

"Absolutely."

"Good. What do you say we both just suck it up for now?"

Patience dropped from the window to the attic floor and nodded back at her uncle. Then she turned toward the stairs, but paused as her eye caught a corner of light on the ceiling, a beam of moonlight reflected by a diamond of broken glass. She bit down on her lower lip and nodded at it.

"If You could help me to find just a speck of Dick's skill, or my uncle's passion for the fight, or even Rutherford's misguided determination, Biz, I'd appreciate it for Zane's sake, not to mention the world's. Please, don't let me screw this up too badly."

She hurried to the staircase without awaiting any response. As she reached the bottom, her phone chimed softly and she froze before the door. She touched a button at her sleeve and scrambled back up again as John's rifle cracked down on the window frame above at her summons. The door flew open and she was caught two-thirds of the way up, staring into the startled eyes of a SolarTech guard.

He raised his gun as she turned back to dash up the last few stairs, and then glass shattered above and Ed leaned in through a window kitty-corner to John. Both their weapons were trained on the guard as Patience spun back. He rushed up toward her, and without thinking, she leapt. A torrent of wind from the second open window meeting its match from the first bent a path around her and drew her forward. She hung suspended over the staircase for one miraculous moment as the shaft of air completed its arc around her body and her foot connected with the man's gun, sending it flying as he crashed through the open door and onto the floor below. She landed on top of him and pulled her revolver from her belt.

He took a swing, but to his credit, he seemed to catch that Patience was serious when she ducked it and cocked the hammer of her gun. She collected his radio and revolver and escorted him up the stairs to Ed, who seemed the less lethal of her options. She passed the radio through the window as John appeared behind him with his rifle raised and a pained expression on his face. He shook his head at his niece before turning his full attention to the guard, who shrank back from the ravenous look in his eye.

John nudged Ed's shoulder as Patience's phone chimed. "More of Rockwell's men are on the move now, courtesy of the ruckus. What's your call, G-man?"

Ed stared at the guard for a moment, and then passed the radio back. He raised his weapon so it fell in line below John's. "What's your name?"

"Stevenson."

"Okay, Stevenson, I'd hate to shoot a man who just showed up for work on an unfortunate day and found himself trapped in a bad situation. Assuming that's what's happened here, I'll give you one second to spare me the disappointment."

The guard didn't hesitate. He clicked the button on his radio with shaking hands. Patience reached up to help him hold it steady.

"Mr. Rockwell, Sir, this is Stevenson. A freaking owl's just flown in through a window of your attic. The thing is huge. Do you want me to take care of it for you?"

There was a pause and they all stared at the silent radio. Stevenson swallowed and flinched a bead of sweat from his face as it crackled at last.

"Everyone, hold your positions!" The radio clicked and the air was dead. Then it crackled again. "What the hell were you doing up there, Stevenson?"

The guard glanced at John and then quickly turned back to Ed. "I was looking for a place to take a leak, Sir. I was on the second floor when I heard the crash."

The radio was silent again for another beat. "There are four johns on the first floor."

"Yes, Sir, it's a big house and I was closest to the stairs at the time. It seemed like the quickest way to get right back to my post. Like I said, I heard the crash and figured I'd better check it out. But, about this owl, Mr. Rockwell... What do you want me to do about it?"

"I want you to shoot the goddamn thing and get back down here! As for the rest of you, return to your posts, and don't anyone else get any ideas about going sightseeing while on duty."

Stevenson exhaled and Ed took the radio back. "I take it you guys are here for the kid?"

Patience's ice cold skin ignited and she pulled him back from the window. She pushed him against the wall and rose up onto her toes.

"You've seen Zane? How is he?"

Stevenson nodded. "Mouthy."

John reached past Ed to pull the guard from her clutches. She turned back, but Ed raised a hand with his eyes set to stun. The guard didn't appear to bear her any ill will, though. He just looked back toward the staircase.

"I didn't sign on for this. We all work security for SolarTech Industries, and a few days ago, the big man offered per diem pay to anyone interested in beefing up security for the Forsyth campaign. It was good money for easy work, so a bunch of us agreed. And then today, a more select group was offered better money to come here and do private work for Mr. Rockwell. We weren't told anything about him bringing that kid here, though. Nobody ever said a word about that."

"All right," Ed said. "So what were you really doing up here?"

He looked the agent directly in the eye. "I was searching for a way out of here. I was going to call the police. I didn't sign on for this."

John stared down at him, then crossed his arms. "He's telling the truth," he said. "He was trying to squirrel out."

Ed gestured toward the stairs. "How organized is it down there? Will Rockwell miss you if you don't return?"

Stevenson paused and then he nodded. "He'll notice. I wouldn't call it organized, but he's pretty worked up about security. He'll notice."

Ed considered this information and took the guard's gun from Patience. He ejected the clip and passed the weapon back through the window with the radio. "I'm sure you understand." He pocketed the clip. "We've got the house wired, Stevenson. If you mention anything about our presence to Mr. Rockwell, or to any of the other men, it will end badly for you. The second anyone down there begins acting differently from what we've come to expect of them, we're coming in and we're coming in hard. I give you credit for telling me the truth just now. You could have lied about whether or not Mr. Rockwell would miss you, in the hopes that we'd have let you continue on your way. We wouldn't have, but I give you credit, nonetheless. We need you to go back to work now, as if nothing's any different from before. Do you understand what I'm saying?"

The guard nodded and reattached the radio to his belt. John reached for his arm as he started toward the staircase. "The other men down there, are any of them loyal to Rockwell or do they feel the same way you do?"

"None of them are loyal to Mr. Rockwell," Stevenson said. "Some are loyal to SolarTech, to varying degrees, and we're all loyal to the money. It's not a brotherhood down there. I'm sure there are others who feel the way I do, but I couldn't point them out to you."

John released his arm with a nod and the guard turned toward the door. He paused halfway across the attic and looked back.

"Whether or not Mr. Rockwell knows it, I don't believe any of those men down there are killers. I've met some pretty scary guys working security for STI, and to a man, they were also selected for special overtime today. But, they were all stationed around the streets of Wellesley. The freakiest among them were sent to something happening out on Cliff Road."

Patience raised a hand to her forehead as Ed stared down at her. Then the agent stepped away to report into his sleeve. The guard disappeared down the stairs and John turned his face from his niece's.

"Don't speak to me."

She smiled and pulled her shirt aside to check out some of the better welts she'd sustained during the tussle. The Biz's trick with the wind had treated her to a rougher landing the second time around. Then she just shrugged back at her uncle.

"It wasn't as exciting as it looked, Uncle John. I promise. Anyway, I've been tossed around by more than the wind since The Biz showed up. It's not as though I was totally unprepared for something like that to occur."

She stopped talking as she realized that what she'd just said was actually entirely true. She'd turned on an armed man twice her size, without hesitation or regard for the fact that only one of them was willing to fire the gun in his hand, and she'd leapt without a shred of evidence that The Biz would save her from a broken neck or bullet in the chest. She'd leapt as though no other outcome was possible.

"Holy hell," she muttered. "Now You're just messing with me."

A smiley chirped onto the screen and she was grateful that there was no time to talk.

Her uncle was still staring when she looked up again, and his expression seemed even less certain than before. Then glass crunched beneath Ed's shoes as he rejoined them from down the roof.

"Things have settled back into to a steady paranoia, now that Stevenson's been accounted for and no one's come crashing down on Rockwell's head. He's still pretty twitchy, but he's stopped threatening to shoot anyone who clears his throat without permission." He turned to Patience and paused a moment before speaking. "Are you all right to do this, Miss Kelleher? That was a nasty tumble you took at the bottom of those stairs."

"I guess that depends, Dick. Is Zane still down there?"

John held a hand up to the agent and pointed his niece back toward the staircase. "Save your breath, G-man. Pax can't back away from a fight, no matter how hard she might try to. Now, let's do this thing. There's something about the sound of breaking glass that always revs me up for a fight."

And with that, Ed O'Brien did something he'd likely never done before in his life.

He sighed.

The rest of the agents followed Mason across once Patience had the line secured. The second-in-command checked her work as soon as he landed, then raised an eyebrow up from the intricate knots tied through the industrial-grade hooks she'd driven into the doorframe.

"My uncle taught me."

"Nice."

Ed and John watched the first few crossings from Rockwell's roof before rappelling to the ground and stealing back across the yard. They climbed up in time to help get Rutherford over safely and then they packed up the last of their gear before coming over last.

Ed landed on the balcony and looked up at his men, crowded still and silent in Rockwell's bedroom, and then his eyes fell to the small green light at the alarm panel beside the door. He turned to Patience as Collins and Mason released the line from the frame.

"You know something, Miss Kelleher..."

"Yes." She sighed. "I do, Dick. I really, really do."

He raised his uninjured hand between them. "I believe you've finally cured me of ever wanting to know the source of your information. At this point, I think I'd probably put a bullet in the kneecap of anyone who tried to tell me."

She looked up at the chief of security, and her smile at him was genuine.

"That's the spirit!"

CHAPTER THIRTY-FOUR

They kept low as Ed and John led them down to the second floor. The hall ended at a wide landing above the foyer, where they hung back to the strains of a Tom Jones tune floating up from the study. Patience rested her battered torso against the wall for a moment, doing all she could not to imagine what might be happening below, and then Zane's voice cut above the music. She dug her fingernails into the carpet to keep from lunging after it, and her uncle took hold of her arm.

Ed leaned in to update him about the latest from the parabolic mic. Rockwell had been unable to shake the owl incident and required nearly constant reassurance from his guards outside. Ed's men were only too happy to oblige via their confiscated radios, but time and inactivity had stoked the fires of his paranoia. He'd left a man at each of the ground-floor doors and moved the rest into the study with him. This development made things much less complicated for the rescue effort, and a hell of a lot trickier.

John nodded and he and Ed reached for their goggles. The men followed suit as Mason passed a pair each to Patience and Rutherford. When all were in place, Ed spoke low into his sleeve.

"Okay, Kirby. Kill 'em."

The lights went out with a whomp and a shudder that reverberated throughout the house, and Tom Jones died mid-croon. Rockwell shouted a stream of expletives as his guards bolted, crashing into each other in the dark under the threat of the hell-bent army rushing at them from above and without. The men at the doors were quickly disarmed and dragged in to join the others and the study filled to capacity. Ed shouted for everyone to get down on the ground and the guards tripped over each other, falling back from his voice as they stumbled through the ghostly green glow of the goggles. None stopped until they were surrounded by a ring of agents and they fell to their knees at the unseen urging of gun barrels, abandoning Rockwell and his hostage at the back of the room.

Zane was tied to a chair with his arms bound behind him. There wasn't a part of him that wasn't battered and bloody. His nose was broken and both eyes were swollen and split. Below him was a pool of blood, being fed by a badly bandaged gunshot wound to each of his biceps. He was conscious though, and grinning at the shouting all around him, despite the Smith & Wesson .44 Magnum at his head.

Ed and John raised their weapons in unison.

"Drop it now."

A humming vibrated through the walls and the lights flickered. They came on again and Tom Jones took it up again from the top as twenty-seven pairs of night-vision goggles hit the floor at their feet. Rockwell smiled at Ed as the agent ran a sleeve over his watering eyes.

"Generator," he said. "I fucking hate New England winters."

Zane blinked at the light a few times and looked up at Patience. He didn't seem the slightest bit surprised to see her. He looked at Ed in pretty much the same way, and then he noticed his father by the door, being held back by three of his agents, and his eyes clouded over. Patience just stared down at him for a moment, quieted by her despair, and then she shut off the phone and pulled her Glock from her coat.

Rockwell stared down at his guards, all lined up on their knees with their hands behind their heads, and pointed to Patience. "What are you waiting for?" he said. "Someone shoot the bitch."

A couple of the men glanced back at the agents, but he otherwise received no response.

"Forget about them, you weaseling pricks. They're eunuchs. As long as I've got the princess, here, none of them will make a move. Pink, on the other hand, is a powder keg. She's goddamned crazy and she's going to kill you all. Shoot her, for fuck's sake, and then shoot the uncle."

When there was still no response, Rockwell reached for his shoulder holster and withdrew a Browning HK. John slid his finger over the trigger of his rifle, but Rockwell bypassed Patience and turned to the closest of his own guards. Zane shouted and rocked back hard in his chair and Rockwell cracked him on the head. Patience heard the wind howl in her ears as Rockwell turned to the guard again.

"I said shoot."

The man looked up at the twenty-four agents, plus John and one pissed-off-looking pink fury, and he jumped up and ran for the door. The agents let him pass, but Rockwell followed him with the Browning and pulled the trigger. Patience froze, horror-struck as the guard fell forward at her feet, his face cloaked by the blood streaming from his wound.

The clamor of the guards' shouting overpowered the clamor in her head as she lowered to one knee and searched his neck for a pulse. She found one, a fleeting flicker of life beneath her fingertips, and then it was gone. She looked up to Ed for help and he shook his head. She looked to her uncle next and he shook his as well. Mason, the physician-agent trained in emergency medicine, took one look at the guard's wound and lowered his eyes. Then he also shook his head and Patience knew there was no hope. She looked to Rockwell, and rage and horror collided inside her like a thunderclap. She stalked toward him with her gun raised as John leapt and Rockwell aimed the Browning again.

Zane grabbed hold of his chair and drove his feet into the floor, pushing up with all the force he had left. The top of the wooden seatback slammed up into the bottom of Rockwell's jaw and he bit through his tongue and fell back. The agents stampeded in, surrounding the youngest Ellison and smashing through the chair as Patience broke from her uncle and ran to him. Rockwell sat up on the floor with blood pouring from his mouth and murder pouring from his eyes as he searched the melee for his prize.

She caught the look in his eye in the same time-burst that she saw him pull back on the trigger. She didn't scream and her life didn't flash before her. Everything just turned very still as she watched him take his last and angriest act of vengeance on the world. She didn't feel dread or fear as the gun discharged, only loss. She thought of her mother, and of Frank, and of Uncle John, who was yards away now and bound to take this failure hard. Then she looked apologetically at Zane as she fell.

The bullet struck her hand as Ed came down hard on top of her. A second shot rang out, followed by an explosion of gunfire so quick and intense it seemed to come from a single weapon of immense size and power. She pushed the agent back, desperate to see who'd been hit, and he stood up without a word. He reached a hand down and helped her to her feet.

Rockwell lay face up on the floor. There wasn't a gun in the room but hers and Ed's that didn't appear to have put at least one bullet into him. Patience stared down at her bleeding hand, and then up again at the chief of Rutherford Ellison's private security force, incapable of productive speech or thought.

The agent just glanced sideways at her and returned his attention to what was left of Alexander Rockwell.

"Please don't look so shocked, Miss Kelleher. I've told you time and again, it's my job to protect Zane."

Her uncle broke between them, but she hardly noticed his cursing at her wounded hand as she gaped at the agent. She just shook her head, struggling to reorder her expectations for a continued existence for the second time in sixty seconds.

Ed appeared somewhat self-amused. He reached into his coat for a handkerchief. "You're dripping."

She nodded her thanks and pulled her wrist from her uncle's clutches, then pressed the handkerchief obediently to her wound and watched it turn from white to crimson. A spot of the same color formed at the corner of the agent's mouth and she screamed. The handkerchief fell to the floor as she grabbed Ed by the arms. He looked confused for a moment, then blood spilled over the side of his chin and he slumped to the floor. The river dammed by the slug in his back found its way past and seeped onto the rug around him.

Zane broke from his agents and fell beside her. He rolled Ed toward him, but the agent looked away, searching the faces above for Mason. The second-in-command pushed toward them, shouting for his bag as Ed caught his eye and nodded to Zane.

"Get him out of here."

Mason signaled to Collins and Polaski and they pulled Zane away. Ed looked to him at last and winked as Mason tore his shirt open. Then his eyes rolled back. He closed them, as his final act of courtesy, and the life disappeared from Ed O'Brien's face.

Zane fought the agents as they barricaded him from Mason's struggle to bring his boss back, until Rutherford stepped between them and took his son by the shoulders.

"Damn it, Zane. Let him work."

Zane just shook his head, and Rutherford pulled him into his arms and held him until the police and paramedics arrived.

CHAPTER THIRTY-FIVE

Patience and John sat on their barstools with their heads low. Frank stood over them, suppressing his anger as best he could and failing in every imaginable way. He lifted Patience's arm up from the bar and shook it at her uncle.

"This is not what I call bringing her back unharmed, John Flaherty. You promised me, man. You promised me."

"I know, Frank," he said. "I let you down and I'm sorry."

Patience pulled the purple cast back from her godfather's grip.

"It doesn't hurt, Frank. Really, it doesn't."

"It's three broken bones and a hole through your hand, Patience Abigail. It hurts."

"Oh no." She brightened. "They gave me a prescription at the hospital, and it's very effective. You're worrying much too much about this. I promise you, I'm fine."

He dropped his face into his hand and then he confiscated her margarita. Patience watched in dismay as it disappeared into the sink, but his look vanquished any thought she had of protest. He slid a glass of water into its place and glanced up as the pub's door opened behind her.

"Holy Christ!"

She turned back and jumped down from her stool. She threw her arms around Zane with more exuberance than judgment. He winced and she backed off, searching him for someplace that looked safe enough to kiss until he grew fed up and grabbed her by the belt loops.

John shook his head at Frank with a sigh. "There now, you see what I've been contending with?"

Frank recovered from his dumbstruck state at the sight of Zane's condition and cleared his throat. They turned back and Patience helped Zane up onto a barstool.

"Nice cast." Zane nodded. "Try to remember that it's not a weapon, though, okay?"

She glanced at the larger, black fiberglass number on his left arm and shrugged. "That would depend on the situation, I suppose. I like yours, too."

He shook his head and then his expression turned serious as he looked up at her godfather. "I'm sorry, Frank. I heard about what happened here with my father's men. I really don't know what to say about that."

Frank studied the rows of stitches across Zane's temple and bruised jaw for a moment and then he turned away. He pulled a bottle of vodka from the top shelf and poured a shot. He slid it in front of Zane and poured himself one as well.

"Alexander Rockwell did all of this to you?"

Zane just nodded and drained the glass.

"The older bruise on my jaw and the abrasion on my forehead are courtesy of my buddy Uncle John, here, but yes, Alexander Rockwell did all of this. It's just a taste of what was to come if he'd been left to his own devices. He had to be stopped, Frank, and not just to save my sorry ass. I promise you that."

Frank just stared down at Zane a moment and then he took John's empty glass from the bar and tossed it into the dish rack. He drew him a fresh beer. "I'll be angry until I'm done being angry, John Flaherty. That's just the way this is going to work."

John wrapped his fingers possessively around the beer. "That's more than fair."

Frank turned back to the mess of Zane's face. "And you're absolutely certain you killed the son of a bitch completely?"

The SCUD stretched his hands behind his head as a slow smile spread across his face. "I'm sure," he said. "It was one thorough killing, Frank. We won't be troubled by that corpse again. Now, with that in my favor, and the kids, here, on the mend, what would you say to a game of darts before I go?"

Frank tossed his towel down and reached for his wallet. "I'd say 'It's nice to see you haven't lost your taste for a beating since you've been gone, John.' And then I'd say 'Let's play for money.'"

John clapped Patience on the shoulder. "I'm just going to go give your godfather the shellacking he's had coming for too long, Pax, and then I'll be back to say goodbye. Please refrain from making out with your boyfriend or speaking to any members of the clergy while we're out of the room."

She waved him off and poured the last of the bottle into Zane's glass once they were alone. His fingers lingered over hers as she slid the glass back.

"How was it with your father today?"

He smiled and tossed the shot back behind the first. "Baby steps. Rutherford is working through alternating waves of anger, fear, guilt, and grief at the moment. Anger is the emotion he's most familiar with, so that's still getting center stage. It's a little different every day. Of course, the press hasn't been making it easier for him."

"No, I don't imagine it has."

"I think once he figures out where to put all the disapproval and disappointment he's so accustomed to feeling whenever I'm around, it'll become easier for him to work through. It seems a little better now that I'm out of the hospital, but he's lost all his comfort zones and he's lost Ed. It's going to take him some time."

She slid down from her stool and ducked beneath the bar for another bottle, ignoring the afternoon bartender's shouts for her to get back to the other side. He was in the middle of a complicated to-go order, so she didn't view him as much of a threat.

"And how is it with you today?"

Zane nodded as she turned back to him. "I'm working through alternating waves of anger, fear, guilt, and grief. Guilt is the emotion I'm most familiar with, so..."

"Yeah," she said. "I know."

"The funeral is tomorrow. Can you come?"

"Can I come?" She paused in her uncapping and looked up at him. "Ed may have been a little stiff for my tastes, Zane, and I've never been too crazy about people who break their promises, as a general rule, but the man died saving my life. I sort of feel inclined to let that stuff slide, under the circumstances."

He pretended not to notice the tears as she wiped them onto her sleeve. She looked away for a moment, then refilled his glass as Frank returned from the back. He paused in the counting of John's money just long enough to point a finger across the bar.

"Patience Abigail Kelleher, get your ass out from behind there or I'll give you a chewing out that won't end until a year after I'm dead!"

She ducked back around with assurances that she'd been nowhere near the tequila. He shot her a final look of warning as he passed and then he returned to his work. John ambled up with a slimmer wallet and a resigned expression on his face.

"Well, Pax, I guess I'm off."

She lowered her eyes. "But you just got here, Uncle John. You didn't even see Mom."

"I know." He dropped his bag to the floor and slid back onto on the stool next to hers. "I'm sorry, kid, but watching you get shot is about as much familial heartache and guilt as I can manage for one visit. I'll be back real soon, though, I promise. You and your mother are going to have plenty of time to scold me for my many atrocities, don't you worry. This is my home base now."

Patience stared at him. Zane leaned across the bar to do the same.

John just grinned and nodded back. "It seems that God's got a new mission in mind for me now, and it's based right here in Allston. I'm not everything He needs in a SCUD at the moment, but I've got a hell of a lot to offer someone who can be. We'll get to work as soon as I come back, so stay on your mark. If you want to nurse your wounds and neck with your boyfriend, this is your chance. You probably won't get too many more in the future."

Patience jumped down from her stool and backed away from him. "Have you lost your goddamned mind?"

He just stood up and dropped a hand on her shoulder. Then he kissed her head and lifted his bag from the floor.

"I work for you now, Pax. He likes that you're unwavering and that you think outside the box. You need a hell of a lot more training to become a safer and more time-efficient SCUD, but that's where I come in. I'm going to make sure you're watched after, as well. You're what He sent me here for. You're my mission now."

"My God," she gasped. "You've finally gone around the bend. There is no way anything like that is going to happen. I don't want it, Uncle John. I won't do it."

He just winked back at her. "I'm sure you two will hash it all out in an explosion of angst and emoticons while I'm gone. I'll be back again when it's time."

She pulled the phone from her pocket and tossed it onto the bar. "Sorry, Uncle John, but you've already lost this one. I haven't received so much as an LOL since I powered down at Rockwell's. He knew what my intentions were back there, and that was a whole lot of blood we spilled, in case you missed it. I'm sorry to disappoint you, but I'm telling you what I know. The Biz has buzzed off."

John cocked his head at her. "Well, I don't know that, kid. I don't know it at all."

Zane laid a hand on her arm. "I don't know that, either."

She turned away from them, fighting the collapse she'd been wishing for since the showdown at Rockwell's, but desperately wanted to avoid in her godfather's pub. John took her by the shoulders and turned her back to face him.

"You don't think God expected you to control every person in that room, do you? Because you can't, and He doesn't presume that you can. Maybe we'll make that lesson number one when I get back— how to avoid developing a God complex when you're working for the Lord."

"You can't be serious," she whispered.

"You're a good girl, Pax, and I'm serious in every way. He knows what happens to our hearts and minds when we see someone we love in pain. It takes a lot more than that to change what's in a person's soul, though. Don't mistake what you felt back there for what you were capable of, and don't worry about The Biz. You'll hear from Him again when you're ready."

"Who said I want to hear from Him? I don't want to be a SCUD. I just want you to go see my mother."

He laughed and turned toward the door. She started after him, but then she gave up arguing with a man so clearly determined not to hear her. She turned back to the bar so he could accomplish the vanishing act he was so fond of performing.

She sat down beside Zane as the door banged shut behind them and she glanced down at the phone. Its face lit up, as if on cue.

"I thought he said when I was ready."

"Are you?"

She picked it up and considered it for a moment. It occurred to her that if she wasn't, she probably owed it to Ed to try to get ready. She owed it to the fallen SolarTech guard as well, and to Joey Forsyth. Even Rockwell's death had been contrary to what she'd set out to do, and while she wasn't finding much space in her grieving for him,

The Biz might have something He'd like to say about that. For the sake of the dead, perhaps she would try to hear Him.

She bit her lower lip and looked up at Zane again. "You were already forgiven?"

He nodded.

She sighed and touched her finger to the screen.

HOW MANY MRTYRS DOES IT TAKE 2 SCRW IN A LGHTBLB? :)

AFTERWORD

The last technician stepped into the darkness a little past eleven p.m. He patted down his pockets, checked for his keys and wallet, and trudged to his car. When he'd driven away at last, John stepped from the shadows and approached the building. His feet and back ached from the hours spent standing around, but sometimes a SCUD's got to do what a SCUD has got to do, and unfortunately for John, what a SCUD has got to do sometimes is wait.

He approached the fire alarm at the main entrance and punched in the glass with his elbow. He pulled down on the handle and the bells sounded throughout the building as he turned the corner and pulled smoke bombs from his bag. He circled the building slowly, shattering windows and lobbing them inside, until the lab's security guards and housekeeping staff spilled out through the doors in droves, some with pieces of clothing pressed against their faces.

Once he'd accounted for every member of the third shift, John slipped back into the shadows and pulled his M32 grenade launcher from his back. He set it upon its stand and braced himself. Then he fired each of its six Hellhound 40mm grenades into the building in lightning-fast succession.

The SolarTech Industries Exploration and Development Laboratory went up in a ball of fire as brilliant as the sun it strove to harness. The night-shift staff all fell back and stared, their amazed faces lit up by the flames.

The beauty of the moment almost made up for the wait.

John turned away from the glorious glow of the SolarTech inferno with the sound of sirens in the distance. It warmed him to know that the executives' sudden courtship of the freshman senator from Nebraska was about to end as abruptly as it had begun, and it was hard to deny feeling a certain satisfaction in the clean and simple elegance of the solution. He walked off into the darkness with a nod up at the sky.

"There Ya go," he said. "No blood."

ABOUT THE AUTHOR

Bower Lewis writes off-beat mainstream fiction, infusing her novels with romance, humor, intrigue, and a touch of sex whenever she can get her characters to sit still long enough. She is the author of *Patience, My Dear* and the forthcoming *Damn It, Jane Damsel*. She lives outside Boston with her husband, three Roombas, and two badly behaved cats. Visit the author at www.bowerlewis.com.

If you enjoyed PATIENCE, MY DEAR,
please be sure to check out

DAMN IT, JANE DAMSEL

by Bower Lewis
Coming Soon From Infinite Words

Turn the page for a sneak preview!

CHAPTER ONE

You don't run a pawn shop within the city limits of Boston without weathering the occasional incident here and there, but holy fuck almighty, Mack had not seen this one coming. The girl wasn't much over five feet tall and she was skinny, but not drug-strung-skinny. She didn't look nervous or too confident. She didn't look a whole lot of anything, really, other than damn good in an interesting and off-setting sort of a way.

The long blonde curls that fell alongside her face to dance above the glass of his display case had been something of a distraction. She looked, kinda bored, down at the rows of jewelry and keepsakes precious to people other than those who'd sold them to him, and her dark lashes brushed lightly across her pale cheeks. Those details had been mitigating factors as well, so it was what it was.

His appreciation for the kind of girl Mack's Pawn saw far too few of was interrupted when she turned her clear blue eyes up to his and asked if he had any antique thimbles for sale. Who the hell comes in to rob a pawn shop in the heart of Allston Center looking for antique thimbles?

Mack leaned forward on the counter and told her not at the present moment. She asked him if he knew of anyone who might, because her grandmother collected antique thimbles. He explained that an item like that was bound to be luck of the draw at any given time, but he did have a pair of one-of-a-kind button hole scissors—solid gold, not plate—in the back that once belonged to a personal seamstress to Queen Victoria. The seller had been a great- or a great-great-grandniece of the seamstress who'd fallen on hard times, so he could probably let them go for two hundred fifty.

The girl said her grandmother didn't sew.

She looked the regular kind of frustrated. It's not a good idea to rely on the pawns if you're looking for something that specific, he advised her. She just shrugged and slipped her arm through the window of his shield.

She had the cutest little Ruger .38 caliber pistol he'd ever seen duct-taped to her hand.

"Aw, what the fuck, honey? Are you kidding me?"

She suggested—earnest and trying to be helpful—that he keep his hands above the counter and come out to the front by her. She was clear that he should use the knob to release the door and not the buzzer.

"You don't really seem like the kind of guy who needs killing," she said. "You'd probably feel obligated to hit the alarm button you've got hidden under there and I'd prefer not to shoot you if it's not absolutely necessary. I'm generally a pretty safety-conscious person."

Mack shook his head and turned away from her. No ninety-pound twitch with her goddamn gun taped to her hand was going to rob his pawn at two-thirty in the afternoon on a Wednesday. He kept a loaded Glock 31 .357 stashed in the cage as a precaution against just this sort of thing. It was kind of a shame this kid—who was a really interesting-looking girl and who, discounting the gun, hadn't been at all unpleasant during their exchange—was going to get an ear full of lead, but what the fuck, man?

He ignored her when she told him to turn his ass back around, and it was as he was reaching for his piece that he heard the hammer cock. He froze, deciding that she might be a little more sincere than he'd initially surmised, and turned back to face her—loused up as hell and still goddamn gunless.

He knew then—the way he knew gold from plate at a glance—that this kid didn't have the desperation or the desire to kill a man, but she'd probably be okay with shooting a guy in the ass if the occasion called for it. She reached through the window and took him by the hand, pulling it not un-gently back to her side of the shield.

"Hang on to that pole there, okay?"

She drew a half-spent roll of duct tape from the pocket of her pink down vest and pulled a strip free with her teeth. "Little lower... lower... okay, perfect." She nodded when he was stretched long and kissing the Plexiglas. She wrapped the tape around his wrist, binding it to the counter pole, and then she motioned for his other hand.

Mack felt like an asshole hanging over the counter of his own pawn with his cheek pressed up against the bulletproof shield like a fifth-grader making faces for the traffic on the school bus. He caught an eyeful of the twitch's chest as she rose again and raised an eyebrow at her T-shirt. It had her name spelled out across the front in letters formed by yogic kittens.

"You're Jane, I presume?"

"I'm Jane." She nodded. "And I presume that you're Mack?"

"That's me."

"Nice to meet you, Mack. What's the best way for me to get back there now?"

Mack considered her question for a moment. "I believe you're going to have to break the handle of the door." He sighed. "I could probably reach the buzzer with my knee, but I'm not sure I can avoid hitting the alarm at the same time, and trust me when I tell you that neither one of us wants that to happen now. Hurry up though, would ya, darlin'? This is fucking uncomfortable."

Jane looked around the shop for something heavy and Mack directed her to a brass urn at the far end of the counter.

"And would you shut those blinds and tape the *Back in Five* sign up in the window? If the cops show up now, you'll pull sixty months' free accommodations and I'll be the laughingstock of Boston. Every wasted fuck with a jones or a grudge will line up to knock me over if word about this fiasco finds its way around the neighborhood."

"I told you to open that door," Jane reminded him. It was awkward work, trying to smash the heavy knob with a pistol taped to her hand. "What did you have to make this so complicated for? I was being pretty nice, considering."

Mack grimaced and flinched as he watched her, until he simply couldn't take the stress of it.

"Jesus Christ, Jane! Would you take that gun off your hand? Even if you don't shoot one of us dead, the cops will drop you in an instant if they catch you in here with a weapon you can't lay down. And darlin', I can't duck at the moment. What the hell did you tape it to yourself for?"

"Don't you read the papers, Mack?" She hit the doorknob a few more times and then set the urn on the floor. She started pulling at the duct tape. "The majority of inexperienced gun owners shot during a highly charged situation are shot with their own weapon. I figured a guy who owns a pawn shop is likely to be pretty handy with a gun, so I'd better make it extra hard for you to disarm me."

Mack looked at Jane and Jane looked back at him as she worked her gun free at last. She tucked it into the waistband of her little skirt as Mack sighed at the door knob.

"You're trying to get at the strongest part of the knob." He nodded. "Hit it at the base so you can knock the spindle off its alignment. All you really need to do is get the spindle free of the pins."

Jane smiled and picked up the urn again. She followed Mack's advice and had the base dislodged in no time. Then she rattled the knob a few times and the door swung free of its frame.

"That was a messed-up story about Queen Victoria," she said. "But I understand that you've gotta make a living." She opened the drawers below the counter and found the envelopes where Mack kept his working cash stashed. She smiled at the bills and slid them into her pocket, then rested her elbows on the counter to look down at him.

"What about the safe?"

Mack's nose dragged against the Plexiglas as he shook his head at her.

"I've got a box in back that contains the cash I keep for changing out money. It's in the metal cabinet in the corner, and it should be easy enough to break into for an inspired girl like you. Go ahead and make yourself at home back there, darlin'. But I'm not giving you the combo to the safe."

"I will shoot you in the ass, Mack."

"You'll have to. I can't absorb the cost of what's in there, and there's no way I'm explaining to the police or to some pointy-headed suit at my insurance company that I handed the combination over to a little girl. I'll take that shot in the ass and be done with it, thanks."

"Can't you tell the cops and the insurance people that you were jacked by a gang or something?"

"You're on video, kid. Your prints are all over the shop, and you're wearing a T-shirt with your goddamn name on it. So, no darlin', I can't tell them I was jacked by a gang or something."

Jane laughed.

"I guess that's all true," she said. "All right, Mack, you can win that one. You've got an ass that's pretty cute for shooting at, and I like you besides. Looks like you're lucky that way. The metal cabinet?"

"Second case on the left, kid. You'll be in gumballs for the rest of your life."

Jane had just about had it with Mack calling her kid. The way she saw it, she had him ass-end-out over his own counter and that alone should have been enough to spare her the dismissive attitude. She pulled her State Liquor ID from her pocket and held it up to his face.

"What does that say?"

Mack studied the ID and then looked back up at her, exasperated.

"Well, it says you're twenty-three years old, dear. It also says your name is Jane Eleanor Damsel and that you live at forty-fucking-seven Dunster Street in Allston. What the hell is wrong with you?"

Jane slid her ID back into her pocket. "Are you gonna come over for some iced tea, Mack?"

"Get your money and get the hell out of my shop, Jane Damsel."

Jane smiled at him. She really did like him all right, and he was a good-looking guy. The money was where he'd said it would be and the lock was indeed easily broken. She pressed the cash flat and zipped it into the lining of her vest with the rest.

The monitors for the security cameras were stacked up on a table in the far corner of the workroom and Jane turned to take a quick look. She stood still for a moment, voyeuristic, transfixed. Watching him in the little black and white televisions—bound up and vulnerable the way he was—made her feel strange in a not-entirely-unpleasant sort of way. It wasn't easy to pull off looking good while duct-taped to a counter, but Mack was doing just that. He had the kind of body that came from working hard, not working out, and his position gave her a very nice view of his ass. But what Jane liked most were his eyes. She wouldn't have minded hanging around to watch him a little while longer if she'd had time to kill.

She returned to the cage and sat down on the floor beside him. He startled as she reached for him, which made her smile. Then she winked and ran her hands over the curves of his ass. Mack was amusing to her now because he finally looked shocked by something she had done.

She found what she was looking for and slid the wallet from his back pocket. She removed his driver's license from its sheath and studied it.

"Hey, we're neighbors, almost." She smiled at that, then turned her eyes to Mack's and her expression became mildly critical. "You look a little older than thirty, Masterson Patrick Chester. You're probably not getting enough fiber in your diet."

She replaced his ID and slid the wallet back into the pocket of his jeans for him. Then she grabbed him by the belt loops and used them to pull herself back up to stand. As she passed back through the distressed door to the service area of his shop, Jane held up a pair of tiny gold scissors.

"Solid gold? Really?"

Mack grimaced a hard grin at her through the Plexiglas.

"They're gold plate, kid, and cheap at that. Try not to be so goddamn gullible."

"I figured as much." She considered the scissors for a moment and then smiled. "I like them." She nodded. "Add them to my tab, all right?"

"Fuck you, darlin'."

Jane used the scissors to snip into the duct tape binding him to the counter poles. She was conscientious about not pulling too hard on his arms as she worked.

"Do you think you'll get free okay on your own if I cut the tape halfway through?"

"I have no idea, Jane. I lost all feeling in my arms about five minutes ago. Why don't you just take my money and get the hell out of here so I can figure out how to clean up this mess?"

Jane stepped back and narrowed her eyes at him through the shield. "You seem like a pretty okay guy, Mack Chester. What the hell would you want to deal in other people's misery for?"

"Money."

She cut the tape the rest of the way through and slipped the scissors into her pocket. Mack's arms pulled free of the counter poles and dangled there for a moment, and then they snaked through the Plexiglas window as his body fell back onto the floor. Jane turned toward the door, then paused and looked back at him.

"I've enjoyed meeting you, Mack." It appeared to her that he was trying to show her his middle finger, but his arms were not yet ready for the job. She just smiled back at that. He hadn't been a bad sport, considering. He was a little bossy maybe—for a guy who didn't have a gun handy—but as she watched the really all right-looking heap squirming on the slate tiles, she decided that she wouldn't mind running into him again if their fates aligned. She couldn't stay and chat just then, of course, because Mack's limbs were not going to stay numb forever, so she waved goodbye with a reluctant smile and turned back toward the door.

"Jane Damsel."

"Yeah, Mack?"

"I am going to kill you dead, kid."

Jane paused with her hand on the knob, considering his words. "That's likely to add some stress to our relationship," she decided.

"Ain't it?"